THE GREAT TALES NEVER END

THE GREAT TALES NEVER END

Essays in memory of

Christopher Tolkien

EDITED BY

Richard Ovenden & Catherine McIlwaine

BODLEIAN
LIBRARY
PUBLISHING

BODLEIAN
LIBRARY
PUBLISHING

First published in 2022 by the Bodleian Library
Broad Street, Oxford OX1 3BG
www.bodleianshop.co.uk

ISBN: 978 1 85124 565 9

Publisher: Samuel Fanous
Managing Editor: Deborah Susman
Editor: Janet Phillips
Picture Editor: Leanda Shrimpton
Production Editor: Susie Foster
Designed and typeset by Dot Little in the Bodleian
Library in 10.5/13.5 Minion

Printed and bound by Gomer Press Limited on
115gsm Munken Print White paper

MIX
Paper from
responsible sources
FSC® C114687
www.fsc.org

British Library Cataloguing-in-Publication Data
A CIP record of this publication is available from the
British Library

CONTENTS

Catherine McIlwaine

INTRODUCTION

you were so special a gift to me, in a time
of sorrow and mental suffering, and your
love, opening at once almost as soon as
you were born, foretold to me, as it were
in spoken words, that I am consoled ever
by the certainty that there is no end to
this … and certain that we have some
special bond to last beyond this life.[1]

TOLKIEN lavished love and praise and time on all his children, making each one feel special, but there is something in these words, written to Christopher during the Second World War, which speaks of the closeness of the bond between them. Like that of his father, Christopher's renown now rests firmly on the shores of Middle-earth, as the scholarly and dedicated editor of his father's unpublished literary manuscripts. But Christopher's first calling (like his father) was to academia, where he studied and edited Old Norse sagas with clarity and skill. His meticulous work on these medieval manuscripts clearly foreshadows his editorial role as his father's literary executor. In 1956 he wrote about a work of 'extraordinary diversity and wealth of material. Many things, of various age and atmosphere, have been sewn together to form a single narrative … the virtue of the work lies indeed not in its structural coherence but in its memorable scenes'. He might have been talking about his father's burgeoning epic, 'The Silmarillion', but in fact he was referring to a Norse saga, the 'most ancient of all extant Germanic heroic lays, the *Hervarar Saga*', for which he wrote this introduction.[2] He continued, 'the account has many inconsistencies and loose ends, and one sees that it would have taken a ruthless rewriting to get rid of them'. This was exactly the problem that he faced himself nearly twenty years later when he took on the role of editing his father's manuscripts and sought to bring 'The Silmarillion' into a publishable form. It is clear that his academic training as a medievalist was to serve him well in his new role. He employed the same

p.2 Christopher Tolkien at home, 2016. Taken by François Deladerrière.
From a private collection.

1.1 Christopher, aged three, asleep with his father in the garden, May 1928. With the rigours of full academic term and three young boys at home, Tolkien's long poem, *The Lay of Leithian*, which he had been working on during the Easter vacation, was now left untouched.
Oxford, Bodleian Library, MS. Tolkien photogr. 5, fol. 20.

close critical examination of multiple versions of the same text produced at different times, the same patient attention to detail as he deciphered rapidly written and sometimes illegible handwriting, and he brought the same linguistic skills to bear on his father's invented languages and scripts as he had on those from the medieval period.

Christopher summarized the scale of the task which lay before him in 1973:

> By the time of my father's death the amount of writing in existence on the subject of the Three Ages was huge in quantity (since it extended over a lifetime), disordered, more full of beginnings than of ends, and varying in content from heroic verse in the ancient English alliterative metre to severe historical analysis of his own extremely difficult languages: a vast repository and labyrinth of story, of poetry, of philosophy, and of philology. … To bring it into publishable form was a task at once utterly absorbing and alarming in its responsibility toward something that is unique.[3]

Alarm was a natural response from a devoted son and a conscientious editor but in fact Christopher was undoubtedly the only person who could have brought his father's legacy to publication so successfully and so faithfully. He had not only the critical academic training in ancient languages and literature but he had inhabited his father's fictional world from his earliest childhood onwards. As a small boy he sat on a footstool in his father's study and listened to the adventures of Bilbo Baggins and the dwarves, sometimes correcting his father when he changed important details such as the colour of Thorin's hood. Long before any tale of Middle-earth had been published, this world was part of Christopher's life: 'Strange as it sounds, I grew up in the world he created. For me, the cities of *The Silmarillion* have more reality than Babylon.'[4]

Christopher Tolkien's life and career
Christopher Reuel Tolkien was born on 21 November 1924 in Leeds, the third son of John Ronald Reuel Tolkien and

his wife Edith. The family moved back to Oxford (where the two elder boys had been born) in January 1926 and he was educated at the Dragon School, a preparatory school close to the family home in North Oxford. He was an able student and his strongest subjects were Latin, Greek, French and English. Despite having to sit his exam papers at home while recovering from an operation for appendicitis, he gained a scholarship to the Oratory School at Caversham Park near Reading, a Catholic boarding school where his two older brothers, John and Michael, had already preceded him. His academic work was of a sufficiently high standard that he started there a year earlier than was necessary, in September 1937, and had the benefit of his brother Michael, some four years older, to 'smooth his path'.[5] When he complained of being homesick, his father wrote, 'I suffer also from "sickness", dear one, – boy-sickness. I miss you very much.'[6] However, he remained at school only one term before being struck down with a heart condition at the beginning of 1938. He spent the following year virtually bedridden as an invalid and did not return to school for almost three years, being educated at home in the interim. This must have been a depressing and frustrating time for a young boy, cut off from friends and unable to take part in any normal physical activities. Initially his father gave him a special task to occupy his time – to find errata in the newly published *Hobbit* 'at twopence a time' – but as the months of illness turned into years, Christopher's literary assistance expanded to include reading, criticizing and typing out chapters of 'the new Hobbit' (as *The Lord of the Rings* was then known).[7] During this long period of ill health, it is certain that Christopher saw a great deal of his father, as a friend, a teacher and, crucially, as an author.

His father recognized from an early age that they shared a great 'degree of intellectual and imaginative sympathy'.[8] This extended beyond his father's literary work to his areas of academic expertise. When Christopher was only eleven years old, his father wrote to him about the BBC's radio broadcast of his translation of *Pearl*, an alliterative Middle English poem written in the fourteenth century: 'The "Pearl" was done very badly (I thought) on Friday night.'[9] This snippet gives a remarkable glimpse of the intellectual life shared by father and son, long before Christopher embarked on his own academic career.

Christopher returned to the Oratory School in 1940, when the future of the school hung in the balance. There were rumours that Reading (the closest town) would be bombed and in fact the town centre was bombed in February 1943 with a significant loss of life. Nevertheless, Christopher completed his final year of schooling unharmed, while at the same time his brother Michael trained with the Royal Air Force (RAF), evacuees were billeted in his family home and London was heavily bombed. He matriculated early at Trinity College, Oxford aged just seventeen, to read English. He was tutored at one time by C.S. Lewis, and also attended his own father's lectures. His studies were interrupted after eighteen months when he was called up for military service in July 1943. He joined the RAF and left for South Africa on New Year's Day 1944, to train as a pilot. He did not see his family for the next fifteen months. Within a year he had qualified as a fighter pilot, receiving his 'wings' and a commission in January 1945. During this gruelling time, with the ever-present threat of death, his father wrote to him constantly, and also began to send out typescript chapters of what became *The Lord of the Rings*. In many ways Christopher's pleasure in these instalments encouraged his father to keep writing, and he confessed, 'I don't think I should write any more, but for the hope of your seeing it.'[10] As the months passed Christopher's father found the separation and uncertainty almost unbearable. 'The time hangs like a stone on me, for my sons are dear to me and this one not the least,' he wrote to his friend, the poet and academic Gwyn Jones.[11] The longed-for news arrived in February 1945, with a letter from Christopher announcing that he had been posted home. 'Truly a red-letter morning', his father declared.[12] Christopher arrived home at Northmoor Road on Easter Saturday (31 March), and after a period of leave spent with his parents and his sister, Priscilla, in Aberystwyth, he was posted to Tern Hill, Market Drayton in Shropshire. In June 1945 he transferred to the Fleet Air Arm, the air force for the Royal Navy, and, although the war in Europe was over, his father

1.2 Christopher, aged twelve, at the family home, 20 Northmoor Road, Oxford, 1937. Although the garage behind him contains only bicycles, the family owned a car from 1932 until the introduction of petrol rationing during the Second World War made it too expensive to run.
Oxford, Bodleian Library, MS. Tolkien photogr. 24, fol. 28.

20 Northmoor Road,
Oxford.

Professor and Mrs. Tolkien

request the pleasure of your company
on Wednesday, November 21st, 1945,

to assist them in celebrating

the Coming of Age of their Son

Sub-Lieut. C. J. R. TOLKIEN, R.N.V.R.

6.30 p.m. onwards.   R.S.V.P. if not coming.

Carriages at midnight.   Ambulances at 2 a.m.
          Wheelbarrows at 5 a.m.   Hearses at daybreak.

previous page **1.3** Christopher (standing, centre), aged nineteen, with his RAF training squadron in South Africa, July 1944. The privations of military life were relieved somewhat by parcels from Oxford containing regular instalments of *The Lord of the Rings*. Oxford, Bodleian Library, MS. Tolkien photogr. 18, fol. 137.

above **1.4** Invitation to Christopher's 21st birthday, 21 November 1945. Guests were requested to depart by midnight or face the ignominy of 'Ambulances at 2 a.m.', 'Wheelbarrows at 5 a.m.' or more ominously 'Hearses at daybreak'. Oxford, Bodleian Library, Tolkien family papers.

now feared that Christopher would be sent to fight in the Far East: 'Fighter-pilot on an Aircraft-carrier in the Japan Seas is not quite what I should choose for my ablest and fieriest son.'[13]

The anxiety continued and even after the end of the war in September 1945, Christopher was not released from service but was kept busy in camp with military courses, or 'time-and-labour wasting eyewash', as his father called them.[14] He was missed not only by his family but by the Inklings, whose meetings he had attended as an undergraduate. 'I overheard CSL telling Mummy … that he and Warnie miss you and will be glad when you're a more regular feature of meetings,' his father told him.[15] The group preferred Christopher's readings of 'The Lord of the Rings', and soon afterwards made him a permanent member with independent rights of admission: 'a quite unprecedented honour', according to his father.[16]

Although still technically in the Navy he was allowed to resume his undergraduate studies at Trinity College in April 1946, and was finally demobilized at the end of that year. He now began to help his father again with his literary work, most notably by creating new maps for *The Lord of the Rings* from his father's draft sketch maps. A period of depression and ill health following a failed love affair led him to graduate with only a third-class degree in 1948, making his pursuit of an academic career a more difficult prospect. However, he completed a B.Litt. at Oxford between 1949 and 1953, under the supervision of E.O.G. Turville-Petre, producing a critical edition and translation of the Old Icelandic *Heiðreks Saga*. The high quality of his work led to its publication in 1960, and his extensive subject knowledge and aptitude for teaching meant that he was increasingly in demand as a tutor in Oxford.

During this time he became engaged to Faith Faulconbridge, an English graduate from St Anne's College,

1.5 Christopher and his father, pipes in hand, at 20 Northmoor Road, Oxford, 1945. Christopher had recently returned from South Africa and is wearing his RAF uniform with his hard-earned 'wings' visible above his left breast pocket.
Oxford, Bodleian Library, MS. Tolkien photogr. 6, fol. 15 (detail).

Oxford, who went on to become a successful sculptor. Her father, Frank 'Laddie' Faulconbridge, and J.R.R. Tolkien had been contemporaries at King Edward VI School, Birmingham and had played rugby together there. Faith was familiar with the Tolkien name having read and loved *The Hobbit* as a child. The couple married in London in April 1951 and settled in Oxford. They took summer holidays in Italy and the south of France, with Provence a favourite destination. In 1954 Christopher was appointed University Lecturer in English Language at St Catherine's Society, Oxford, and later at New College, Oxford. At the same time he worked as an English language tutor for various Oxford colleges, and his academic reputation continued to grow. His lectures on the Norse sagas in particular drew undergraduates from beyond the English faculty, attracted by his vivid style of presentation. In 1959 the couple's only son, Simon, was born.

Christopher was elected a Fellow of New College in 1963. Shortly afterwards his marriage began to fail, and he and Faith separated the same year. Faith and Simon continued to live in Oxfordshire and remained close members of the extended Tolkien family. Later Christopher met Baillie Klass, in Oxford. She was a Canadian scholar, 'both beautiful and highly qualified academically', who had attended McGill University and the University of Manitoba, and was studying for a Masters in English Language and Literature at St Hilda's College, Oxford.[17] She worked as Tolkien's secretary from 1965 to 1966 before leaving to work for the philosopher Isaiah Berlin. She and Christopher married in September 1967 and moved to a spacious Georgian house in the village of West Hanney, Berkshire, fourteen miles south-west of Oxford, where they had two children: Adam, born in 1969, and Rachel, in 1971. During this period Christopher collaborated with Nevill Coghill on various editions of Chaucer, which are still required reading for Oxford students today.

In 1967 Tolkien named Christopher as his literary executor and co-author of 'The Silmarillion', thereby acknowledging that he was unlikely to complete the work and giving his son the authority to finish and publish it. When he died in September 1973, Christopher was faced with a mass of manuscripts accumulated over more than fifty years of disconnected work on the First and Second Ages of Middle-earth. During 1974 and 1975 he began to work on the manuscripts at his home in West Hanney, transforming the barn into a large study space and sorting the papers on a huge dining table in the centre. He was helped by a young Canadian undergraduate and family friend, Guy Gavriel Kay (now a successful fantasy author). As the scale of the task became clear he resigned his Fellowship at New College in September 1975 to work full-time on his father's papers, and moved with his wife and younger children to France. They had always enjoyed holidays in the French countryside, and both he and Baillie were fluent French speakers. In France he was able to find the peace and, crucially, the privacy he needed to carry out his mission as literary executor.

He spent the next forty-five years working tirelessly on his father's papers, eventually bringing the complete legendarium of Middle-earth to publication. He died in France on 16 January 2020.

The Tolkiens and the Bodleian

The historic buildings of the Bodleian Library in central Oxford were a familiar landmark in Christopher's childhood, and the dome of the Radcliffe Camera, the circular reading room of the library, features prominently in a drawing from 'Father Christmas' received when he was eight years old. In the accompanying letter Father Christmas explains that the location of the Tolkien house is marked by three black lines, on the far right of the Oxford skyline. Christopher's formal relationship with the library began as an undergraduate when he 'illegally accorded' himself a seat in Duke Humfrey's Library, the fifteenth-century reading room, which was then strictly off-limits to undergraduates. Many times over the following years he had recourse to use the Bodleian's vast resources and hushed reading rooms, following in his father's footsteps up the winding stairs.

After his father's death, Christopher received a letter from David Vaisey, the library's Keeper of Western Manuscripts, keen to acquire Tolkien's literary manuscripts.

Vaisey wrote, 'As a reader, a curator of manuscripts, and as a fellow of Exeter College, I need no persuading of J.R.R. Tolkien's literary eminence … nothing would delight me more than if an example of J.R.R. Tolkien's work could find its permanent home here.'[18] Christopher was 'enormously pleased' with the suggestion and, after consultation with his brothers and sister, agreed that the Bodleian would be an eminently suitable home for his father's papers.[19] The first of numerous deposits was made in 1979, and the process was aided by Christopher's willingness to work from photocopies rather than originals, a decision which made his editorial work considerably more difficult, particularly when deciphering a difficult passage or attempting to date a page from the type of paper or writing implement used.

The Bodleian's pride in its association with the Tolkiens, both father and son, was confirmed by the award of the Bodley Medal to Christopher Tolkien in 2016, for his outstanding contribution to the world of literature. Richard Ovenden, Bodley's Librarian, described his editorial work as immense: 'Without his dedication and commitment, his father's works would not have reached such a broad public audience and without his erudition and scholarship J.R.R. Tolkien's work would not have been presented so fully and with such authority.'[20] Christopher accepted the award with characteristic humility, saying 'I have never looked for anything remotely of such a kind', but he acknowledged his pleasure on his father's behalf: 'it affirms the unique significance of my father's creation and accords a worthy place in the Republic of Letters to Tolkien scholarship.'[21] His last phrase acknowledges the international nature of Tolkien studies but also echoes Sir Thomas Bodley's vision of the Bodleian as a library not just for Oxford but for the whole scholarly world, 'the Republic of the Learned'.

1.6 This drawing by 'Father Christmas', 1932, features the dome of the Radcliffe Camera (one of the Bodleian's reading rooms) prominently in the centre.
Oxford, Bodleian Library, MS. Tolkien Drawings 57.

The history of Middle-earth

> Looking back over my work, now concluded after some
> forty years, I believe that my underlying purpose was
> at least in part to try to give more prominence to the
> nature of 'The Silmarillion' and its vital existence in
> relation to *The Lord of the Rings* – thinking of it rather
> as the *First Age* of my father's world of Middle-earth
> and Valinor.[22]

These words, from Christopher's preface to his final work,
The Fall of Gondolin, published in his ninety-fourth year,
summarize and simplify a quite astounding achievement.
The scale of his endeavour can best be seen in the
bibliography published here (see pp. 206–9), which lists
eighteen books relating to Middle-earth alone, as well as
scholarly editions of his father's work on *Beowulf*,
Sir Gawain and the Green Knight, *The Fall of Arthur* and
others. Although he confided to David Vaisey in 1976 that
'it looks to me as though the task will outlast me', this
proved not to be the case.[23] His work ethic was so prodigious
that he fulfilled his obligations as literary executor beyond
anyone's wildest expectations; never faltering in his
determination to publish his father's work 'in forms as
accessible and as accurate as I could make them'.[24]

The tale of Gondolin is a perfect example of what
Christopher Tolkien's extraordinary editorial efforts have
brought to light. *The Fall of Gondolin* was one of the first,
perhaps the very first, of the 'Great Tales' written by Tolkien
during the First World War but in his lifetime only brief
references to it appeared in his published works. The first
is found in *The Hobbit* (1937), when Elrond explains the
significance of the swords found in the trolls' cave:

> These are not troll-make. They are old swords, very old
> swords of the elves that are now called Gnomes, my
> kin. They were made in Gondolin for the Goblin-wars.
> They must have come from a dragon's hoard or goblin
> plunder, for dragons and goblins destroyed that city
> many ages ago. This, Thorin, the runes name Orcrist,

the Goblin-cleaver in the ancient tongue of Gondolin;
it was a famous blade. This, Gandalf, was Glamdring,
Foe-hammer that the king of Gondolin once wore.
Keep them well![25]

The words hint at ages past, at ancient languages no longer
spoken and great cities destroyed by evil races. They are
meant to thrill the reader, and they do, but they are not
just allusions created to give an impression of depth to this
children's story, but references to a weighty history which
Tolkien had been writing for over twenty years.

In *The Lord of the Rings* (1954–5) several more references
to Gondolin come to light, the first made once again by
Elrond: 'my memory reaches back even to the Elder Days.
Eärendil was my sire, who was born in Gondolin before its
fall.'[26] The second is in Gimli's song in the mines of Moria:

The world was fair, the mountains tall,
in Elder Days before the fall
Of mighty kings in Nargothrond
And Gondolin, who now beyond
The Western Seas have passed away:
The world was fair in Durin's Day.[27]

The third comes from Galadriel in Lothlórien: 'ere the fall of
Nargothrond or Gondolin I passed over the mountains, and
together through ages of the world we have fought the long
defeat'.[28] In all these passages, Gondolin is used as a byword
for antiquity, a once great place now long since passed away.
Further 'facts' are given in the appendices. 'Idril Celebrindal
was the daughter of Turgon, king of the hidden city of
Gondolin', and also the second Elf to marry a mortal Man,
a union which created the Half-elven.[29] Here we have actual
names and a royal lineage but this information raises more
questions than it answers: why was the city hidden, and how
and why did it fall?

Tolkien's contemporary readers had to be content with
these 'endless untold stories: mountains seen far away,
never to be climbed, distant trees (like Niggle's) never to be
approached'.[30] Today's readers have access to so much more;

they are the beneficiaries of Christopher Tolkien's painstaking editorial work spanning more than forty years. They can trace the evolution of this tale from the earliest version onwards: marvel at the beauty of the city rising up out of the mountain-circled plain, understand the treachery of Maeglin (the enemy within), oversee the city's final destruction by Orcs and Balrogs, and watch as desperate refugees flee across the plain.

Christopher's monumental legacy is the publication of the entire legendarium, placing the events of the Third Age, recounted in *The Hobbit* and *The Lord of the Rings*, into the context of the long and enthralling history of Arda. From his meticulous and skilful handling of his father's manuscripts, the First and Second Ages of Middle-earth have arisen. Readers can now look down on the whole of Tolkien's world from its creation by Ilúvatar to the fall of the Elves from paradise, their doomed struggle to retrieve the Silmarils, and the overthrow of Morgoth at the end of the First Age. They can chart the rise of the Númenóreans, the duplicity of Sauron as he encourages their hubris and the destruction of Númenor at the end of the Second Age. Not only can the whole history of Middle-earth, and the scale of Tolkien's vision, be appreciated but unforgettable passages of great narrative power have been brought to light.

The essays

This volume was planned as a *festschrift*, a collection of essays in honour of Christopher Tolkien. As such, contributors were invited to write about the work of both father and son, viewed from the vantage point of Christopher's final publication in 2018. Many chose to explore Christopher's contribution to our understanding of the whole legendarium while others took the opportunity to illuminate previously dark corners in the field of Tolkien studies, but the main intention was always that Christopher himself would enjoy reading them. Sadly events overtook us and the volume is now published in memory of Christopher and in appreciation of his immensely valuable work on his father's literary papers over many decades.

With the generosity of spirit she displayed throughout her life towards her father's legions of fans, **Priscilla Tolkien** contributed some personal reminiscences of her brother.

As the last of J.R.R. Tolkien's children and the closest in age to Christopher, she was able to give a precious first-hand account of life growing up in the Tolkien household.

The French poet and close family friend **Maxime Pascal** wrote a beautiful, moving and highly personal eulogy which was delivered at Christopher's funeral in January 2020. It has been translated for this volume by **Baillie Tolkien**, Christopher's wife and constant companion for fifty-three years.

Based on an in-depth analysis of the publications of Middle-earth, **Vincent Ferré** questions whether the term 'editor' is sufficient to encompass his work. He argues that Christopher's contribution went beyond the merely editorial and is sufficiently inventive and creative to be considered original literary work in its own right.

Verlyn Flieger begins by exploring Tolkien's description of *The Lord of the Rings* as 'a monster: an immensely long, complex, rather bitter, and very terrifying romance, quite unfit for children'. Her illuminating analysis of these words positions the book as the endpoint of Tolkien's legendarium, and examines how his projected but unused ending would have linked it back explicitly to his creation myth, *The Music of the Ainur*, written almost forty years earlier.

Taking up Christopher Tolkien's mantle as 'literary archaeologist', **John Garth** uses meticulous research to build a case for an earlier date of composition for *The Music of the Ainur*. Garth's research places its creation alongside the three 'Great Tales' written in 1916–17, and in doing so puts the tale of Middle-earth's genesis at the heart of the *Lost Tales*.

Wayne G. Hammond and Christina Scull's review of Tolkien's maps of Middle-earth and Arda shows clearly that his cartography was an integral part of his story-telling, and was indeed central to the development of his tales. As Tolkien wrote about Middle-earth, he mapped it as well. His maps were an indivisible part of the mythopoeic process as well as a means of authenticating the world he had created.

Using previously unpublished manuscripts, **Carl Hostetter** shows the range of problems facing the editor of Tolkien's work, from deciphering his 'challenging and sometimes defeating handwriting' to prising clues from the materiality of the texts in order to date them. In this editorial masterclass Hostetter reveals the meticulous and painstaking work undertaken by Christopher Tolkien as he brought his father's manuscripts into a publishable form.

Delving into the BBC's archives, **Stuart Lee** reconstitutes a lost radio production of *The Lord of the Rings*. This was the first dramatization of the work, and the first six episodes were written before all three volumes had even been published. In the essay Lee not only looks at Tolkien's response to the adaptation, the actors and their accents but also unearths the views of listeners, recorded by the BBC's Audience Research Department.

Tom Shippey explores Tolkien's unfinished time-travel story 'The Lost Road', looking for clues as to how it might have been completed and seeking answers in the related poem 'King Sheave', which was to have been part of 'The Lost Road' tale. He finds fertile ground in Tolkien's lectures on *Beowulf*, and sets out the connections between the Anglo-Saxon epic and Tolkien's projected work.

Brian Sibley's journey with the hobbits through the doorways of Middle-earth lays bare the extraordinary number and variety of portals used by Tolkien in *The Hobbit* and *The Lord of the Rings*. He explores the meaning and significance of doorways in Tolkien's work, revealing their importance as indicators of what lies beyond but also the role they play in the personal growth of individual characters.

The great tales never end

Rayner Unwin, 'the original hobbiteer', a supporter of J.R.R. Tolkien's work from childhood onwards, a contemporary of Christopher's at Oxford, and a publisher throughout his life of both father and son, summarized Christopher's achievements thus: 'no other author has ever had the advantage of a literary executor with the sympathy, the scholarship, and the humility to devote half a lifetime to the task of unobtrusively giving shape to his own father's creativity. In effect one man's imaginative genius has had the benefit of two lifetimes' work.'[31] The field of Tolkien studies would have been very thin indeed without Christopher

Tolkien's unstinting work as editor: a lasting gift to the world.

> [Sam] 'Why, to think of it, we're in the same tale still!
> It's going on. Don't the great tales never end?'
>   'No, they never end as tales,' said Frodo. 'But the
> people in them come, and go when their part's ended.'[32]

Christopher Reuel Tolkien ∴ 1924–2020 ∴ Man of Letters.

TIMELINE

1924	21 November: Born in Leeds.
1929-30	Listens to 'The Hobbit' told by his father in instalments in the evenings.
c.1932–37	Educated at the Dragon School, Oxford.
1937	Gains a scholarship to the Oratory School, Caversham Park, Michaelmas term.
1938–40	Educated at home due to ill-health.
1940	Michaelmas term: Returns to the Oratory School.
1942	January: Matriculates at Trinity College, Oxford.
1943	July: Enlists in the Royal Air Force.
1944–45	Trains as a fighter pilot in South Africa.
1945	March: Posted home and stationed with the RAF at Tern Hill, Shropshire.
1945	June: Transfers to the Fleet Air Arm.
1946	April: Resumes undergraduate studies at Trinity College, Oxford.
1946	December: Discharged from the Fleet Air Arm.
1948	December: Graduates B.A. at Oxford.
1949	Awarded M.A. at Oxford.
1949	Michaelmas term: Commences B.Litt. under E.O.G. Turville-Petre.
1950	Works as a freelance tutor in Oxford.
1950	Announces engagement to Faith Faulconbridge.
1951	2 April: marries Faith Faulconbridge in London.
1953	Michaelmas term: Awarded B.Litt. for an edition and translation of *Heiðreks Saga*.
1954–59	University Lecturer in English, St. Catherine's Society, Oxford.
1957	Appointed lecturer in English Language at New College, Oxford.
1958	Publication of Geoffrey Chaucer, *The Pardoner's Tale*, co-edited with Nevill Coghill.
1959	12 January: Birth of son, Simon.
1959–64	Lecturer in English Language, University College, Oxford.
1959–75	University Lecturer in English, New College, Oxford.
1959	Publication of Geoffrey Chaucer, *The Nun's Priest's Tale*, co-edited with Nevill Coghill.
1960	Publication of his translation and edition of *The Saga of King Heidrek the Wise*.
1963	October: Elected Fellow of New College, Oxford and lecturer in English Language.
1967	Divorced from Faith.
1967	18 September: Marries Baillie Klass.
1969	3 March: Birth of son, Adam.
1969	Publication of Geoffrey Chaucer, *The Man of Law's Tale*, co-edited with Nevill Coghill.
1971	13 February: Birth of daughter Rachel.
1973	2 September: Death of his father, J.R.R. Tolkien, in Bournemouth.
1974–5	Begins work on the first version of 'The Silmarillion'.

1975	Publication of his edition of J.R.R. Tolkien, *Sir Gawain and the Green Knight, Pearl and Sir Orfeo.*	1988	Publication of his edition of J.R.R. Tolkien, *The Return of the Shadow.*
1975	September: Resigns Fellowship of New College, Oxford.	1989	Publication of his edition of J.R.R. Tolkien, *The Treason of Isengard.*
1975	September: Moves to France and begins to edit his father's papers full-time.	1990	Publication of his edition of J.R.R. Tolkien, *The War of the Ring.*
1977	Publication of his edition of J.R.R. Tolkien, *The Silmarillion.*	1992	Publication of his edition of J.R.R. Tolkien, *Sauron Defeated.*
1979	Publication of *Pictures by J.R.R. Tolkien.*	1993	Publication of his edition of J.R.R. Tolkien, *Morgoth's Ring.*
1980	Publication of his edition of J.R.R. Tolkien, *Unfinished Tales of Númenor and Middle-earth.*	1994	Publication of his edition of J.R.R. Tolkien, *The War of the Jewels.*
1981	Publication of *The Letters of J.R.R. Tolkien,* edited by Humphrey Carpenter with Christopher Tolkien's assistance.	1996	Publication of his edition of J.R.R. Tolkien, *The Peoples of Middle-earth.*
1983	Publication of his edition of J.R.R Tolkien, *The Monsters and the Critics and Other Essays.*	2007	Publication of his edition of J.R.R. Tolkien, *Narn I Chîn Húrin: The Tale of the Children of Húrin.*
1983	Publication of his edition of J.R.R. Tolkien, *The Book of Lost Tales, Part I.*	2009	Publication of his edition of J.R.R. Tolkien, *The Legend of Sigurd and Gudrún.*
1984	Publication of his edition of J.R.R. Tolkien, *The Book of Lost Tales, Part II.*	2013	Publication of his edition of J.R.R. Tolkien, *The Fall of Arthur.*
1985	Publication of his edition of J.R.R. Tolkien, *The Lays of Beleriand.*	2014	Publication of his edition of J.R.R. Tolkien, *Beowulf: A Translation and Commentary together with Sellic Spell.*
1986	Publication of his edition of J.R.R. Tolkien, *The Shaping of Middle-earth.*	2016	Awarded the Bodley Medal.
1987	Publication of his edition of J.R.R. Tolkien, *The Lost Road and Other Writings.*	2017	Publication of his edition of J.R.R. Tolkien, *Beren and Lúthien.*
		2018	Publication of his edition of J.R.R. Tolkien, *The Fall of Gondolin.*
		2020	16 January: Dies aged 95 in France.

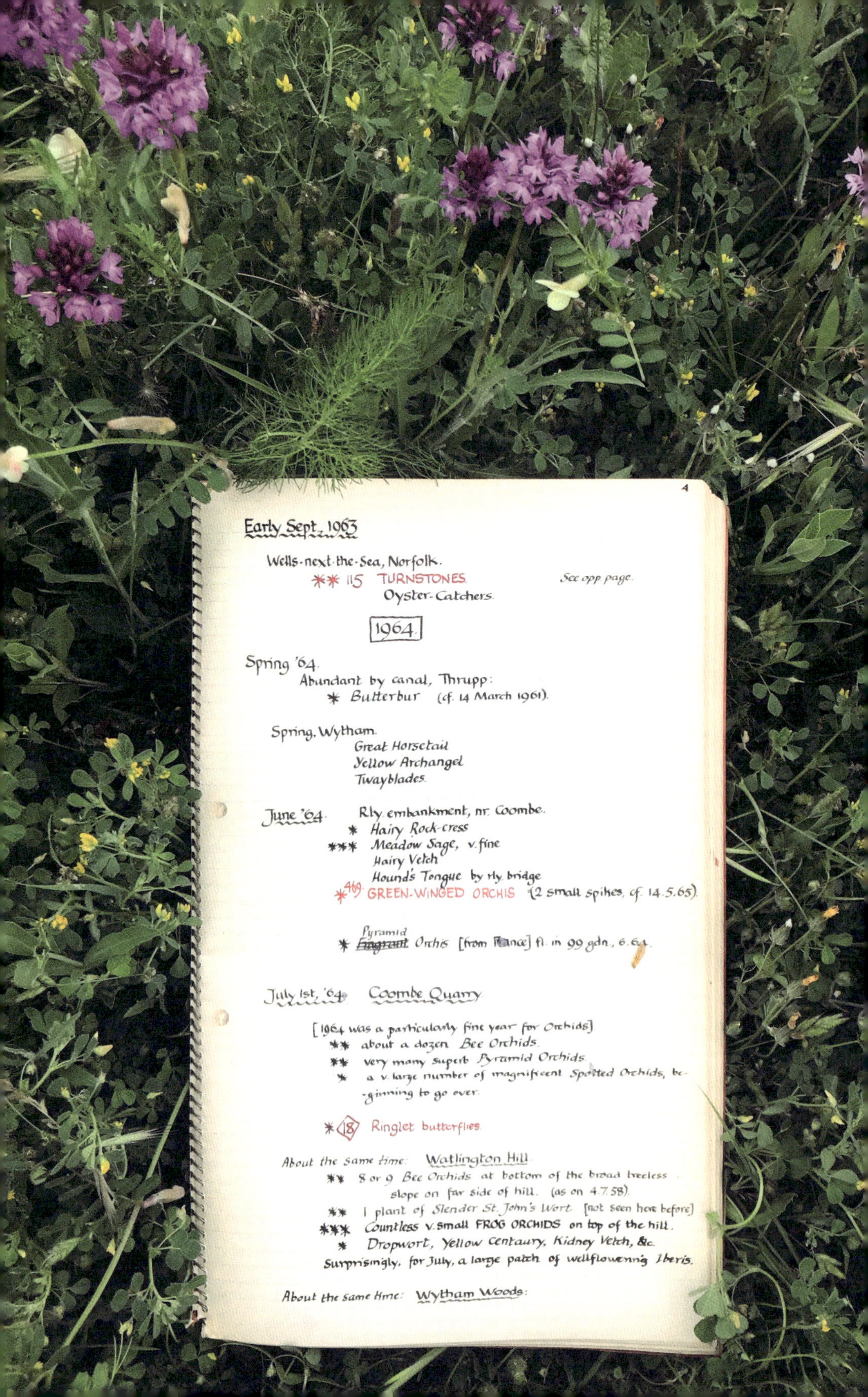

Early Sept., 1963

Wells-next-the-Sea, Norfolk.
** 115 TURNSTONES.   See opp. page.
Oyster-Catchers.

1964.

Spring '64.
Abundant by canal, Thrupp:
* Butterbur (cf. 14 March 1961).

Spring, Wytham.
Great Horsetail.
Yellow Archangel.
Twayblades.

June '64.   Rly. embankment, nr. Coombe.
* Hairy Rock-cress
*** Meadow Sage, v. fine
Hairy Vetch
Hound's Tongue by rly. bridge
*469 GREEN-WINGED ORCHIS (2 small spikes, cf. 14.5.65).

Pyramid
* ~~Fragrant~~ Orchis [from ~~France~~] fl. in 99 gdn., 6.64.

July 1st, '64   Coombe Quarry

[1964 was a particularly fine year for Orchids]
** about a dozen Bee Orchids.
** very many superb Pyramid Orchids.
* a v. large number of magnificent Spotted Orchids, be-
-ginning to go over.

*18 Ringlet butterflies

About the same time: Watlington Hill
** 8 or 9 Bee Orchids at bottom of the broad treeless
slope on far side of hill. (as on 4.7.58).
** 1 plant of Slender St. John's Wort [not seen here before]
*** Countless v. small FROG ORCHIDS on top of the hill.
* Dropwort, Yellow Centaury, Kidney Vetch, &c.
Surprisingly, for July, a large patch of well-flowering Iberis.

About the same time: Wytham Woods:

Maxime H. Pascal

EULOGY

2

Delivered in French at CHRISTOPHER TOLKIEN's Funeral

*Parfois les mots se taisent et ce n'est
pas le silence*

Il manque un battement au cœur

L'aube ne voudrait pas se lever

*Christopher vient de s'endormir, toute
la chair du monde en est changée*

*Les oiseaux ne le savent pas encore, ni
la rosée sur les canopées*

*Mais Deneb et Vega sont là, au
Nord de la Grande Ourse, Cassioppé
s'attarde et sans aucun doute l'étoile
Polaire t'attendait*

*Cet horizon stellaire tu l'as si souvent
partagé*

*L'été était accueillant dans les champs
sonores et nocturnes où allongé
dans l'herbe tu aimais indiquer les
ressources de l'esprit qui sont écrites
dans le ciel*

*C'est que tu as regardé le monde en
face, la lumière le traverse*

*C'est important la lumière, c'est une
consolation*

*Tu as dialogué avec elle depuis la
source simple et souveraine qui
respirait en toi*

*Cette lumière intérieure dont tu as été
le passeur ne te quitta jamais*

*Tu l'as servi avec une fidélité qui ne
connut aucune éclipse*

2.1 A page from one of
Christopher's botanical
notebooks, kept meticulously
throughout his life, recording 'a
particularly fine year for Orchids'
in Oxfordshire, July 1964. Taken
by Baillie Tolkien.
From a private collection.

Lorsque ta réflexion creusait des questionnements de haute portée, tu demandais à chacune de tes pensées, de tes gestes ce supplément d'être qui pouvait embellir la compréhension et rendre éloge à la vie

Tu as été ce seuil incarné où les philologies anciennes venaient bruisser leurs ailes dans les langues de féeries constructives pour instruire de solides concepts

Ta sollicitude les a transmises et rendues accessibles

Tu as été le protecteur, la sentinelle et le gardien de sapiences qui s'effacent et qui participèrent aux questions concrètes que l'humanité ne cesse de se donner

C'est que ton érudition aussi rare que généreuse a traversé des siècles de connaissance et de savoirs, faisant de toi le témoin irremplaçable et précieux d'époques disparues tout en interrogeant avec acuité la modernité

Ta présence vigile fut cette inlassable lueur dans l'obscurité des jungles d'aujourd'hui

Dans le présent de la mémoire, tu souris et le monde s'ouvre

Ton sourire d'accueil, d'humour, de connivence, d'émerveillement, je le garde

La lumière dans ton regard, je la garde

Ce regard venu de l'observation
rêveuse et perspicace de la course
du temps vient du monde aîné de la
contemplation, cet exercice patient
de l'esprit que tu as quotidiennement
pratiqué pour relever l'exactitude des
éléments du réel, recenser la beauté du
monde afin de lui donner une chance
de poursuivre, déchiffrer les signes,
les indices, les formes, les fleurs, les
insectes, les champignons, les oiseaux,
les personnes, tous ces immenses
chapitres à relier pour éclaircir
l'énigme du monde par la lecture du
visible

Lire la nature, cette spacieuse
bibliothèque, lire les sagas du
Septentrion, lire la cartographie de
la Terre du Milieu, lire les parcours
imaginaires et rectifier les chemins
creux de ceux qui errent et ne sont pas
perdus

Lire et lire et relire les manuscrits
qui ressemblent quelques fois à des
palimpsestes

Lire entre les lignes interrompues, les
branches abandonnées et composer
des phrases à l'écriture cristalline pour
accorder les fragments et les traces

Lire inlassablement une œuvre,
veiller à son chevet quelles que soient
les tempêtes, en gardant intact ton
appétit du lien inattendu, de la
prochaine découverte

*Lire avec sagacité et finesse pour
préserver les étincelles d'intelligences
et arpenter les sentiers ouverts par la
poésie*

*Lire, depuis ta bienveillance, dans le
cœur des autres*

*La lecture fut pour toi une exploration
questionnée, un privilège décisif*

*Tu es resté ce plus jeune et premier
lecteur de ton père dont tu as
augmenté le bonheur de vivre en te
révélant au fil des années ce complice
sensible et ce compagnon de création
doué de discernement subtil et de
cette profondeur de vue singulière
que tu ne cessas de déployer dans
l'approfondissement du langage*

*Ce champ infini de ta curiosité vive,
le point de départ de ta première
escapade hors de réalités absurdement
nommées*

*Ton voyage fut inépuisable à la
recherche du mot juste, congruent,
celui qui délivre le sens et déplie une
joie pour célébrer la splendeur des
êtres et réjouir l'intellect*

*La lumière de Christopher toujours
est un élan appelé à faire aller et
retour*

*On parlera très longtemps de ton
travail magistral, unique dans
l'histoire de la littérature, de ta
modestie infaillible, pour ne pas*

*dire ton humilité, de l'éminente et
minutieuse et amoureuse tâche de
chacun de tes jours où ta conscience
vigilante était requise pour réunir ce
qui avait été laissé séparé*

*Du monde de Tolkien, les livres
fondateurs avaient été édités*

*Ils prospéraient tels de très grands
arbres, mais c'est toi qui a révélé la
forêt*

*Une œuvre dans une œuvre dans la
grandeur de l'existant, voilà ce qui
s'est passé*

*Cependant la plus verticale de toute,
la plus essentielle, le centre vital et
rayonnant de tes jours et de tes nuits,
est dans l'heure qui vient à inventer la
vie avec Baillie*

*Elle est ton Nord, ton Est, ton Ouest, le
sol sous tes pieds, ton horizon absolu,
la pulpe de chaque minute, la voix qui
sait te répondre, l'air que tu respires*

Elle est l'or de tes jours, ton ciel étoilé

*Lorsque ta pensée élégante déplora la
trajectoire du monde occidentalisé et
la maudite invention de la roue qui
nous menace de la domination des
machines, Baillie, ton rempart contre
le pessimisme persuasif, saura dissiper
les ombres et les rendre fugitives*

*La fin du jour se déploie, tu es assis
près de la fenêtre, ton profil est tourné
vers le grand dehors où se tiennent les
interrogations qui comptent*

Quelle est la direction du vent, celles des nuages, la pluie est-elle en route vers le champ d'oliviers, quelle est l'intention de cette phalène, quel est le songe en approche

Tu te rappelles avoir pisté la lumière dans les pierres romanes, la naissance des vingt trois espèces d'orchidées sauvages, le désir des papillons, la puissance de l'ouest au crépuscule, l'éclosion des boutons d'or sous le pont romain dans cette vallée de Vidauban que tu contribuas à sauver d'une exploitation minière délétère, en révélant et cataloguant la spécificité de sa flore

Petites fleurs joyaux que tu étudiais et photographiais avec ferveur

Tu as tellement chéri l'univers de la végétation spontanée et sans hiérarchie

Tu restes immobile et pensif, tu espères le vol d'un geai, l'appel du petit duc, le passage du renard vespéral, les nouvelles des collines

Ces évènements considérables sont parmi les rendez-vous discrets de tes journées

Bientôt tu diras 'I think it's time for a drink'

Le soir s'installe, tu rejoins la cheminée, c'est l'heure de la disposition des pommes de pin, la préparation du feu, le temps de la conversation que tu élèves au rang d'art de vivre

Les enfants sont là et les petits-enfants, les merveilleux petits-enfants

Tu constates que merveilleux est cet adjectif que tu utilises le plus souvent en anglais et en français

Les amis vivants et morts visitent la douceur dans l'air

A nouveau, tu te mets à sourire, le front clair légèrement penché

Une conclusion remarquable vient à ta rencontre, elle te murmure jusqu'au bout de la nuit que tu n'as jamais usé d'une langue étrangère mais seulement parlé et connu et vécu et partagé un seul langage, trésor inépuisable que tu nous laisses en héritage et qui se nomme l'amour

Lorsque les choucas se sont mis à dessiner des pistes d'envol par-delà la fenêtre, tu te rappelles avoir noté qu'à la Carrière de Coombe, début juin 1964, il y avait des Bee Orchids, des Pyramid Orchids, des Yellow Rattle, des Meadow Sage, des Woolly Thistles, des Yellow Archangels, des Lamb's Lettuce, et des Marsh Marigolds en bord de rivière

Tu te souviens du théâtre des peluches
et des batailles d'oursons Red Ted

Tu te souviens des belles assemblées,
de tous les rires, des traits d'esprit,
des country folk songs, de chacune de
tes lettres écrite dans le silence animé
de la maison où tu entrais dans le
temps infini de la lucidité active afin
qu'aucune de tes phrases ne puisse
blesser le monde

L'amour ne tient pas en place

Il est inespéré, il est libre, il est vivant

2.2 Christopher, aged 81, at work in his study in France, May 2006. He wrote without the aid of a computer, which points to both a prodigious memory and astonishing intellectual and organizational abilities. *The Tale of the Children of Húrin* was published the following year. Taken by Georgia Klass.
From a private collection.

Sometimes words cease and it is not silence

What is missing is a heartbeat

Dawn will not come

Christopher has just gone to sleep, all the flesh of the world has changed

The birds don't know it yet, nor does the dew on the treetops

But Deneb and Vega are there, to the north of the Great Bear, Cassiopeia tarries, and there's no doubt the Pole Star was waiting for you

The stellar horizon you so often shared

The summer was welcoming in the sonorous nightime fields where stretched out in the grass you liked to point out the resources of the spirit that are written in the sky

You looked the world in the face, the light shines through it

It is important, the light, it is a consolation

You conversed with it from the simple and sovereign source that breathed within you

That interior light of which you were the ferryman never left you

You served it with a loyalty that knew no eclipse

When your reflection delved into questions of high import, you asked of each of your thoughts, each of your gestures this supplement of being, that could embellish understanding and give praise to life

You incarnated that threshold where
ancient philologies rustled their wings
in the tongues of faierie that enhance the
teaching of solid concepts

Your solicitude transmitted them and
rendered them accessible

You were the protector, the sentinel and
the guardian of knowledge that is fading
away and which participated in concrete
questions that humanity never ceases to
ask itself

Your erudition, so rare and generous,
covered centuries of knowledge and
learning, making you the irreplaceable and
precious witness of vanished epochs while
sharply questioning modernity

Your guardian presence was that
unflagging light in the darkness of the
jungles of today

In present memory, you smile and the
world opens

Your smile of welcome, of humour, of
complicity, of wonder, this I keep

The light in your eyes, this I keep

This light arising from the dreamy and
perceptive observation of the passage
of time comes from the elder world of
contemplation, this patient exercise of the
spirit that you practised daily to determine
the exactitude of the elements of reality,
record the beauty of the world in order to
give it a chance to carry on, decipher the
signs, the clues, the shapes, the flowers,
the insects, the mushrooms, the birds,

the people, all these immense chapters to bind together to clarify the enigma of the world by the reading of the visible

To read nature, that spacious library, read the sagas of the North, read the cartography of Middle Earth, read the imaginary courses and the deep pathways of those who wander and are not lost

To read and read and reread the manuscripts that sometimes resemble palimpsests

To read between the uninterrupted lines, the abandoned branches, and compose sentences of crystalline writing to match fragments and traces

To read unflaggingly a written work, keep watch by its side whatever the storms, keeping intact your appetite for the unexpected link, the next discovery

To read with sagacity and finesse to preserve the sparks of intelligences and roam the paths opened by poetry

To read, from your benevolence, into the heart of others

Reading was for you a questioned exploration, a decisive privilege

You remained that youngest and first reader of your father whose joy of living you increased by revealing yourself over the years as the sensitive accomplice and companion in creation gifted with subtle discernment and that singular depth of vision that you never ceased to deploy in the enhancement of language

The infinite field of your keen curiosity, the starting point of your first escapade away from absurdly named realities

Your voyage was inexhaustible in its
search for *le mot juste*, congruent, that
which delivers meaning and unfolds a joy
to celebrate the splendour of beings and
delight the intellect

Christopher's light is ever an impulse to go
there and back again

It will long be spoken of your masterly
work, unique in the history of literature,
of your unfailing modesty, not to say your
humility, of the eminent and meticulous
and loving task of each of your days where
your watchful consciousness was required
to reunite what had been left scattered

Of the world of Tolkien, the founding
books had been published

They prospered like tall trees, but it is you
who revealed the forest

A work within a work in the grandeur of
the existent: that is what came about

Meanwhile the most vertical of all, the
most essential, the vital and shining centre
of your days and your nights is in the hour
that came to invent life with Baillie

She is your North, your East, your West,
the earth under your feet, your absolute
horizon, the substance of each minute, the
voice that knows to answer you, the air
you breathe

She is the gold of your days, your starry sky

When your elegant thought deplored the
trajectory of the westernized world and the
cursed invention of the wheel that threatens

us with the domination of the machine, Baillie,
your rampart against persuasive pessimism,
knew how to dissipate the shadows and render
them fugitive

The end of the day unfurls, you're seated near the
window, your profile is turned towards the great
outdoors, where linger the questions that matter

What is the direction of the wind, the clouds, is
the rain heading for the olive field, what is the
intent of that moth, what dream approaches

You remember having tracked the light in the
romanesque stones, the revelation of twenty-
three species of wild orchids, the desire of
butterflies, the power of the west at dusk, the
blooming of buttercups under the Roman bridge
in that plain of Vidauban you helped save from
the threat of a mine by revealing and cataloguing
its remarkable flora

Small flower jewels that you studied and
photographed with fervour

You so cherished the universe of spontaneous
vegetation without hierarchy

You remain still and pensive, you hope for the
flight of a jay, the call of the Scops Owl, the
passage of an evening fox, news of the hills

These important events are among the discreet
appointments of your days

Soon you will say 'I think it's time for a drink'

The evening settles in, you go over to the
chimney, it's time to place the pinecones, prepare
the fire, time for the conversation that you raise
to the level of an art of living

The children are there and the
grandchildren – the marvellous
grandchildren

You note that marvellous is the adjective
that you use most often, in English and
in French

Friends living and dead visit the softness in
the air

Again you smile, your clear forehead slightly
inclined

A remarkable conclusion comes to you, it
murmurs to you till the end of the night
that you have never made use of a foreign
language but only spoken and known
and lived and shared a single language,
inexhaustible treasure that you leave to us as
a heritage and which is named love

When the jackdaws began to draw flight
paths beyond the window, you remember
noting that at Coombe Quarry, in early
June 1964, there were Bee Orchids, Pyramid
Orchids, Yellow Rattle, Meadow Sage,
Woolly Thistles, Yellow Archangel, Lamb's
Lettuce and Marsh Marigold by river's edge

You remember the Red Ted theatre and the
battles of the stuffed animals

You remember the happy gatherings, all the
laughter, the wit, the country folk songs,
each of your letters written in the animated
silence of the house where you entered the

infinite time of active lucidity so that none of your
phrases could wound the world

Love does not stand still

It is unhoped-for, it is free, it is alive

following page **2.3** 'I believe
when Chris turned the scaled
sketch into the beautiful new
map he sat at it from 9 p.m.
to 6 a.m. continuous!' In this
letter to a family friend, J.R.R.
Tolkien describes the map
drawn by Christopher Tolkien
for publication in *The Return of
the King*, 1955.
Oxford, Bodleian Library,
25615 d.33

ROHAN

= Entwade

* Dunharrow
* EDORAS

Snowbourn

Falls of Rauros

FOLDE

EASTFOLD

N.I.

We

ERED

Great West Road

River ENTWASH

Border of Rohan

MOUTHS of

* MORTHOND

ERECH

Tarlang's Neck

NIMRAIS

FENMARCH

MERING STREAM

* Halifirien

?? FIRIEN WOOD

ENTWASH

ANÓRIE

LAMEDON

River KIRIL

* Calembel

Calenhad

Min-Rimmon

Erelas

Nard

RINGLO

River

* Ethring

River KELOS

R. Sie

GONDOR

LEBENNI

Dor-en-Ernil

River GILRAIN

River SIRITH

Linhir

River SERNI

Belfalas

ETHIR ANDUIN

[Mouths of Anduin]

Miles   Scale
        10   20   30   40   50   60

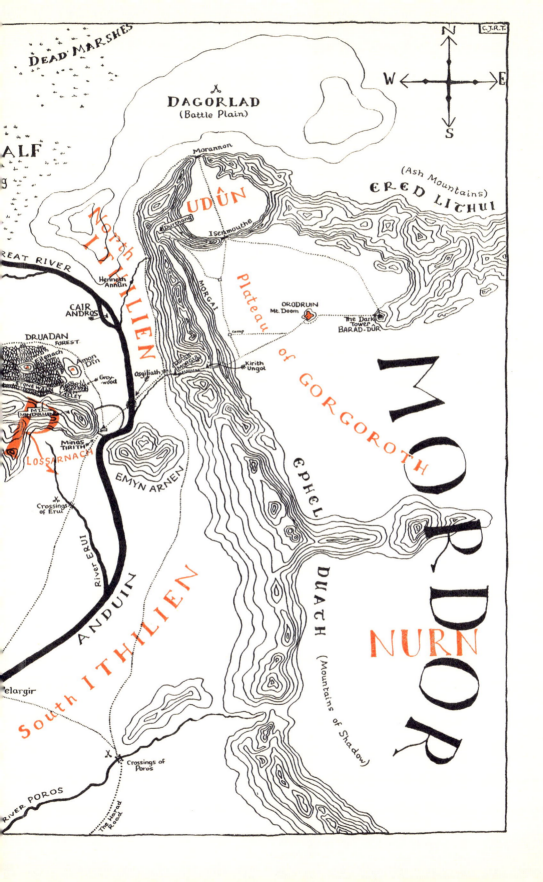

Ernest Hall Oxford

Priscilla Tolkien

A PERSONAL MEMORY

3

M Y RELATIONSHIP with my brother, Christopher, goes back in my memory to the early 1930s, to the years before I went to school when we shared the nursery at 20 Northmoor Road. This period was marked by a strong sense of territory, and conflicts inevitably arose over sharing the nursery table and the shelves in the toy cupboard.

As he was four and a half years older his life was increasingly lived in the outside world and so differed from mine, but we continued to share much imaginative life and play around my toys and in the excitement in the weeks before Christmas as we wrote letters to Father Christmas. On Christmas Eve we chose stockings under our father's guidance, and on Christmas morning shared the discoveries in our stockings and our pleasure in receiving an illustrated letter from Father Christmas with news from the North Pole.

As time went on, we shared some of the excitement outside the nursery, and I became aware of the growing intensity of his interests, in particular in the natural world. Even in his boyhood his knowledge of plants and flowers was considerable, with the result that he has for many years been an impressive botanist. One incident from more recent years struck me forcibly, when he described a hawk moth basking in the sun outside his study window in France and how such an experience helped him to 'cope with the beauty of the world' (his phrase).

Our father took both of us on botanical expeditions around Oxford, and a special excitement was discovering the bee orchid, then I think an uncommon species. I believe that Christopher always maintained a particular interest in orchids.

During this period of our growing up I also became aware of his interest in weather and in aspects of astronomy, particularly the stars. This became significant when he was given a telescope, which he used constantly, and which

3.1 Priscilla and Christopher (aged five) taken in Oxford on Priscilla's first birthday, 18 June 1930.
Oxford, Bodleian Library, MS. Tolkien photogr. 18, fol. 1.

encouraged his interest in flying.[1] An extremely dramatic event we shared was seeing an RAF Lancaster bomber on a fine Sunday afternoon in May 1941, flying low over us on a training exercise, catch fire and crash at the bottom of the next road, killing all the crew but, amazingly in a heavily populated residential area, only one civilian.[2] Christopher was watching the whole event through his telescope and later remarked on what an effect this had had on him.

It was no surprise, therefore, as his call-up time approached that he applied to join the RAF and then trained as a fighter pilot, first in this country and then in South Africa, where he remained for about a year, returning in the spring of 1945, when the war in Europe was coming to an end.

It was a big change in family life while Christopher was overseas, but his absence was eased by his letters: there was a type of letter, an aerograph, which was photographed, thus reduced in weight and carried by air. Here I think he developed his gift for letter-writing, which over the years he has used generously.

A·Merry·Christmas

3.4 Christopher, Priscilla and
Michael on the promenade
at Weston-super-Mare,
during their last holiday taken
together as a family, 11 April
1940. Christopher had recently
returned to school after an
absence of two years due to a
heart condition.
Oxford, Bodleian Library,
MS. Tolkien photogr. 18, fol. 118.

3.5 Christopher, aged twenty, in his black and gold Fleet Air Arm uniform, July 1945. His father kept this photograph framed on his mantelpiece. Oxford, Bodleian Library, MS. Tolkien photogr. 24, fol. 49.

One of my most vivid memories of growing up was Christopher's return home from South Africa after a long and difficult journey by sea.[3] He arrived back in Oxford early in the morning, and from my window I saw him walking down the road towards our house carrying a very heavy kit bag.[4] His return had been prepared for by the arrival of an immensely weighty cabin trunk, together with parcels of food, deeply welcome at a time when we were still strictly rationed, so there was of course great excitement on many levels![5]

Another powerful memory I have from his undergraduate student days was when he became absorbed with reading Milton and decided to learn some of *Paradise Lost* by heart. I can still hear his voice at the top of the long garden at Northmoor Road clearly audible from the entrance of the garden, declaiming the grandeur of the blank verse.

In succeeding years, Christopher's giving up his academic career in order to take up the role of our father's literary executor inspired my continuing admiration for his dedication and scholarship. He showed a great ability in conveying his considerable learning in works of clarity and disciplined enthusiasm, which have already received distinguished academic recognition, but now with the publication of a volume in his honour I am delighted to have been asked to write this memoir.

4.1 Christopher in 2009. Taken by Bob Cohn.
From a private collection.

Vincent Ferré

THE SON BEHIND THE FATHER 4

CHRISTOPHER TOLKIEN AS A WRITER

And whether all these tales be feigned,
or whether some at least be true, and by
them the Valar still keep alight among
Men a memory beyond the darkness
of Middle-earth, thou knowest now,
Ælfwine, in thyself. Yet haply none shall
believe thee.[1]

T HIS ESSAY considers Christopher Tolkien's
achievement as a writer in his own right, and not
only as an 'editor' of his father's manuscripts, as he
has often been presented.[2] My hypothesis is that his own texts
in the *History of Middle-earth* series, in *The Silmarillion* and
in his last published volumes (*The Fall of Gondolin, Beren
and Lúthien*) qualify as literature, for two main reasons. The
first is his style and the choices he made in 'constructing' *The
Silmarillion* as a narrative, which will be examined according
to Gérard Genette's conception of 'conditional literarity'.[3]
The second is related to the presence of a fictional dimension
in his writings: Christopher Tolkien had to invent elements
when the narrative was deficient or threads were impossible
to weave together.

In such a prolific list of publications, from 1975 (*Sir
Gawain and the Green Knight*) to 2018 (*The Fall of Gondolin*),
distinctions have to be made. In *The Silmarillion* (1977),
Christopher Tolkien edited his father's manuscripts but he
also wrote some parts, especially in the last chapters of the
volume. In the *History of Middle-earth* series (1983–96), he
edited and commented on the original material according to
'a general principle'[4] but he also created a sort of biography of
a work in progress. This constitutes a common point with the
third group of volumes – *Beren and Lúthien* (2017) and *The
Fall of Gondolin* (2018) – in which he assembles a puzzle and
guides the reader through a narrative.[5]

In the beginning: the father, the son and
The Silmarillion

The partnership formed by Christopher and J.R.R. Tolkien is unique in our modern literary history, and much has been said on the former's extraordinary achievement as an editor of the *Unfinished Tales of Númenor and Middle-earth* (1980) and of *The History of Middle-earth* series, to name only a few of his publications. In the case of *The Silmarillion*, at the start of his forty-five-year-long enterprise, the real nature of Christopher Tolkien's work was a matter of debate, before a more simplistic consensus began to prevail.

Indeed, as early as 1981, commenting upon the publication of *Unfinished Tales*, Randel Helms reckoned that 'its relationship to [*The Silmarillion*] provides what will become a classic example of a long-standing problem in literary criticism: what, really, *is* a literary work? Is it what the author intended (or may have intended) it to be, or is it what a later editor makes of it?' As Helms argues, the authorship is clear: '*The Silmarillion* in the shape that we have it is the invention of the son not the father.'[6] What Helms considers as an unequivocal statement on this matter by Christopher Tolkien is to be found in his foreword to *The Silmarillion*:

> It became clear to me that to attempt to present, within the covers of a single book, the diversity of the materials – to show *The Silmarillion* as in truth a continuing and evolving creation extending over more than half a century – would in fact lead only to confusion and the submerging of what is essential. I set myself therefore to work out a single text, selecting and arranging in such a way as seemed to me to produce the most coherent and internally self-consistent narrative.[7]

It is remarkable that Christopher Tolkien took Helms's interpretation so seriously that in his next book he decided to quote it in order to reject it: 'this is a serious misapprehension to which my words have given rise'.[8] This response sounds unquestionable; yet, it would be misleading to quote it without saying that Christopher Tolkien does not discuss Helms's statement, nor does he put forward any argument:

what a sharp contrast with the previous pages (six of them!) dedicated to discussing Tom Shippey's comparison between *The Lord of the Rings* and *The Silmarillion*.[9] On the contrary, he immediately quotes other remarks (by Tom Shippey and Constance B. Hieatt) that echo Helms's judgement, before embarking on the importance of the 'Silmarillion' for J.R.R. Tolkien.[10] In other words, Christopher Tolkien's rejection is firmly stated but in a single sentence, without any argumentation. The discussion launched by Helms remains open.

Almost forty years later, Christopher Tolkien made a very strong declaration in another context: not in English this time, nor in a scholarly introduction to a learned edition. Breaking a long silence in the media with an interview in the French newspaper *Le Monde*, he shared exceptionally intimate thoughts in a retrospective judgement on *The Silmarillion*:

'Right away I thought that the book was good, but *a little false*, in the sense that I had had to invent some passages,' he explains. At the time, he even had a worrying dream. 'I was in my father's study at Oxford. He came in and started looking for something with great anxiety. Then I realized in horror that it was *The Silmarillion*, and I was terrified at the thought that he would discover *what I had done* [emphases mine].'[11]

Does this expression of concern, even guilt, over what he had done with the 'Silmarillion' show that in 2012, after completing the publication of *The History of Middle-earth*, Christopher Tolkien felt no further need to defend *The Silmarillion* (as published), nor the twelve volumes of his *magnum opus*, which could speak for themselves? And that he no longer had to accept the public's view regarding his exact role in the publishing process? For the time being, let us not simply rely on this statement either, as strong as it is. But it is sufficient to incite us to examine the 'part' that Christopher Tolkien really 'played' (Helms) and his 'editorial freedom' in publishing *The Silmarillion*, to compare it to *The History of Middle-earth* and to his last volumes.[12] I shall argue first that a common point between the 'construction' of *The Silmarillion*, the rewriting of some chapters of that volume, as well as the narrative perspective of *The Fall of Gondolin* and *Beren and Lúthien*, is the style, visible or more discreet, of the same writer.

Christopher Tolkien as a storyteller: rewriting and 'constructing'

A comparison of *The Silmarillion* published in 1977 with J.R.R. Tolkien's original manuscripts as edited in *The History of Middle-earth* provides many examples of rewriting, alteration or condensation, from which one may judge Christopher Tolkien's stylistic qualities. Readers should turn for instance to the fascinating step-by-step commentary on his father's and his own texts that Christopher Tolkien offers in 'The History of the *Akallabêth*', in *The Peoples of Middle-earth*.[13] Presenting the first manuscript of the 'Fall of Númenor', he gives us the opportunity to observe the reorganization (for stylistic reasons) of phrases and groups of words in the version published in *The Silmarillion*. See for instance this paragraph:

> (1) The summit of the Meneltarma, the Pillar of Heaven, / *in the midst of the land,* / (2) had been a hallowed place, and even in the days of Sauron none had defiled it. Therefore / (3) among the Exiles many believed that / (4) it was not drowned for ever, but rose again above the waves, a lonely island lost in the great waters, *unless haply a mariner should come upon it.* / (5) And some there were / (6) that after sought for it, because it was said among lore-masters that the farsighted men of old could see from the Meneltarma a glimmer of the Deathless Land.[14]

which has been reworked in *The Silmarillion*:

> (3) Among the Exiles many believed that / (1) the summit of the Meneltarma, the Pillar of Heaven, / (4) was not drowned for ever, but rose again above the waves, a lonely island lost in the great waters; for it / (2) had been

a hallowed place, and even in the days of Sauron none had defiled it. / (5) And some there were of **the seed of Eärendil** / (6) that after**wards** sought for it, because it was said among loremasters that the far-sighted men of old could see from the Meneltarma a glimmer of the Deathless Land.[15]

Most elements have survived (except for the two expressions in italics) from the original paragraph but they have been rearranged to create another rhythm; the periphrase 'the seed of Eärendil' comes from another paragraph of the *Akallabêth*, and this transplantation is also Christopher Tolkien's decision. This example of stylistic interventions in *The Silmarillion* is one among many. In the *Valaquenta* (the second part of *The Silmarillion*) he changed verbal tenses,[16] and in the *Akallabêth* he replaced 'thou' with 'you'.[17] To track every such choice made by Christopher Tolkien would require a whole essay, in order to delineate particular features of his literary style. Then the results might be compared to an authentic sample of Christopher Tolkien's narrative writing, like his retelling in prose of the legend of Sigurd and Gudrún first presented in verse by his father: 'There was a king in the North, a descendant of Óðin, who was named Völsung. Sigmund was his eldest son, and Signý was his sister: she was wise and could foresee much that would come to pass. There were nine other sons besides.' As Adam Tolkien writes, this 'prose summary of the legend as recounted by J.R.R. Tolkien, [was] written exclusively for [the Tolkien Estate] website by Christopher Tolkien'.[18] It stands as such as a testimony to his style, which deserves to be analysed with a close-reading approach.

On a structural level, Christopher Tolkien's *manière* is to be seen in the very form of *The Silmarillion*, of *The History of Middle-earth* and of his last works. To begin with, one should not under-estimate the changes that J.R.R. Tolkien's stories have undergone during the process of publication: first told in prose (*The Book of Lost Tales*), rewritten in verse (*The Lays of Beleriand*), then in prose again (in the *Quentas*, along with other narrative texts), many stories exist in several versions, and not as 'a fixed text'.[19] As Christopher Tolkien clearly shows in *The History of Middle-earth* by presenting successive manuscripts, 'the object of the study [the manuscripts] was not stable, but exists, as it were "longitudinally" in time (the author's lifetime), and not only "transversely" in time, as a printed book that undergoes no essential further change'.[20] To a modern reader's eyes, their instability, their mutability, may evoke the medieval practice of retelling stories. In this context, Paul Zumthor's concept of *mouvance*[21] as applied to medieval manuscripts might (taking all due precautions in the transposition) be of help in apprehending the fundamental transformation of manuscripts written by J.R.R. Tolkien into a 'fixed point of reference', as Christopher Tolkien himself describes *The Silmarillion*, as opposed to the 'variants and rival versions'.[22]

The original, mutable texts, 'a creation of unceasing fluidity', are also extremely diverse in their status and nature.[23] The *Quenta Noldorinwa*, for instance, is not in the same 'unfinished' state as the lays published in two versions in *The Lays of Beleriand*. Moreover, in the late 1930s 'The Silmarillion' was made up of several texts, as demonstrated by one of the title pages accompanying the *Quenta Silmarillion* edited by Christopher Tolkien:

> *The Silmarillion*
> The history of the Three Jewels, the
> Silmarils of Fëanor, in which is told
> in brief the history of the Elves from
> their coming until the Change of the
> World.
>
> 1. *Qenta Silmarillion*, or *Pennas Hilevril*
>   To which is appended
>   The houses of the princes of Men and Elves
>   The tale of years
>   The tale of battles
> 2. *The Annals of Valinor*   *Nyarna Valinoren*
> 3. *The Annals of Beleriand*   *Nyarna Valarianden*
> 4. *The Lhammas* or Account of Tongues.[24]

This table of contents reveals a heterogeneity that lies at the core of J.R.R. Tolkien's project. In the new phase of his work on 'The Silmarillion' after the publication of *The Lord of the Rings*, he even considered adding essays such as 'Laws and Customs among the Eldar', 'Athrabeth Finrod ah Andreth' and 'Quendi and Eldar'.[25] As Jason Fisher remarks, J.R.R. Tolkien's purpose may have been 'to create an illusion of historically conditioned diversity' with the coexistence of prose, poems, annals and essays in his 'Silmarillion'.[26] Thus, whether or not 'to reflect that diversity' (Fisher) in *The Silmarillion* was Christopher Tolkien's choice: he eventually decided to offer as unified a volume as possible, 'the most coherent and internally self-consistent narrative'.[27]

This choice remains one of his distinctive marks on the book – along with his decision to add 'two short separate works', *The Downfall of Númenor* and *Of the Rings of Power*.[28] The volume is a striking combination of J.R.R. Tolkien's projects and Christopher Tolkien's artistic licence, given the obligation to rework 'the legends of the earlier age', as stated (for instance) in a letter written by his father to a reader in 1963: 'I am afraid all the same that th[eir] presentation will need a lot of work.… The legends have to be worked over … and made consistent … and they have to be given some progressive shape.'[29] In other words, Christopher Tolkien's *Silmarillion* is not similar to any of the successive versions of 'The Silmarillion' written or imagined by J.R.R. Tolkien.

Christopher Tolkien as a literary critic: a question of style

'[A] completed and cohesive entity', as Christopher Tolkien retrospectively described *The Silmarillion*, was not the only option: his original idea, 'an historical study, a complex of divergent texts interlinked by commentary', was superseded by the choice of consistency and simplicity, when he decided not '[to burden] the book further with any sort of commentary or annotation'.[30] But the original idea was carried out in the volumes that followed, revealing the deep coherence of his literary enterprise. Published between 1983 and 1996, the *History of Middle-earth* series shares even more features with *The Silmarillion* than one might expect, as well as with *The Fall of Gondolin* and *Beren and Lúthien*. What follows is a reading of these books according to the criteria of literarity as discussed by Gérard Genette in *Fiction and Diction*: according to him, a text may be considered as literary either because of its style (its 'formal features') or because of its fictional status and content, in a post-Aristotelian perspective.[31]

Despite obvious differences between *The Silmarillion* and the twelve scholarly volumes, especially the presence of a critical discourse in the latter, the whole interpretation by Christopher Tolkien of the birth and evolution of his father's writings creates a global narrative, a 'story' of Middle-earth, behind the recreated history. And the storyteller, our guide, is the one responsible for this specific type of 'progressive shape' taken by the narrative, by the story 'of the changing literary conceptions in the passing years' – as a sort of biography of a literary work.[32] Christopher Tolkien's input and touch are conspicuous when *The History of Middle-earth* is compared with his editions of essays or translations written by J.R.R Tolkien: the act of deciphering, annotating, gathering and presenting the texts in *The Monsters and the Critics* is similar to his philological task in *The History of Middle-earth*. Yet, in the latter, the nonfictional discourse creates a narrative movement, or flow, through the forewords, the numerous commentaries and each introduction to each section of the twelve volumes.

Thus, a form of continuity exists between the series and his last two books through their prefaces, prologues, introductions and 'notes', whose tone is very similar to that in *The History of Middle-earth*. To begin with, one may observe that the last two books cannot be dissociated from the series, since 'the treating of one legend as a developing entity' demands a context against which that development may be followed.[33] In Christopher Tolkien's mind, the last two books were intended to make more visible stories that would otherwise have remained just two among many others in the twelve-volume series: 'To follow the story of Beren and Lúthien, as a single and well-defined narrative, in *The History of Middle-earth* is … not easy,' as he remarks in his preface.[34] In order to achieve this, he presents, comments and discusses the previously edited texts, quoting his father's letters and his own publications: *Beren and Lúthien* refers for instance to the foreword to the *Lost Tales*, which in turn quotes his foreword to *Unfinished Tales*, eventually resulting in a web of cross-references and overlapping echoes.[35] All this creates not only a dialogue between his books but also a persona, an image of a narrator.

The main features of the literary critical discourse related to this persona that emerge are a modest yet thorough approach to presenting (in *Beren and Lúthien* and in *The Fall of Gondolin*) a wider audience with 'one single particular narrative from its earliest existing form and throughout its later development'; and a determination to establish in *The History of Middle-earth* the most authentic reconstruction of his father's literary career, even if this means acknowledging some earlier interpretations and choices as mistakes.[36] In the foreword to *The War of the Jewels*, for instance, Christopher Tolkien explains that, with the recent publication of all the relevant material, 'a criticism of the "constructed" *Silmarillion* becomes possible … it will be apparent in this book that there are aspects of the work that I view with regret.'[37]

The most distinctive feature of his style is indeed the presence of a voice, in the last two volumes as well as in *The History of Middle-earth*; a voice that we identify as that of 'our Vergil' (as David Bratman puts it), our guide in this textual maze.[38] In the more intimate introductions to *Beren and Lúthien* and *The Fall of Gondolin* the voice is in the foreground, as in a personal essay. But even the more scholarly commentaries of the whole series recall the voice perceived by readers of other texts written by Christopher Tolkien that are also discursive and nonfictional: his letters.[39] In two recent tributes, Willam Fliss presents Christopher Tolkien as 'a masterful letter writer with a prose style delightful to read', as he appears in the letters exchanged in the 1980s with the archivist at Marquette University, Chuck Elston, and two researchers, Taum Santoski and John Rateliff. The same John Rateliff remarks forty years later that 'when I pulled one of his volumes off the shelf and began to read … I could hear it in his voice'.[40] Thus, the stylistic qualities of Christopher Tolkien's nonfictional texts – forewords, commentaries, notes – characterized by the presence of his voice and belonging to the essayistic genre, call for an acknowledgement of their literary status. Not only because it is now admitted that literary criticism is literature in its own right, but because of the 'formal features' (Genette) of Christopher Tolkien's style itself.

As Tom Shippey has remarked, 'the characteristic activity of the philologist [is…] "reconstruction"', in the sense of recreating something 'which no longer existed but could with 100 per cent certainty be inferred'.[41] Obviously, Christopher Tolkien treated his father's manuscripts as a philologist, and even commented on the difficulty of the task, on his efforts to decipher 'the layer upon layer of changes in a single manuscript page', in order to understand his father's texts.[42] *The History of Middle-earth* series also gives a retrospective account of his task in preparing *The Silmarillion*, of 'his efforts to bring together all the parts of *The Silmarillion* at the earliest time consistent with the painstaking accuracy he is seeking', as Clyde Kilby put it in 1976.[43] But did Christopher Tolkien only act as a philologist, and did all the 'reconstructions' that he achieved reach the '100 per cent certainty' that Tom Shippey rightly considers as a criterion?

From 'construction' to invention:
Christopher Tolkien as a fiction writer
Raising this issue seems all the more important when we consider statements by Christopher Tolkien that require interpretation without over-simplification, such as this passage in *The War of the Jewels*: 'the published work [*The Silmarillion*] is not in any way a completion, but a *construction* devised out of the existing materials [emphasis mine]'.[44] The term 'construction' is echoed in later books, with some variations that deserve our attention, for instance in the foreword to his final work: '*The Silmarillion* that I published in 1977 … was composed, one might even say "*contrived*" to produce narrative coherence [emphasis mine].'[45] For a writer as precise as Christopher Tolkien, the choice of words is of course crucial and the use of the verb 'contrive' at the end of his literary career gives an inkling that his role had been greater than merely editing manuscripts. And as early as 1977, in a more confidential publication, he had combined two significant terms (instead of choosing only

one) when he mentioned that he had 'work[ed] out a single text, by *selection* and *arrangement* [emphases mine]', in order to produce *The Silmarillion*.[46]

Unfortunately, only a few critics have remained as careful as Verlyn Flieger when she refers to 'the one-volume book selected, arranged, and edited by Christopher Tolkien and published in 1977'.[47] Too often in the mainstream critical discourse on *The Silmarillion*, only the last word ('edited') has remained. Yet in his foreword to *Unfinished Tales* (published after *The Silmarillion*, in 1980), Christopher Tolkien placed small stones that the reader (as in the well-known fairy-tale) may find in the huge forest of texts: 'I have indeed treated the published form of *The Silmarillion* as a fixed point of reference of the same order as the writings published by my father himself, without taking into account *the innumerable "unauthorised" decisions* between variants and rival versions that went into its making [emphasis mine].'[48] Still, since it is common for an editor to choose between versions, in what way should such a task be considered as 'unauthorised', except if one goes beyond the editorial role? The self-contradictory description should induce us to investigate the kind of liberties Christopher Tolkien decided to take in the process of publishing *The Silmarillion*, that later seemed to him 'overstepping the bounds of the editorial function'.[49]

It appears that there are two main types of interventions – in the plot and the actual writing – and both correspond to the definition of fiction. The latter is usually defined as the product of imagination, of invention, according to the interpretation of Aristotle's *Poetics* as applied to literary studies in the past decades.[50] A writer is indeed characterized in the *Poetics* by the invention and conception of plots: 'the poet [= the writer] must be a maker of stories rather than verses, in so far as it is representation that makes him a poet, and representation is of actions'.[51]

Modifying and constructing the plot, inventing events and elements, is precisely what Christopher Tolkien has done in *The Silmarillion*, extending his activity beyond the publication of a book from existing manuscripts and into the production of fiction. In *A Brief Account of the Book and Its Making* published in 1977, he himself described *how he had to* 'develop the narrative out of notes and rough drafts' written by his father, and had in places to 'modify the narrative to make it coherent'.[52] In this text, more confidential than a preface to *The Silmarillion*, the objective description sheds light on an interesting allusion present in the latter: 'In this work the concluding chapters (from the death of Túrin Turambar) introduced peculiar difficulties, in that they had remained unchanged for many years, and were in some respects in serious disharmony with more developed conceptions in other parts of the book.'[53] Thus, especially from Chapter 22 ('Of the Ruin of Doriath') onwards, the last parts of the book are reputed to bear the imprint of the so-called editor more distinctly. The most interesting example, because it is in the public domain and provides a striking illustration of Christopher Tolkien's qualities as a writer, is to be found in the scene of Thingol's death:

> Then the lust of the Dwarves was kindled to rage by the words of the King; and they rose up about him, and laid hands on him, and slew him as he stood. So died in the deep places of Menegroth Elwë Singollo, King of Doriath, who alone of all the Children of Ilúvatar was joined with one of the Ainur; and he who, alone of the Forsaken Elves, had seen the light of the Trees of Valinor, with his last sight gazed upon the Silmaril.[54]

This passage has been praised as an artistic climax by readers such as Tom Shippey, who distinguishes in *The Silmarillion* 'two of Tolkien's great strengths'. The first one is '"inspiration": he was capable of producing, from some recess of the mind, images, words, phrases, scenes in themselves irresistibly compelling – Lúthien watched among the hemlocks by Beren, Húrin calling to the cliffs, Thingol's death in the dark while he looks at the captured Light'.[55] Yet, taking his cue from a statement by Christopher Tolkien,[56] another critic has argued for a different authorship of this dramatic scene, located at the heart of a five-page passage. For Douglas Kane reckons that the paragraphs 'which tell of Húrin's coming to Nargothrond, his slaying of Mîm the petty-dwarf … are complete editorial inventions'; and that the following paragraphs are respectively 'mostly editorial invention' and 'almost entirely editorial inventions'.[57] Kane notes the difference between the plot in J.R.R. Tolkien's manuscript and 'Christopher [Tolkien]'s solution – to eliminate the gold altogether ... and to create a whole new history for the Nauglamîr'.[58] Not only one of the key scenes of *The Silmarillion*, but whole sections of this chapter, have been written by Christopher Tolkien.

He was in fact the first to indicate the transformation of the original material in *The Silmarillion*, in which 'the story told ... is fundamentally changed, to a form for which in certain essential features there is no authority whatever in my father's own writings'.[59] 'No authority' is an elegant euphemism to avoid claiming his own status as the author of the said passage. It is quite moving to see Christopher Tolkien's efforts to remain behind his father, by using a passive voice that masks him in the very sentence where he explains what he has done: 'the outlaws ... *were removed*, as also *was* the curse of Mîm; and the only treasure ... was the Nauglamîr – which *was here supposed* to have been made by Dwarves.... Húrin *was represented* as ... [emphases mine]'.[60] The whole paragraph uses the same device, even when the fictional invention is justified and the creative process confirmed: 'This story was not lightly or easily conceived, but was the outcome of long experimentation among alternative conceptions.'[61]

What is important here is not to repeat Christopher Tolkien's own conclusion, in which he expresses regrets about his supposed 'mistake' in 'alter[ing] the story',[62] and his hope that another solution had been found; but rather to keep a good, critical distance. This inevitably leads us to identify Christopher Tolkien's writing as fiction writing, in some chapters.[63] This status of writer of fiction constitutes the counterpart of his persona as a literary critic and editor; and their common point is subjectivity.

Looking back in 2007, Christopher Tolkien explained in these terms the composition of a (then) non-existing narrative in Chapter 21 of *The Silmarillion*: 'I undertook ... the strange task of trying to simulate what he [J.R.R. Tolkien] did not do: the writing of a "Silmarillion" version of the latest form of the story, but deriving this from the heterogeneous materials of the "long version", the *Narn*.'[64] The subjectivity at work is all the more visible since Christopher Tolkien acknowledges here that some choices made in order to compose the chapter published in 1977 were not the right ones:

> the text in this book [*The Children of Húrin*] that fills the long gap in the story in *Unfinished Tales* is derived from the same original materials as is the corresponding passage in *The Silmarillion* ... but they are used for a different purpose in each case, and in the new text with a better understanding of the labyrinth of drafts and notes and their sequence.[65]

What Christopher Tolkien could not 'understand' at that time (but did after three more decades of hard work on his father's manuscripts), he just had to replace by selection, invention (fiction), in a text that became partly his own.

Is it a problem if parts of *The Silmarillion* are not by J.R.R. Tolkien but by Christopher Tolkien? Not in so far as the latter's aim was faithfully to edit his father's manuscripts and, in some cases, to fulfill his father's intentions, which he knew better than anyone else – even if this led him to write fiction, to fill the gaps in some chapters, to 'invent some passages', as he admitted in 2012.

Twenty years ago, David Bratman expressed regrets that scholars tended to underestimate *The Silmarillion*.[66] The situation has changed, but not enough, despite effort by scholars such as Allan Turner and his colleagues, whose *The Silmarillion: Thirty Years On*, published in 2007, was aimed at filling a gap in Tolkienian studies.[67] My own intention here has been to reassess some facts taken for granted and to address some simplifications. Each of the elements examined here – Christopher Tolkien's 'construction' of *The Silmarillion*, his rewriting and even invention in some chapters, his style as a narrator in his later volumes – obviously deserves an article to itself. Nevertheless, the idea was to bring them together in this essay because, combined, they compose a portrait of Christopher Tolkien as a writer in his own right, given the stylistic qualities of his prose and the fact that he had to invent, to create fiction as part of his critical work, in order to shed a light on his father's creation. As Helms observed in 1981, 'If the work [*The Silmarillion*] was to be printed at all, the editor had to play his part'; it appears that Christopher Tolkien in fact played many 'parts', and not only in *The Silmarillion*.[68]

Among other questions that need to be fully investigated, one may count Christopher Tolkien's role in the writing of *The Children of Húrin* (2007), bearing in mind his intriguing statement: 'while I have had to introduce bridging passages here and there in the piecing together of different drafts, there is no element of extraneous "invention" of any kind, however slight'.[69] The conclusion of the sentence contradicts the rest, since to 'introduce bridging passages' (even if they are not 'extraneous') means modifying the plot, hence writing fiction. A further investigation might try to explain to what extent 'The text [published in *The Children of Húrin*] is nonetheless artificial' in the original and strongest sense: made by art … constructed and contrived.[70]

Thus, Christopher Tolkien's enterprise may be described in the same words that J.R.R Tolkien used in a famous letter written to Milton Waldman: 'always I had the sense of recording what was already "there", somewhere: not of "inventing"'.[71] There is a moving echo of this sentence in a recent letter from Christopher Tolkien to Carl Hostetter: 'As I see it, I have called myself a "literary archeologist". I have never been more than a discoverer, and interpreter of what I discovered.'[72] Still, it would be a mistake to forget that his father was describing in his letter his conception of creation and fiction; and if the same words may be accurate to describe Christopher Tolkien's achievement, it is only by taking into account the presence of fiction, of invention, in his case as well.

For decades, his achievement has been oversimplified. And to be fair, this has been largely due to Christopher Tolkien's own humility. His perception of his accomplishment appears ambivalent, varying from one statement to another: but why he felt it important to minimize his role while publishing his father's manuscripts is easy to understand. Many other statements expressing his desire to respect the integrity of his father's manuscripts may be found; but this essay is also meant to remind us that, between a writer's intention and his achievement, a discrepancy is always to be observed – for the better. Placing such statements in the context of a literary career spanning more than forty years (let alone his academic publications preceding 1975) reminds us that a writer's words cannot be taken for granted, even when they are sincere.

In other words, Christopher Tolkien's statements about his own work do not do him justice. To paraphrase a sentence written by Proust about another creator, Christopher Tolkien was bolder as a writer than as a commentator on his own work; and not all his statements should be taken for granted by general readers and literary critics.[73]

Let us observe, in conclusion, how complex and ambivalent his view of his own work may appear, in a passage coeval to the publication of *The Silmarillion*:

> I set myself, therefore, to work out a single text, by selection and arrangement. To give even an impression of the way this has been done is scarcely possible in a short space, and it must suffice to say that in the result *The Silmarillion* is emphatically my father's book and in no sense mine.
>
> Here and there I had to develop the narrative out of notes and rough drafts; I had to make many choices between competing versions and to make many changes of detail; and in the last few chapters (which had been left almost untouched for many years) I had in places to modify the narrative to make it coherent. But essentially what I have done has been a work of organization, not of completion.[74]

The full quotation is even more interesting since the original term used by Christopher Tolkien was not 'organization' but 'composition': when the text was published in 1977, the publishers decided to change 'composition', which, in American English, 'mainly implies creation',[75] while it is more polysemic in Great Britain.[76] Indeed Christopher Tolkien may have chosen this word for its polysemy, as a signpost; it is now clear that many of his interventions in *The Silmarillion* belong to fiction as defined in this essay.

Once his literary duty as a son and as a 'literary executor' (in the fullest sense of the expression) was fulfilled, he appeared more and more inclined to recognize that he had played a greater part than the one that he would admit in the first place – perhaps because he had fully succeeded in his project, by publishing books of several kinds: editions (*The Monsters and the Critics*), volumes interlacing his own voice with his father's texts (*The Fall of Gondolin*, *Beren and Lúthien*, as well as *The History of Middle-earth*) and the 'unique' and fascinating work, *The Silmarillion*, parts of which he 'wrote'[77] by combining his skills in philology and his talent for writing fiction.

5   LISTENING TO THE MUSIC

ON 24 FEBRUARY 1950, J.R.R. Tolkien wrote to his publisher Stanley Unwin concerning his long-overdue but by then completed manuscript of *The Lord of the Rings*. 'My work has escaped from my control,' he cautioned Unwin, 'and I have produced a monster: an immensely long, complex, rather bitter, and very terrifying romance, quite unfit for children ... and it is not really a sequel to *The Hobbit*, but to *The Silmarillion*.'[1] His work had not, in fact, escaped from his control, but he seemed concerned that it might have escaped from Unwin's. 'The Silmarillion' he referred to was a vast, as-yet-unpublished mythology Tolkien wanted to 'dedicate ... to England'.[2] He had laboured over it – in what time he could spare from academic duties – for over thirty years, and now wanted very much to see it in print. At the time he wrote to Unwin he was in concurrent (but unmentioned) discussions with Milton Waldman, an editor at the London publishing firm of Collins, about publishing 'The Silmarillion' and the 'monster' together as 'one long Saga of the Jewels and the Rings'.[3] In the end we can be grateful that that this did not happen, for it was the separate and prior appearance of *The Lord of the Rings* that created a readership for 'The Silmarillion' and thus paved the way for its publication. Nevertheless, Tolkien's letter of 24 February seems to have been part of a strategy to dissuade Unwin from accepting *The Lord of the Rings* as a sequel to *The Hobbit* so that Collins could publish it as a sequel to 'The Silmarillion'.

The monster
In point of fact it was a sequel to both, and that hybrid origin (for the two source works are poles apart in tone and treatment and audience) has complicated its reception. How you approach *The Lord of the Rings* depends to a great extent on what context you place it in and what prior knowledge

(if any) you bring to it. Begun as a follow-up to *The Hobbit*, it soon grew beyond that book to be 'captured', as Tolkien described it, by the older, continuously evolving but as yet unknown legendarium that was his life's work.[4] It was thus an amalgam – 'as indivisible as I could make it', he wrote in another letter to Unwin – of narrative types ranging from Grimmsian fairy tale to Edwardian children's story to medieval myth on the order of *Beowulf* and the Icelandic Eddas.[5] It grew beyond any of these, however, to become something unlike anything that had gone before. The only term available was fantasy, a genre at that time confined largely to pulp magazines and the by-then out of favour stories of William Morris and Lord Dunsany, to which it bore a superficial resemblance. Aside from the Frankenstein allusion and the 'unfit for children' comment (challenged by over six decades of children who've found it quite fit), Tolkien's own description of his masterpiece was and is spot on. It is long. It is complex. It is terrifying. And it is a good deal more than 'rather' bitter.

At over a thousand pages and half a million words *The Lord of the Rings* is not just 'immensely' long, it is enormous. Its six interlaced books with their overlapping time schemes and storylines, competing voices and styles, and multiple shifts in point of view are complex in the literal meaning of the word, derived from Latin *complexus*, 'braided', 'comprised of different interrelated parts'. The sniffing, un-bodied Black Riders, shadow-men on real horses, the dismal chant of the Barrow-wight whose groping arm walks through the tomb on its fingers, the half-world of the Ring that engulfs Frodo, are images out of nightmare. So far, so good. *Long* describes dimension, it is measurable, concrete. *Complex* describes structure, narrative organization; it is a technical term. *Terrifying* describes the effect on the reader, the *pathos* of Aristotle.

Bitter shifts the focus from the work to its author. It is self-referential, describing not the size or structure or effect of a work but its tone, the attitude that informs it. Depending on the context, 'bitter' can describe reaction – unpleasant, unpalatable, hard to accept; and can also convey emotion – anger, resentment, disappointment, regret. The *Oxford*

following page **5.1** Map of the north-west of Middle-earth, drawn for *The Lord of the Rings*, late 1940s, showing the Grey Havens to the west of Hobbiton and the Shire. Oxford, Bodleian Library, MS. Tolkien Drawings 124.

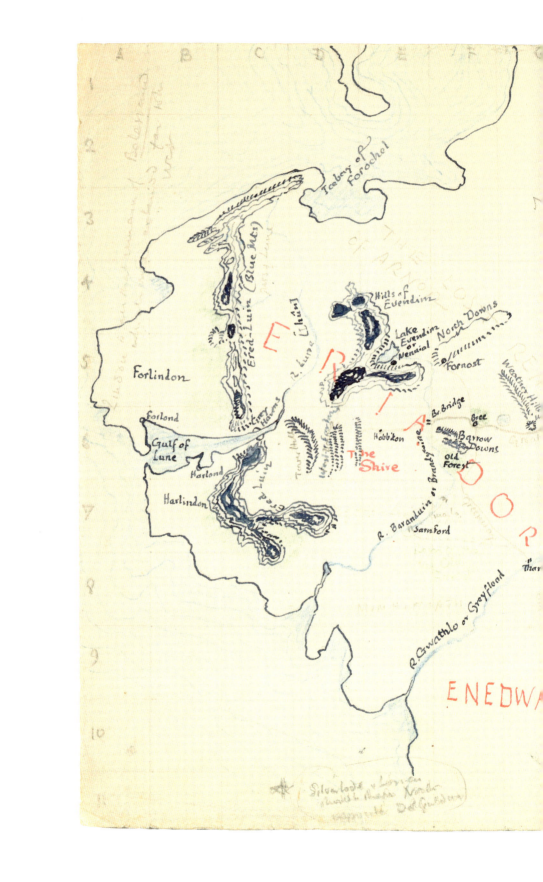

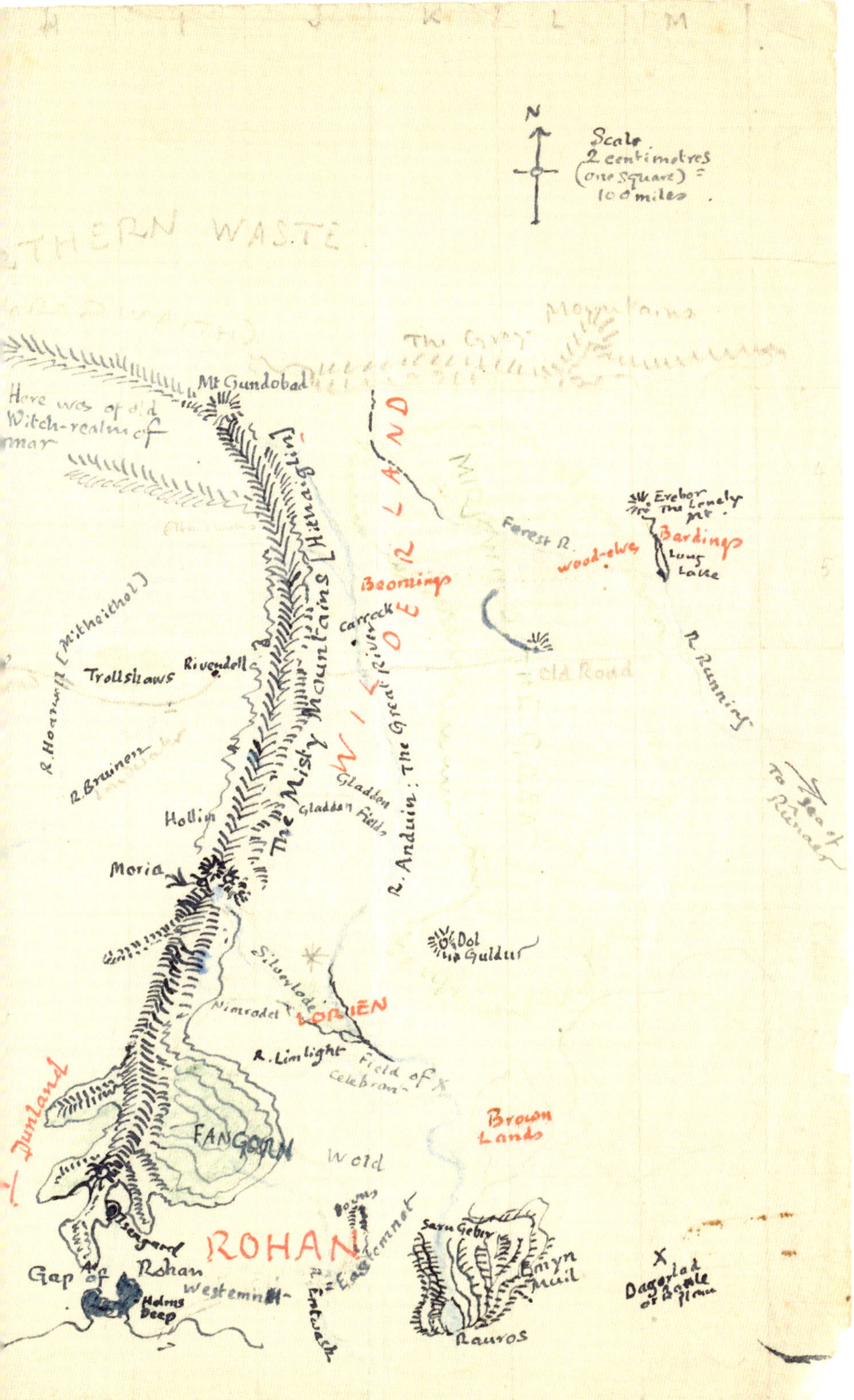

N

Scale
2 centimetres
(one square) =
100 miles .

...THERN WASTE

...RDWAITH?

The Grey   Mountains

Mt Gundobad

Here was of old
Witch-realm of
...mar

The Misty Mountains [Hithaeglir]

W I L D E R L A N D

Beornings

Forest R.

W. Erebor
The Lonely mt.

wood-elves

Bardings
Long
Lake

Carrock

R. Anduin: The Great River

Trollshaws   Rivendell

Old Road

R. Running

R. Hoarwell (Mitheithel)

R. Bruinen

To Sea
Rúnaer

Hollin

Gladden

Gladden Field.

Moria

O: Dol
na Guldur

Silverlode

Nimrodel   LORIEN

R. Limlight   Field of
Celebrant

Dunland

FANGORN   Wold

Brown
Lands

Isengard

ROHAN

Sarn Gebir

Emyn
Muil

X
Dagorlad
or Battle
Plain

Gap of
Rohan

Westemnet

R. Eastemnet

R. Entwash

Helms
Deep

Rauros

English Dictionary (*OED*) traces 'bitter' back to 'bite', with the primary definition of 'cutting, sharp', and a secondary definition of 'unpalatable to the mind; unpleasant, hard to swallow or admit'.

Tolkien's qualifying 'rather' takes some of the sting out of 'bitter', and to be sure not all in *The Lord of the Rings* is dark. There are light-hearted moments and flashes of humour. The legacy of *The Hobbit* bestows bread and cheese and feasting and song and companionship to brighten the picture. These episodes, however, as readers tend to notice, occur mostly in Book I of *The Fellowship of the Ring*. By the time the Company gets to Rivendell at the opening of Book II the tone has darkened perceptibly. With a few intervals for comic relief – the hobbits' reunion with Legolas and Gimli at Isengard; and with Aragorn in the Houses of Healing – it continues to do so over the following five books.

Written between two world wars, the bitter message of Tolkien's monster is that every win is temporary and what is lost is gone forever. 'I am a Christian,' he wrote in response to a reader, Amy Ronald, in December 1956, 'and indeed a Roman Catholic, so that I do not expect "history" to be anything but a "long defeat" – though it contains (and in a legend may contain more clearly and movingly) some samples or glimpses of final victory.'[6] While *The Lord of the Rings* offers both the 'long defeat' of history and also 'samples or glimpses' of victory, readers have on the whole tended to prefer and to emphasize the victory over the defeat. Not so Tolkien, for whom the long defeat simply met expectations, while the victory was only a glimpse, a fleeting, partial vision.

Four years after the letter to Unwin and following considerable back-and-forth between Tolkien and the two publishers, volume I of the monster was finally published in July 1954 – by Unwin, and without 'The Silmarillion' – as *The Fellowship of the Ring*. Volume II, *The Two Towers*, followed later that same year, and volume III, *The Return of the King*, in 1955. The book was generally well received, though it was inevitably and misleadingly read by the light of *The Hobbit*. Critical opinion ran the gamut from glowingly positive – 'lightning from a clear sky', 'beauties that pierce like swords or burn like cold iron', 'a book that will break your heart';

to condescension – 'boys masquerading as adult heroes'; to outright calumny – 'juvenile trash'.[7] There was in addition some perplexity about exactly what species of animal it was – science fiction? modern novel? adventure story? all of the above? But despite the attempts at classification none of the early reviewers I am aware of found *The Lord of the Rings* to be 'bitter'. In that respect, I submit they missed Tolkien's point.

Two years later, in 1957, Douglass Parker, a professor of classics at the University of California, Riverside, wrote an article in the *Hudson Review* that came close. Though Parker was off the mark in some regards – he called the book a trilogy, dismissed the hobbit names as 'ridiculous', put the Shire in *The Hobbit*, and left out Merry and Pippin – nevertheless, he correctly pegged the book as fantasy, calling it 'probably the most original and varied creation ever seen in the genre, and certainly the most self-consistent'.[8] Himself the designer and teacher of a course in parageography, the study of imaginary worlds, Parker was well qualified to judge Tolkien's invented world against that of others. He also pointed out that *The Lord of the Rings* does what an imaginary world can do better than a realistic one, which is to estrange the familiar, like a looking-glass held at an unfamiliar angle. The fantastic elements of Tolkien's world, he argued, its elves, dwarves and hobbits, show us ourselves in an angled mirror and thus from a new perspective.

It was in his summation that Parker came closest to Tolkien's description, writing that, 'Tolkien's whole marvelous, intricate structure has been reared to be destroyed, that we may regret it.'[9] Parker didn't use the word 'bitter', but 'regret' was not far off the mark. 'Regret', after all, carries the notion of pain for something not done that should have been, or for something done that should not have been. If Tolkien got ahead of himself in saying his monster was unfit for children, Parker was ahead of his time in recognizing that beneath the fantasy elements – and even more effective in contrast to their enchantment – there lies a deep stratum of pain, of sorrow for loss. Though *The Lord of the Rings* has comedic elements and happy moments, some bordering on what Tolkien called 'Joy beyond the walls of the world', it is not at bottom a happy book.[10] It is more than anything a lament, a cry of grief for a lost and unrecovered world, re-created only so that it may be lost again, and lost so that it can be mourned. It is to Parker's credit that he perceived the long defeat in Tolkien's story before he or anyone had knowledge of its larger but equally defeatist parent mythology.

Christopher Tolkien's serial publication from 1977 to 2018 of his father's entire legendarium has given us that larger framework. We now have the interior history of Tolkien's fictive world from its lofty creation in celestial music to Sam Gamgee's homely return to Bag End at the end of the Third Age. Christopher repositioned the looking-glass, thereby putting *The Lord of the Rings* in longer perspective to show it as something more than itself. It is the culmination of a multivalent narrative that Tolkien himself called an 'evil-aroused story'.[11] Taken entire, the 'Silmarillion', like *The Lord of the Rings* it encompasses, is not a happy story but a catalogue of losses piled one upon another upon another. To be sure, there are, as in *The Lord of the Rings* by itself, 'some samples or glimpses of final victory', but they remain glimpses only, potential but not actual. Tolkien's mythology did not withhold the possibility of hope from his readers, but he was too honest to guarantee it.

With the whole of Tolkien's mythological world now displayed, many components of the complex fabric of Middle-earth, not just Lórien and Moria and the Entwives and the trees along Bagshot Row but those far in the past of the legendarium – Númenor and Gondolin and Nargothrond and Doriath – all provide context for one another as 'reared to be destroyed', so that we may feel their loss. More than seventy years after Tolkien's caveat to Unwin and sixty years after Parker's melancholy summing-up, we can see how the 'Silmarillion' supports and underscores both Tolkien's and Parker's key words, 'bitter' and 'regret'. *The Lord of the Rings* is the culmination, narrative end-point and realization of a long, terrifying, bitter saga. But fully to understand this end-point we must go back to the starting-point of the whole long story.

The beginnings

Conceived when he was still at school and carried on throughout his life, Tolkien's legendarium had starts and stops before it settled down (to the extent that it ever did), and its compositional history is intertangled, complex and confusing. There have been many efforts (some of them Tolkien's own after-the-fact attempts at dating) to pinpoint the earliest burgeoning of his myth-making impulse. The actual genesis of an idea can be hard to locate, especially in retrospect after the notion has already taken shape. In Tolkien's case there are paintings, poems, references in letters, all evidentiary, none conclusive. His invention of languages, begun with his earliest stories, is also a major factor in his myth-making, since he felt that a culture's language encodes its myths just as the myths inform the languages; they are co-temporous and coeval.

5.2 'The Shores of Faery', one of the earliest poems relating to Tolkien's legendarium, written when he was a student at Oxford, 1915.
Oxford, Bodleian Library, MS. Tolkien Drawings 87, fol. 21v.

5.3 'Gondolin & the Vale of Tumladin from Cristhorn', September 1928. The tale of 'Tuor and the Exiles of Gondolin' was the earliest prose story from Tolkien's mythology, written during the First World War. Oxford, Bodleian Library, MS. Tolkien Drawings 90, fol. 12.

In the exterior, real-world chronology of his writing life, his earliest attempts at mythology seem to have been two poems, the 1914 'Voyage of Earendel' and the 1915 'Shores of Faery'. Written before his 1916 military service in France, the poems are in spirit and essence largely Edwardian and thus to some degree retrogressive to the nineteenth-century prettification of faërie that Tolkien later deplored and abjured. Not till his military service had ended with trench fever and sick-leave in England, and at the suggestion of his friend Christopher Wiseman that he 'ought to start the epic', did Tolkien begin in 1916 or 1917 his first serious attempt to write a story in which both Middle-earth and Valinor were taking shape in his mind. By that time his invented world was neither Edwardian nor pretty. It was contemporary and realistic.

'I shall never write any ordered biography', Tolkien wrote to Christopher on 11 July 1972, 'it is against my nature, which expresses itself about things deepest felt in tales and myths'.[12]

So it was in his early life. The first serious story of Tolkien's mythological world followed directly his own war experience on the Somme in 1916–17. 'Tuor and the Exiles of Gondolin', later renamed 'The Fall of Gondolin', is a tale of war with accounts of battles, the sack of a great city and the subsequent wanderings of its refugees. It is not hard to see 'things deepest felt' in this mythic start of 'the epic' that mixed elves and humans and gods of the sea with the technology of Tolkien's own war. The bronze dragons with orcs inside them and the 'creatures of pure flame' reconfigured the tanks and flame-throwers of the Western Front.[13] It was fantasy doing what Parker said it does best, reflecting reality at an angle. For all its mythological elements and epic tone, the story's content came close to the deeply felt war poetry of such fellow veterans as Wilfred Owen and Siegfried Sassoon.

The story of Tuor and Gondolin was the start of Tolkien's mythology and the first of its three 'Great Tales', the other two being the bitter, tragic story of Túrin Turambar and the bittersweet love story of Beren and Lúthien. Written and rewritten again and again, sometimes in prose and sometimes in verse and now published in their entirety by Christopher, the 'Great Tales', together with the story of the Silmarils, form the backbone of Tolkien's mythology. They are not happy stories. The Túrin story ends in a double suicide. 'The Fall of Gondolin' tells of the overthrow and sack of a city, and the wanderings of its refugees. Only the Beren and Lúthien story has what might be called a happy ending, and even that ends in death.

But Tolkien's world also had its own interior timeline, one that began with creation. Christopher assigned the earliest version of the creation story, the 'Ainulindalë' or 'Singing of the Ainur', to the period of Tolkien's work on the *OED* (at that time called *The New English Dictionary*), between the years 1918 and 1920, that is to say after but not long after 'The Fall of Gondolin', suggesting that Tolkien may have had the arc of the story already sketched out.[14] Since he was an observant Catholic it is noteworthy that his creation story omits the Fall of Man. It has no prohibition, no temptation, no disobedience, no punishment; none of the elements that make up the foundation story of Judaeo-Christianity.

This is a hugely significant change, removing original sin (therefore guilt) and replacing it with cosmic disharmony that misshapes the world before humanity comes on the scene. The 'Ainulindalë' tells how the godhead Eru gives to his offspring the Ainur a musical theme and invites them to develop it together. Their harmony is interrupted when the chief among them, Melkor, intrudes a competing theme of his own, causing some of the Ainur to abandon Eru's theme and join his instead.

The result is musical war in heaven as the two themes contend. The resultant discord prompts Eru to call a halt and start over with a second theme, which gets the same treatment. In a final attempt Eru incorporates Melkor's disharmony into yet a third theme, this one described as 'wide and beautiful but slow and blended with an immeasurable sorrow' that weaves the rebellious theme 'into its own solemn pattern'.[15] It is with and through this third theme that the created world comes into being, a history at once divinely inspired and 'evil-aroused', flawed in its inception through the Music that plays out both its beauty and its evil, the theme and variations of the long defeat. It is well to remember that Tolkien was neither writing religious apologetics nor creating an allegory. Rather, he was telling a history of the world as he imagined it might once have seemed, but also as he experienced it, as a long defeat.

The interior history underwent a shift of direction, however, with the intrusion of *The Hobbit* in the 1930s. Starting as a playful story first told, then read to Tolkien's children, this was not a mythology *per se* but a children's book that strayed from its genre into the older legendarium. Its popularity sparked the commissioning of a sequel, *The Lord of the Rings*, which in turn took *The Hobbit* along as it attached itself to 'The Silmarillion'. The huge physical and mental endeavour of pushing *The Lord of the Rings* to completion, towing *The Hobbit* in its wake, took Tolkien twelve years. It was his final great effort and he succeeded in bringing it to a close, but the interruption broke the rhythm of 'The Silmarillion' and he was never able to go back and finish the parent mythology satisfactorily. The result is that for all practical purposes *The Lord of the Rings* stands as that mythology's zenith, narrative climax and effective finish. Tolkien's foreword to that work's second edition declared that it 'became an account … of [the] end and passing away' of the older world 'before its beginning and middle had been told'.[16]

The endings

That end and passing away comes not with its protagonist Frodo, who is sent offstage before it happens, but with his friend and follower Sam Gamgee. It was Sam on whom Tolkien bestowed the story's dual ending that brought the exterior and interior chronologies together. The exterior chronology of Tolkien's composition, the arc that sprang up in 1916–17 from Gondolin's defeat and the exile of its inhabitants, may be said to come back to earth with Sam's homecoming and his laconic 'Well, I'm back.' For it was here that Tolkien for all practical purposes brought his story to a close. This was not Tolkien's original ending, however, which in draft continued into material that became the later discarded Epilogue, with much conversation between Sam and his children Elanor and Frodo-lad. It ends with a conversation between Sam and Rosie about the King's impending visit, after which they 'went in and shut the door, but even as he did so Sam heard suddenly the sigh and murmur of the sea on the shores of Middle-earth'.[17] The directly following editorial comment by Christopher Tolkien, 'It cannot be doubted that this was how he [Tolkien] intended at that time that *The Lord of the Rings* should end', must mean that Tolkien intended the book to end with the sigh and murmur of the sea.[18]

Persuaded that the tying-up of loose ends was anticlimactic, Tolkien decided to omit the Epilogue. He wrote to Katherine Farrer in October 1955, shortly after the publication of *The Return of the King*, 'I still feel the picture incomplete without something on Samwise and Elanor, but I could not devise anything that would not have destroyed the ending.'[19] He discarded the Epilogue but he wanted to keep the sigh and murmur, so he moved that episode back to the scene of Frodo's departure at the Havens. Here, after Frodo's ship has gone beyond his sight, Sam stays 'far into the night, hearing only the sigh and murmur of the waves on the shores of Middle-earth, and the sound of them sank deep into his heart'.[20] Tolkien's retention of that moment in very nearly the same words makes it clear that something was going on that he considered essential. He was not just creating atmosphere; he had something specific in his mind. It was not until 1977, however, when Christopher Tolkien published *The Silmarillion* and we read the 'Ainulindalë' that we were able to learn what it was.

Thanks to Christopher we now know that 'in water there lives yet the echo of the Music of the Ainur'.[21] So what Sam is hearing is the echo, the repetition of the Music. As to why he is listening, that is because 'many of the Children of Ilúvatar' – of whom Sam is one – 'hearken still unsated to the voices of the Sea, and yet know not for what they listen'.[22] This is a moment packed with meaning for Tolkien's 'rather bitter' story. The Children of Ilúvatar, Elves and Men, come into being only with Eru's third theme, whose message – the voices of the sea carrying the echo of the Music that Sam is hearing – is that the world is inherently imperfect, flawed in its inception, therefore flawed in its realization. The scene with Sam makes the Music part of the story, and is clear evidence that Tolkien felt he had written 'one long saga' whose beginning was contained in its end.

We are not told whether Sam understands what it is he is hearing, only that the sound 'sank deep into his heart', but we do know – thanks to Christopher – that the waves Tolkien has chosen as the vehicle for his message are themselves recurrent and endless, telling and retelling the tragedy of the creation story, a world that began with harmony and wound up in discord. Sam hears the echoic repetition, the re-verberation, the re-statement (as in a musical theme) and playing out of the Music of creation. In thus reconnecting his world to its intentionally flawed beginning, Tolkien was using fantasy to do what Parker says it does best, to show his readers their actual world reflected in his invented one, a place where things go wrong and even the most promising start will be affected by the founding flaw. Readers in 1956, however, had no access to that knowledge. Back then the scene with Sam was unexplained. Yet even then it was clear that something was going on to which readers were meant to respond, even though the actual significance was beyond their knowledge.

5.4 'Cove near The Lizard', drawn on holiday in Cornwall at the outbreak of the First World War, 12 August 1914. Oxford, Bodleian Library, MS. Tolkien Drawings 85, fol. 13.

In thus referencing unrevealed information Tolkien was taking a page from his own scholarship and blending it with his invention. In his landmark 1936 lecture 'Beowulf: The Monsters and the Critics' he talked about 'the mood of the author, the essential cast of his imaginative apprehension of the world' as essential to understanding of that poem, particularly what he called its 'fusion' of Christian and pagan elements.[23] Pondering the fragments of pagan mythology still remaining in Beowulf, Tolkien twice lamented the present lack of knowledge about it. 'Of English pre-Christian mythology', he said in his lecture, 'we know practically nothing.'[24] He returned to the subject a few pages later, saying again and more explicitly that, 'we may regret [my emphasis] that we do not know more about pre-Christian English mythology'.[25]

In the primary context of English mythology in Beowulf this fits his lecture's argument. But a second circumstance makes it equally apposite to The Lord of the Rings. That is the fact that at the time Tolkien was regretting a lost English mythology, he had been for twenty years engaged in creating one invented expressly to fill in the gap. Seen in this light the word 'regret', used in similar contexts by both Tolkien and Parker, packs a triple whammy. It describes (1) Tolkien's regret for the lost pre-Christian myth in Beowulf; (2) his regret for the parallel and as yet unread mythos behind his own work; and (3) the very similar regret for loss that Parker felt The Lord of the Rings was intended to arouse.

'One long Saga'

Knowledge of this gives added meaning to Sam and the waves wherever the scene occurs, with the then unpublished 'Silmarillion' as the lost history of which at the time Tolkien's readers knew 'practically nothing'. The important thing is that its author knew, and built that 'nothing' into the emotional subtext of his narrative. And now we know practically everything. We now have Tolkien's 'Silmarillion' in its entirety to illuminate what then was unclear. With the whole corpus now available for survey, we can see how and why Tolkien wanted to make the two narratives into 'one long Saga'. He used this wordless moment with Sam and the Music to do just that, to connect the story's ending back to its distant beginning in Eru's third theme, 'wide and beautiful but slow and blended with an immeasurable sorrow', and bring it forward again to show how Frodo's departure was also part of that theme.

But Tolkien added a coda which he also gave to Sam, the simple and moving account of his return to Rosie after his farewell at the Havens:

> Sam turned to Bywater, and so came back up the Hill, as day was ending once more. And he went on, and there was yellow light, and fire within, and the evening meal was ready, and he was expected. And Rose drew him in, and set him in his chair, and put little Elanor upon his lap.
>
> He drew a deep breath. 'Well, I'm back,' he said.[26]

These are the last words in the narrative as published. The rest of the page is blank. Tolkien chose to shift from the melancholy vigil at the Havens with the sigh and murmur of the waves to the cozy domesticity of the homecoming – the yellow light, the fire, the evening meal, the reunited family. The paratactic sentence structure with its succession of 'ands' (there are eight over the course of two sentences) is emblematic of continuity. The legendarium that began with refugees fleeing a fallen city ends with Sam's return to a restored and revitalized Shire, a happy ending if ever there was one. At first glance his understated 'Well, I'm back' seems to reinforce this.

A second glance suggests another possibility. Sam's announcement is so bare, its message so unnecessary as to imply hidden depths, profundity cloaked in simplicity, a world in a grain of sand. We know Sam is back, we have just been told that. We don't need to be told again. Nor does Rosie. Tolkien must have had a purpose beyond the obvious in having Sam tell us what we already know. He had. 'Well, I'm back' is there both to evoke Bilbo's return at the end of *The Hobbit* and to invoke the there-and-back-again motif that rounded that book. But in the context of the larger legendarium, in the context of the Music that Sam has just been hearing with its reverberation of the long defeat, above all in the context of Frodo's departure, Sam's final words could be about more than there and back again. They could also, like Tolkien's regret for the lost pre-Christian mythology, be a 'rather bitter' reminder of all those who are not back, most especially those unlike Sam who cannot come back, who will never come back.

Not just Frodo but the anonymous Man of Harad whose death far from home so distressed Sam at the battle of Ithilien. Not just Frodo but the heroes dead on the Pelennor Fields whose names are preserved in the song of the Mounds of Mundberg: Harding and Guthláf and doughty Grimbold and Hirluin the fair and Forlong the old, all those who fought and 'fell … in a far country' and now lie 'under mould … under grass in Gondor by the Great River' nor ever to their own country 'returned in triumph'.[27] Not just Frodo but the other exiles and outcasts of Tolkien's imaginary and all too real world – Húrin and Túrin and Morwen and Nienor and Fili and Kili and Thorin Oakenshield. Sam's 'Well, I'm back' stands in contrast to all of these. His last words bring to a close both *The Lord of the Rings* and the larger myth to which the Music reconnects him. These words – which are also Tolkien's – are not the 'rather bitter' ones of their author's description to Unwin, but in the context of all that has gone before and of all that is lost and will never come back they are at best bittersweet. They make a fitting finish to this long, complex and rather bitter story, Parker's marvellous, intricate structure reared expressly to be destroyed that we may regret its loss.

These two scenes with Sam illustrate how knowledge of Tolkien's background can change our reading of the foreground. Effective in themselves, one for its melancholy, the other for its cheer, both episodes are also tied into a web of implicit meaning that reaches beyond their immediate placement to put them in the context of and make them relevant to the larger mythology. They bring to a close *The Lord of the Rings* but they also mark the *de facto* ending of the whole legendarium that surrounds it. For though Tolkien wrote and rewrote till almost the end of his life, he never succeeded in carrying his mythology to its projected but never fleshed-out conclusion. In terms of the whole story, then, the scenes we have looked at must stand not just as Sam's farewell but in a practical sense also Tolkien's. Freighted with implications that we can now fully grasp, they are emblematic of both Tolkien's and Parker's words for the story, words that give deeper insight into a book and a world we thought we already knew.

Now that we have it all we can begin to evaluate the breadth and depth as well as the height of an extended history within which *The Lord of the Rings* still stands out as the masterpiece and enduring monument to Tolkien's genius. The legendarium was Tolkien's for the sixty or so years during which it grew under his hands in ways not even he could have anticipated. 'The Silmarillion' has been Christopher's for the last forty-six years, during which he made the enormous task of editing and making the whole corpus available his life's work. His contribution to his father's vision and to the field of Tolkien studies is incalculable.

Christopher's publication in 2018 of *The Fall of Gondolin*, Tolkien's first foray into his mythology (which Christopher announced would be his last), both closed and reopened the book of Tolkien's legendarium. With it, Christopher laid down his pen. He said to the many fans, critics, lovers and scholars of his father's work who have had the benefit of his own life's work, 'Over to you.'

It is thanks to him that we are, like Sam, listening to the Music.

John Garth

THE CHRONOLOGY OF CREATION 6

HOW J.R.R. TOLKIEN MISREMEMBERED
THE BEGINNINGS OF HIS MYTHOLOGY

S TARTING the *Lost Tales* soon after the Battle of the
Somme, J.R.R. Tolkien set out as he would go on all
his life: developing the stories of his world alongside its
invented languages, with a creative drive and a perfectionism
that ultimately ruled out actually finishing the work. He
left his papers in disorder, and it is only thanks to his son
Christopher that we now have not only *The Silmarillion* but
also a twelve-volume *History of Middle-earth* tracing the
evolution of the whole legendarium. The creative process is
epitomized by the small book dated 1917 in which Tolkien
compiled a lexicon of the so-called Gnomish language,
'emending, rejecting, adding, in layer upon layer,' as
Christopher puts it, 'so that in places it has become very hard
to interpret'.[1]

It has been our great fortune that Christopher inherited
his father's scholarly instinct and expertise, as well as his
passion for Middle-earth, but not his disorderly work
practices. In his edition of *The Book of Lost Tales* (the first two
volumes of *The History of Middle-earth*), he gives a readable
text of each tale as it stood at a significant point, a careful
record of variant readings, and an editorial commentary
cautiously tracing the evolution of the main ideas. For
stories never actually written, he provides his father's drafts
and notes.

Christopher later aptly described himself as a 'literary
archaeologist'.[2] These two volumes are the report of a major
literary-archaeological 'dig'. Plot points, key concepts and
variant names are all examined and analysed, with particular
attention to determining the order of composition, 'layer
upon layer'. Just as layers of deposition can help archaeologists
understand a past culture and its material remains, layers
of composition helped Christopher shed light on his father's
artistry and aims.

6.1 Tolkien in his shared
army cubicle at 'Withernsea
(Thirtle Bridge) 1917', where
he was posted to the
garrison defending the
east coast while he was
recovering from trench fever.
Oxford, Bodleian Library,
MS. Tolkien photogr. 11, fol. 25.

But his attempt is cautious – and with good reason. Some of the manuscript texts were erased, or they lapsed into illegibility; very few carried a date of composition; and a mass of linguistic papers, though potentially illuminating, was too extensive and complex for Christopher to edit. The *History of Middle-earth* is an astonishing, unique achievement in 'literary archaeology'; but one of its most unexpected virtues is Christopher's frankness where a question eluded all efforts at resolution.

Yet he has laid the path for others to press forward where he could not. *The Book of Lost Tales* sets out a wealth of data for study. With his encouragement, the Gnomish Lexicon and other contemporary linguistic papers have since been edited meticulously in the journal *Parma Eldalamberon*. In the last year of his life, Christopher allowed me to examine the restricted *Lost Tales* papers at the Bodleian Library for my investigation into the most vexing question about when they were written.

A chronological conundrum

These are the chief fixed points in the chronology of composition of *The Book of Lost Tales*. A few pieces were composed between Tolkien's return from the Somme in late 1916 and the end of 1917: 'The Cottage of Lost Play', which introduces the location where the stories will be told; 'The Fall of Gondolin'; 'The Tale of Tinúviel'; and (according to Humphrey Carpenter) 'The Tale of Turambar'. The fair copy of 'The Cottage of Lost Play', written out by Edith, is dated by her 12 February 1917 – the sole contemporaneous date on any of the *Lost Tales* narratives.

The rest of the tales were written – and earlier ones rewritten – after 'The Music of the Ainur', the cosmogonical creation myth. This remainder comprises the full story of Valar and Elves up to and including the creation of the Sun and Moon, together with the abortive 'Gilfanon's Tale' about the arrival of mortal Men (almost all of *The Book of Lost Tales, Part 1*); plus the last-written story, 'The Tale of the Nauglafring'; along with rewritten versions of the 'Music', 'Turambar', 'The Fall of Gondolin' (one or two) and 'Tinúviel' (two). *The Book of Lost Tales* seems to have gone into almost

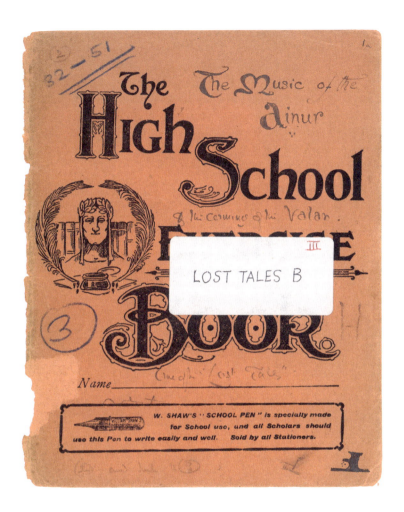

permanent hiatus around the middle of 1919, as Tolkien's free time was swallowed up either by tutoring or by compiling *A Middle English Vocabulary* for Oxford's Clarendon Press.

There is no reason to question any of these generally accepted points. But a 1964 letter from Tolkien creates a major difficulty. He recalled writing 'The Music of the Ainur' 'after escaping from the army: during a short time in Oxford, employed on the staff of the then still incomplete great Dictionary' – which means December 1918 or later, but let us call it 1919 for brevity's sake.[3] If this memory is correct, it suggests a curiously lopsided picture. After that initial burst of three or four tales totalling about 69,000 words, the two years to late 1918 must have been largely barren of story-making.

6.2 High School Exercise book containing 'The Music of the Ainur & the coming of the Valar', [1917]. Tolkien has added at the bottom, 'One of the "Lost Tales".'
Oxford, Bodleian Library, MS. Tolkien S 1/III, fol. 1a.

That is despite continued periods of convalescence in military officers' hospitals when he was below par rather than seriously ill – the very situation that had fostered those earliest tales. And the bulk of work on the *Lost Tales* – roughly 65,000 words of original story and much the same amount again in rewrites – must have been squeezed into the next six or seven months, when he was working full-time for the *Oxford English Dictionary* and living with Edith and their one-year-old son John.

Why does this difficulty matter, aside from the simple issue of biographical accuracy? First, it matters for what Christopher would call 'literary-archaeological' reasons: to understand a creative process we must get the sequence of composition right. Second, it matters for what I would call literary-historical reasons: to understand creative motivations, we need to know the original context. Two years may not be long during settled peacetime, but there was an enormous gulf between 1917 and 1919, both universally and, I would suggest, for Tolkien personally.

Christopher found 'no evidence to set against' his father's memory of writing the 'Music' in Oxford after leaving the army.[4] But by allowing me to re-examine the *Lost Tales* manuscripts at the Bodleian, he has enabled me to find such evidence. As he showed in *The History of Middle-earth*, the changing forms of names are particularly useful for dating a composition; but they are even more useful now that they can be checked against the language texts in *Parma Eldalamberon*. Most unexpectedly, the paper on which Tolkien wrote the 'Music' turned out to tell its own story.

For what follows, I have examined almost all the original *Lost Tales* manuscripts. I cite here name-forms I have checked in 'The Cottage of Lost Play' (MS. Tolkien S 1/I, pencil draft fols 19–25, ink fair copy 26–37), 'The Music of the Ainur' (original draft MS. Tolkien S 1/III, fols 2–8, rewritten in ink 9–26), and 'The Fall of Gondolin' (original version 'Tuor A', MS. Tolkien S 1/VIII–IX, and fair copy 'Tuor B', MS. Tolkien S 1/X). I only give folio numbers where needed for clarity; and I give vowel diacritics as Tolkien wrote them here rather than the forms published later, for example, *Ilūvatar* rather than *Ilúvatar*.

6.3 Text for the Music of the Ainur showing Linqil and Sūlima, early name forms for Ulmo and Manwë, [1917]. Oxford, Bodleian Library, MS. Tolkien S 1/III, fol. 6v.

and Ainur were ... very great

... here ... a ... ... the music the

... with full heard ... in any ... in the world; ... in the deeps ...

Iron and ... Stone and Gold ... and

much else. But ... the music ... no water

held its ... and ... ... and ... life ...

... their ... ... and ... ...

Long ... and ... the Sea said ... him that

the ... ... mercy ... out ... but had

not destroyed ... ...

... ... whose ... and the exquisite

good ... ... ice.

Melko desired under heat and excessive cold and

yet has not destroyed your ... nor ... ... the

music of your seas. Behold the power and glory

of ... the ... ... and vapours; and

even so ... not all ... . and Ainur said

... ... that Sea rather is ... fairer now

... ... for there is ... of

a loveliness ultra marvellous. albeit it has no music

... ... that comes in the end of ...

... is not ... Beautiful indeed but has a ...

... ... my heart and I am glad that ...

... ... even ... ... sadness is among

... saddest of all things, and I will go seek

Sulimo ... ... that he and I

play melodies for ever and ever ... ...

... ...

While the journey may seem arid at times, the destination can be reached no other way – and it promises to be fruitful.

Anomalies in 'The Music of the Ainur'

Tolkien drafted the 'Music' in pencil, emended the draft in pencil and ink, and then made a new version in ink. Compared to other *Lost Tales* writings, the story contains relatively few names; notably it names very few individuals among the divine beings who populate it. Yet in the pencil draft, several names differ from the forms that they take in other *Lost Tales* and that were to endure.[5] The most salient are these:

– The Creator, God, is named *Ilu* as well as *Ilúvatar*. Everywhere else in the *Lost Tales* we see the form that Tolkien retained all his life, *Ilúvatar*.

– The angelic beings who sing with Ilu are the *Ainu*, here both singular and plural; indeed, the creative choiring is called 'the music of the Ainu'. In the pencil 'Music', haphazardly, plural *Ainu* is twice emended or replaced by insertions in ink as *Ainur*. The pencil layer of 'Tuor A' likewise gives plural *Ainu* twice, emended to *Ainur* in ink at the second mention, and *Ainur* in four ink insertions further on.[6] This plural form *Ainur* is standard everywhere else in the legendarium narratives.

– The elven Shoreland Pipers are named the *Solosimpe*, plural, in both the pencil and ink versions of the 'Music'. This form, in Tolkien's handwriting, is written into three blank spaces left by Edith in her February 1917 fair copy of 'The Cottage of Lost Play' (Tolkien later emended each instance to *Solosimpi*). The forms in all other literary texts are *Solosimpe* singular, *Solosimpi* plural.

– The Ainu of the deeps is named *Linqil*, only appearing as the familiar *Ulmo* by emendation or on a replacement page. (The pages are disordered, but it is clear that 6v, with *Linqil*, ran on to 6r with *Linqil* emended to *Ulmo* before Tolkien turned back, struck out 6v, and replaced it with 5v, where *Ulmo* is the form as first written.) *Linqil* is unique to this pencil manuscript. Even the original pencil layer of 'Tuor A' has *Ulmo*.

– The Ainu of the airs is named *Sūlima*, three times clearly and once probably (the ending is obscured by archival tape). The pencil layer of 'Tuor A' has *Sūlimo*, employing what became a standard masculine ending in Tolkien's invented Qenya or Quenya language. Notably he is not called *Manwe*, a name which 'The Cottage of Lost Play' – pencil draft and February 1917 copy – assigns instead to an Elf. On the 'Cottage of Lost Play' copy, Tolkien emended this elf-name *Manwe* to *Valwe*.[7] By ink changes to 'Tuor A' and in the ink 'Music', he gave *Manwe* and the combination *Manwe Sūlimo* to the Ainu of the airs.

The simplest explanation for all this would be that the draft 'Music' predated the first writing of 'Tuor A' and belonged in the same phase as 'The Cottage of Lost Play'. This would also explain straightforwardly why 'Tuor A' can mention 'the great music of the Ainur'.[8]

Yet Christopher was mindful of his father's recollection that the 'Music' was written in the later, Oxford period. He noted that this reference to 'the great music of the Ainur' appears in an ink addition and surmised that 'Tuor A' was emended in that period too. Furthermore, having once (in *Unfinished Tales*) accepted that Edith made her fair copy 'Tuor B' in 1917, in *The History of Middle-earth* Christopher reassigned that copy to the 1919 phase too.[9]

All the data mentioned above can indeed be squared with Tolkien's recollection, but not straightforwardly. It demands that we picture him repeatedly making creative decisions in 1917 and then undoing them in 1919, only to revert to his first position thereafter. When it comes to *Ulmo/Linqil*, *Sūlima/Sūlimo* and *Manwe* as Elf or Ainu, the inferred order of changes becomes headspinningly convoluted and counterintuitive.

Fortunately, there is little need to pursue the twists and turns of these speculative processes. Tolkien's recollection of writing the 'Music' in Oxford comes under decisive challenge from the linguistic texts in *Parma Eldalamberon*, published since Christopher finished his work on *The Book of Lost Tales*.

The 'Music' and the lexicons

The earliest of these language-focused documents is a dictionary of Qenya, probably begun in early 1915. It acquired many accretions over the next few years, so that some items match the draft 'Music' and others match the ink version. Like the draft 'Music', this Qenya Lexicon (QL) has the plural *Solosimpe*. On the other hand, QL has *Ilúvatar* for God (but *Ilu* as 'ether'); *Ulmo* but not *Linqil*; *Manwe* as the Ainu of the airs, with the title *Súlimo*.[10] Work on QL seems to have fallen away during the writing of the *Lost Tales* as other lists took up the strain of recording Tolkien's prolific linguistic invention.

Most extensive is the Gnomish Lexicon (GL), recording the language of the people of Gondolin and others. Out of the jumble of GL, described by Christopher Tolkien above, the *Parma Eldalamberon* editors distinguish a first pencil layer, mostly erased, overwritten by a second ink layer. A matching ink dateline on the cover says *Tol Withernon ar lim gardin arthi, 1917*: 'Tol Withernon and many places besides, 1917'.[11] *Tol Withernon* is clearly an Elvished version of Withernsea, the town nearest Tolkien's army posting from 19 April that year. As will be seen, the initial pencil layer can have been no older than 1917 either.

The Gnomish Lexicon's ink layer cites plenty of Qenya forms too, and these can be compared directly against the forms in the pencil 'Music'. While *Ilu* and *Ilúvatar* alike appear in both texts, GL gives singular *Solosimpe*, plural *Solosimpi* (rather than *Solosimpe* as a plural); GL has *Ulmo* (but nothing equivalent to *Linqil*); and GL has *Súlimo* (not *-ma*) and *Manwe* as his forename.[12] A later, third layer of additions and emendations was made to the lexicon, but none of these Qenya forms was touched, so there is no support there either for the idea that the 'Music' was written later than 1917.

The 'Music' and the name-lists

Among the other linguistic lists from the *Lost Tales* era are two derived from 'The Fall of Gondolin', both of which mention the cosmogonic myth. The first is an 'Official name list' (ONL), compiled from 'Tuor A' after most of the emendations to the tale had already been made. It has plural *Ainur, Ulmo, Manwe (Súlimo)* and *Ilúvatar*, like the second, ink version of the 'Music'; but it also has *Ilu*, intriguingly, in a set of abbreviations for four items:

C = Cottage of Lost Play.
Al. = Ilu's music.
T = Tuor.
E = Earendil.[13]

It is evidently a title catalogue, and the *Parma Eldalamberon* editors reasonably surmise that it lists the texts for which name-lists had been or would be made. Edith compiled such a name-list (MS. Tolkien S 1/XIV, fol. 104v) from her February 1917 ink fair copy of 'The Cottage of Lost Play'. 'Tuor' means 'The Fall of Gondolin' (which Tolkien called in full 'Tuor and the Exiles of Gondolin'). I take 'Earendil' (*sic*) to mean the long poem or body of poems about the mariner which he had been writing since 1914. 'Ilu's music' can only mean 'The Music of the Ainur', and the name *Ilu* suggests this list was made before the ink version of that tale, which uses *Ilúvatar* exclusively.

Equally noteworthy are the omissions. If this mini-catalogue were compiled in 1919, when Tolkien recalled writing the 'Music', we would expect it to list also 'The Tale of Tinúviel', which was written in summer–autumn 1917, and probably 'The Tale of Turambar' too.

Tolkien used ONL as the basis for an encyclopaedic 'Name-list to The Fall of Gondolin' (NFG). One entry describes the *Ainur* (not *Ainu*):

> Now these were great beings who dwelt with *Ilúvatar* or *Enu* as the elves name Him (but the gnomes *Âd Ilon*) ere the world grew, and some of these dwelt after in the world and are the Gods or *Ainur* as say the elves; but thereof may more be learnt in the tale told by Rûmil in the "Music of the Ainur", or in those sayings of his to Eriol in the garden of Lindo.[14]

Note this time the use of *Ilúvatar* (besides *Enu* but not *Ilu*). The last clause perfectly describes what Tolkien called the 'Link between Cottage of Lost Play and Music of Ainur' that runs into the second, ink version of the 'Music'.[15] It sounds very much as if the 'Link' and its tale were in existence when the entry was written.

So Tolkien's memory of writing the 'Music' in 1919 suggests that we should put ONL and NFG in 1919 too. Yet comparing their name forms against the Gnomish Lexicon shows beyond reasonable doubt that both of these 'Fall of Gondolin' name-lists were made in 1917.

It is instructive to look at close correspondences between the two name-lists and the 1917 ink lexicon layer. They reveal a pattern of progressive shifting of forms by revision and replacement. The comparison of forms makes it clear that ONL (compiled from 'Tuor A') and NFG (enlarged from ONL) cannot have postdated the 1917 Gnomish Lexicon entries. If they had, it would mean for example that Tolkien had invented a form *Teld Quing Ilon* in 'Tuor A', abandoned it for *Ilbranteloth* in GL, then reverted to *Cris o Teld Quing Ilon* in ONL, then more-or-less copied that into NFG, only to emend the NFG entry to *Cris Ilbranteloth* – essentially going back to the GL form.[16] And he would have had to have made similar steps forward and then back again, methodically, across several related and unrelated entries.

Words for the Eldarin elves and their language in NFG and GL show clearly what the correct chronology must be. NFG first has *Egol* for an Elda, emended to *Egla*; *Eglothlim* for the Eldar, emended to *Eglothrim*; *Lam Eglon* for their Qenya language, emended to *Lam Eglathon* or *Egladrin*. Every time, GL has the later forms: *Egla, Eglothrim, Egladrin* respectively.[17]

So ONL predated NFG, which predated the 1917 Gnomish Lexicon. Both ONL and NFG mention the 'Music'. If the 'Music' were not written until 1919, we would be forced to imagine Tolkien planning the tale two years in advance; indeed, planning both of its successive versions! We would have to suppose that in 1917 he looked that far ahead and (in ONL) foresaw a draft of that tale naming *Ilu* that speaks of the *Ainu* in the plural; and also (in NFG) foresaw a fair copy naming *Ilúvatar* and the *Ainur*. The idea does not stand up to the kind of close scrutiny that the published linguistic papers now make possible.

The lion and the unicorn

A final piece of evidence connecting the 'Music' with 1917, and specifically with the period of 'The Cottage of Lost Play' and 'The Fall of Gondolin', made itself apparent as I pored over the names and other points in the loose-leaf pencil draft of the cosmogonic myth.

Indeed, it positively leapt into focus – a small lion-and-unicorn crest on the second and sixth sides of Tolkien's text. Embossed but now barely raised, sideways in the margin, this is easy to miss. So are the watermark lines, 2.8 centimetres apart, that run parallel to Tolkien's writing. Two sheets of this paper have been turned sideways and folded or torn to make four pages (eight sides of writing). The remaining three pages are on a different stock, watermarked with a large crown and the (rather surprising) words SUPERIOR INVADER | LONDON.[18]

Tolkien tucked the pencil draft into a stapled, lined book in red card covers carrying the printed title *The High School Exercise Book*, in which he wrote the ink version of the 'Music' and began the next tale, 'The Coming of the Valar'. That tale continues in a further, identical exercise book (MS. Tolkien S 1/II). The same brand of notebook was used for most of 'Tuor A' and for the ink version of 'The Cottage of Lost Play'.[19]

But like the draft 'Music', 'Tuor A' begins on loose leaves – and remarkably, the same lion-and-unicorn stock is used for its opening page. Furthermore, the other kind of paper used for the draft 'Music', watermarked SUPERIOR INVADER, is the same stock used for the whole of the pencil draft of 'The Cottage of Lost Play'. I have examined almost all the *Lost Tales* papers but find no further examples of either stock. Archivist Catherine McIlwaine has kindly examined the remainder (MSS. Tolkien S 1/XI and XII) for me and likewise finds none. Of course, a supply of various paper or notebook brands might be used over any number of years. But here is a very striking constellation, fully supporting the linguistic evidence that all three tales belong in 1917.

'My father erred'

Tolkien's memory about the circumstances of long-ago writing could be unreliable. To the BBC in 1968 he described a vivid memory of beginning to write *The Hobbit* at 20 Northmoor Road, where the family moved on 14 January 1930. But his son John's diary records that it was already being read aloud on 1 January. Tolkien said elsewhere that the 1930s story of Númenor was 'originally unrelated' to 'the main mythology'; but Christopher, finding the very earliest outline already entrenched in the legendarium, judges it 'inescapable that my father erred when he said this'.[20] In his 1965 foreword to the second edition of *The Lord of the Rings*, Tolkien recalled that he wrote the beginnings of Book V in 1942, 'and there as the beacons flared in Anórien and Théoden came to Harrowdale I stopped', only resuming in 1944; and yet (despite this stirring image) Christopher again finds 'very clear evidence that my father erred in this recollection'– a 1944 letter stating that in recent days he had 'actually begun Book Five'.[21] He had not begun in 1942 at all. It was this 1944 beginning that proved a false start, and the delay that stuck in Tolkien's memory had actually been between then and 1946, when the book got properly under way.

I believe it is now plain that Tolkien likewise erred in 1964 when he remembered writing 'The Music of the Ainur' in Oxford after the Armistice. We can only speculate how the idea came to lodge in his mind. But when he made a new version of the cosmogonic myth in the mid-1930s – living in Oxford – it 'was composed with the "Lost Tale" in front of him, and indeed he followed it fairly closely', says Christopher.[22] Of all the *Lost Tales*, it was indeed the only one he ever used directly in this way to make a further full version.

Starting 'the epic'

We have no 1917 letter from Tolkien saying he has just written the 'Music', but there are contemporary letters from Christopher Wiseman (the friend after whom Tolkien would later name his own son) that shed further light on progress on *The Book of Lost Tales* early in that year. This has been made possible by permission from the Tolkien Trust to look again at these items in the Tolkien family papers at the Bodleian.[23]

We can infer from Wiseman's comments that by 18 January 1917 he knew Tolkien was planning some new and ambitious overarching narrative. On that date, returning some poems that Tolkien had sent him from hospital in November–December 1916, Wiseman told him, 'You ought to start the epic.' Tolkien wrote to him on or after 27 February, and Wiseman replied on 4 March:

> As to the burning question of epics, I am delighted to have touched you off. Please don't think I expect you to make any better attempt at an epic than Pope or Matthew Arnold.… But I want you to get it done.… This stage, if it doesn't produce an epic, will produce, I have no doubt whatever, a great poem, and I should think probably, as is your ambition, a mythology.

A little further on, Wiseman refers to Tolkien's many poems on Eärendel and other matters and says: 'The reason why I want you to write the epic is because I want you to connect all these up properly, and make their meaning and content tolerably clear.'

Without the other side of the correspondence Wiseman's words are, themselves, not quite tolerably clear. Perhaps he thought Tolkien had begun a verse epic in the classical mode of Homer's *Odyssey*. Perhaps Tolkien (characteristically) had quibbled with the word 'epic'. But it is clear enough that no connective narrative project had been begun by mid to late January.[24] We know 'The Cottage of Lost Play' was already written by 12 February; but we do not know whether, since Wiseman urged him in mid-January to make a start, he had begun any of the tales that were to be told in the Cottage. Nonetheless, Wiseman's comments suggest that Tolkien erred, too, when he later recalled writing 'The Fall of Gondolin' at the end of 1916.

However, they mesh with other points that stuck in Tolkien's memory: that the story was written 'in hospital and on leave', 'during sick-leave', or specifically 'during sickleave from the army in 1917'.[25] Tolkien had been on leave since before Wiseman told him to 'start the epic'. He was still debilitated and suffering occasional returns of trench fever contracted at the Somme. On 27 February, a military medical board sent him for a month to a comfortable sanatorium, the Furness Auxiliary Hospital in Harrogate, Yorkshire.

Discharged from there on 28 March, he spent three weeks on convalescent leave in nearby lodgings at 95 Valley Drive, with Edith. Here he was apparently in the thick of writing when Wiseman declared on 15 April that he was about to 'burst in on your literary solitudes'. Four days later, Tolkien was sent to join the Humber Garrison near Withernsea, Yorkshire.

Could it be that the paper with the lion-and-unicorn crest – the royal coat of arms of the United Kingdom – was official stock obtained by Tolkien at this military hospital? During the war years, stationery embossed with official crests was characteristically used by military hospitals and regiments, according to Ellen Parton, archivist at the Imperial War Museum.[26] The royal coat of arms was widely used by any such organizations with royal affiliations. The Furness Auxiliary Hospital was the patriotic gift of local Harrogate peerage: it had been converted from Harrogate's Grand Hotel by the generosity of Lord Furness of nearby Nidd Hall, and was presided over by Lady Furness.

If Tolkien did indeed get his lion-and-unicorn paper at the Harrogate hospital, we may suppose that 'The Cottage of Lost Play' (on SUPERIOR INVADER paper) was the only narrative written before Wiseman's 4 March letter; that Tolkien wrote the 'Music' (on a mixture of the two stocks of paper) in the hospital; and that he began 'Tuor A' (on lion-and-unicorn paper) in the hospital, completing it while on leave at Valley Drive. Such name-evidence as exists – mostly too slight to justify presenting here – offers no contradiction to the idea that 'The Cottage of Lost Play' preceded the 'Music'. At least it is clear that the 'Music', with *Linqil* emended to *Ulmo* for the Ainu of the deeps and with *Sūlima* for the Ainu of the airs, was written before 'Tuor A', with *Ulmo* and *Sūlimo*.

Implications

But this investigation is not about applying a magnifying glass to a couple of months in 1917; it is about getting a clear view of the evolution of *The Book of Lost Tales* from then until Tolkien largely set it aside in mid-1919. Moving 'The Music of the Ainur' from 1919 to 1917 has ramifications for it all.

The opening phase comes into clearer focus, gaining in artistry and practical purposefulness. It has always seemed

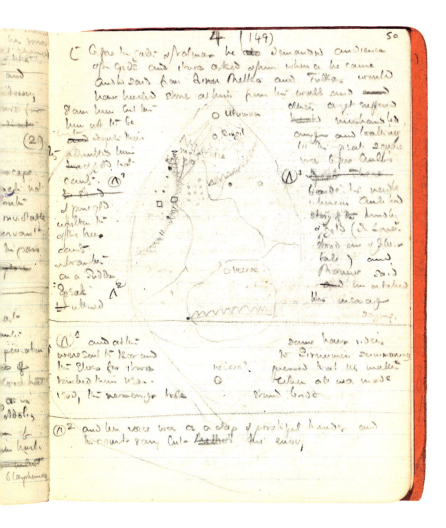

logical that Tolkien would write 'The Cottage of Lost Play'
early on. Now it seems reasonably clear that this introductory
narrative was the very first thing he wrote. 'The Music of the
Ainur' and 'The Fall of Gondolin', previously understood to
be separated by two years, can now be seen as a product of
just two months or so; the story of revolt in heaven virtually
a twin to the tale of tyrannical assault on earth. As I have
written elsewhere, in a paper discussing some of the literary
implications of this revised chronology, 'They form a diptych
of theory and practice, problem and outcome, with two falls:
the cosmic and the earthly, the mythic and the epic, each with
the satanic figure of Melko as instigator.'[27]

6.4 Rough map of the
world set amid text for 'The
Darkening of Valinor' [1917].
See Chapter 7, 'I Wisely Started
with a Map': J.R.R.Tolkien as
Cartographer by Wayne G.
Hammond and Christina
Scull for a description of this
map (pp. 106–7).
Oxford, Bodleian Library,
MS. Tolkien S 1/IV, fol. 50r.

Previously, when 'The Fall of Gondolin' appeared to predate all the other tales, it seemed that Tolkien was driven primarily by impulse. With the revised chronology, it can be seen that he made three parallel beginnings. 'The Cottage of Lost Play' provides the setting for the telling of the stories. 'The Music of the Ainur' recounts the creation and the angelic fall that sets mythological history in motion. 'The Fall of Gondolin' is the long-overdue origin story for the hero who 'sprang up from the ocean's cup / in the gloom of the mid-world's rim' in Tolkien's earliest mythological poem in September 1914: Eärendel, whom the tale finally establishes as the son of the union of elven Idril and mortal Tuor in Gondolin.[28] Each beginning was a vital entry point into just the kind of project that Wiseman was urging at the time: an 'epic' or mythology that would connect up all the ideas that had only been glimpsed in the disconnected poetry of 1914–16.

Looking beyond the opening phase and these three earliest tales, the rearranged chronology has profound ramifications. It has always been clear that the majority of the tales, most notably those of Valinor, were written after the 'Music'; but the notion that this cosmogonic myth belonged to 1919 has artificially corralled all those tales into an almost unfeasibly busy six months or so. Now we know the 'Music' was written in 1917, it is as if a dam has been removed. It may take a while for the waters to settle; it has certainly taken me painstaking work to begin to see how they will lie. But I think we can now make the working assumption that Tolkien was most productive when he had most time: in 1917–18 during his long, enforced gaps between military duties.

He told W.H. Auden in 1954 that after 'The Fall of Gondolin' he 'wrote a lot else in hospitals before the end of the First Great War'.[29] Up till now, that seemed an odd thing to say, because the tales of Tinúviel and Turambar – though astonishing in themselves – hardly amounted to 'a lot else'. These two tales seemed as much the products of impulse as 'The Fall of Gondolin' had: disconnected episodes during the tyranny of Melko in the 'Great Lands' east of the sea, one tale joyous and the other grievous, like comedic and tragic theatrical masks. Melko lurks behind the stories of Tuor, Tinúviel and Turambar, but none of them really explains who he is, where he comes from and why he acts as he does. Now, we know that Tolkien had begun to explain all these things in 'The Music of the Ainur' at the outset. But what of the rest of Melko's progress, from his fall in heaven to his enthronement as iron-crowned king of a slave empire in the North of mortal lands? And what of the divine cohort, the Ainur, who descend into the world in the 'Music' but whose names and natures remain largely undefined in this cosmogonic myth? There is not a great deal to be gleaned about this, either, from Tinúviel's, Turambar's and Tuor's stories. All three tales refer to the Valar in the West, but between them they give only fragmentary glimpses. If Tolkien had indeed written nothing but these tales before 1919, it would mean that for the intervening two years he simply went on making new bits to be connected up – aggravating rather than alleviating the confusion that Wiseman had urged him to resolve with an overarching 'epic'.

In fact, after the original three stories, Tolkien moved from beginnings to a primary phase of world-building – and the writing of the Valinor narrative that would form the backbone of the 'epic'. The evidence of changing nomenclature will demonstrate that the tales describing the coming of the Valar, the building of Valinor, the chaining of Melko, and the coming of the Elves were all written during 1917, beginning in High School Exercise Books like the ones used for the earliest tales. Name-lists of the Valar and the creatures of the Earth will be found to be the products of this same phase, along with the now well-known diagram of the 'World-Ship'. So too will the 'earliest map' of the world, still exquisite behind a veil of pencil smudges that show how often Tolkien consulted it.[30]

I hope to be able to publish these and further findings in due course. The methods I have used here, particularly the close comparison of literary with linguistic material, are slow and painstaking. Yet they are indispensable for understanding the real sequence in which the *Lost Tales* emerged, and for shedding a clearer light on how Tolkien began constructing his mythology.

Wayne G. Hammond and Christina Scull

7

'I WISELY STARTED WITH A MAP'

J.R.R. TOLKIEN AS CARTOGRAPHER

MORE THAN sixty maps by J.R.R. Tolkien survive among his papers. These include, by our subjective count, sketches and plans (such as one of the citadel at Minas Tirith), which may be considered maps by another name and of different degree. In at least one instance – the 'world-ship' drawing *I Vene Kemen*, discussed below – we have perhaps stretched the definition of what might be considered a map. But however defined, the number of maps Tolkien drew indicates the notable extent to which he used cartography in connection with his tales of Middle-earth.

It seems likely that he became familiar with the reading and making of maps already in boyhood, as a Scout in Birmingham. Later, as an undergraduate member of the Officer Training Corps at Oxford (1914–15), he took classes in map-reading. In 1916, having entered the Army, he was tested on the reading of maps, among other subjects, to qualify as a signalling officer. A map of the area around Regina Trench, an objective of Tolkien's battalion at the Somme, is preserved in his family papers; he did not draw it, but he understood its signs and conventions, as well as the grid-reference system then recently introduced in British military map-making. This knowledge, combined with the skills he had developed as an amateur artist, with pen, inks, watercolours and coloured pencils (chalks or crayons), would be of use to him when he returned from France and began to write the stories for which he became famous.

Mapping 'The Silmarillion'
The two earliest of Tolkien's literary maps are associated with *The Book of Lost Tales*, the first prose treatment of his 'Silmarillion' mythology. One, a rough sketch drawn on

a page of the manuscript of 'The Theft of Melko and the Darkening of Valinor' (see fig. 6.4), fits the world of the story within a narrow pointed oval, in appearance like that of the mandorla or almond-shaped maps found in copies of the medieval *Polychronicon* edited by Ranulf Higden.[1] A view from above oriented to the north, the map contains features of importance such as Utumna (the dwelling of Melko), the Mountains of Valinor and the Great Sea, as well as others (such as the Magic Isles) which had not yet entered the tales. The Two Trees are marked, but also their predecessors, the Two Lamps mounted on pillars of ice, Ringil and Helkar. Another drawing of about the same time, *I Vene Kemen* (meaning perhaps 'Ship of the Earth' in the Elvish language Qenya), in contrast is a longitudinal view of the world from west to east, surrounded by the Outer Ocean (Vai) and with layers of air above; Tolkien shows the relative locations and elevations of features such as the mountain Taniquetil and the island Tol Eressea. Remarkably, *I Vene Kemen* has the appearance of a Viking ship, with a mast, sail and curved prow, though these elements may have been added later.

Tolkien made the early sketch of the world and *I Vene Kemen*, both compact in scope, probably in 1919. He had not yet made a small-scale map for his fiction (that is, a large map covering extensive territory), though the 'lost tales' were numerous and their setting complex, and it is remarkable to think of him carrying the geography of his stories in his head; but that may well have been the case. Not until the 1920s did he make a larger map for 'The Silmarillion', perhaps in association with the *Sketch of the Mythology* he began probably in early 1926. (The map is drawn on a sheet of University of Leeds examination paper, and therefore could not have been made earlier than autumn 1920, when Tolkien took up his Leeds readership.) This became his working map for several years. 'Names were emended and places re-sited', as Christopher Tolkien describes; 'the writing is in red ink, black ink, green ink, pencil, and blue crayon, often overlaying each other. Lines representing contours and others representing streams tangle with lines for redirection and lines cancelling other lines. But it is striking that the river-courses as drawn on this first map were scarcely changed at

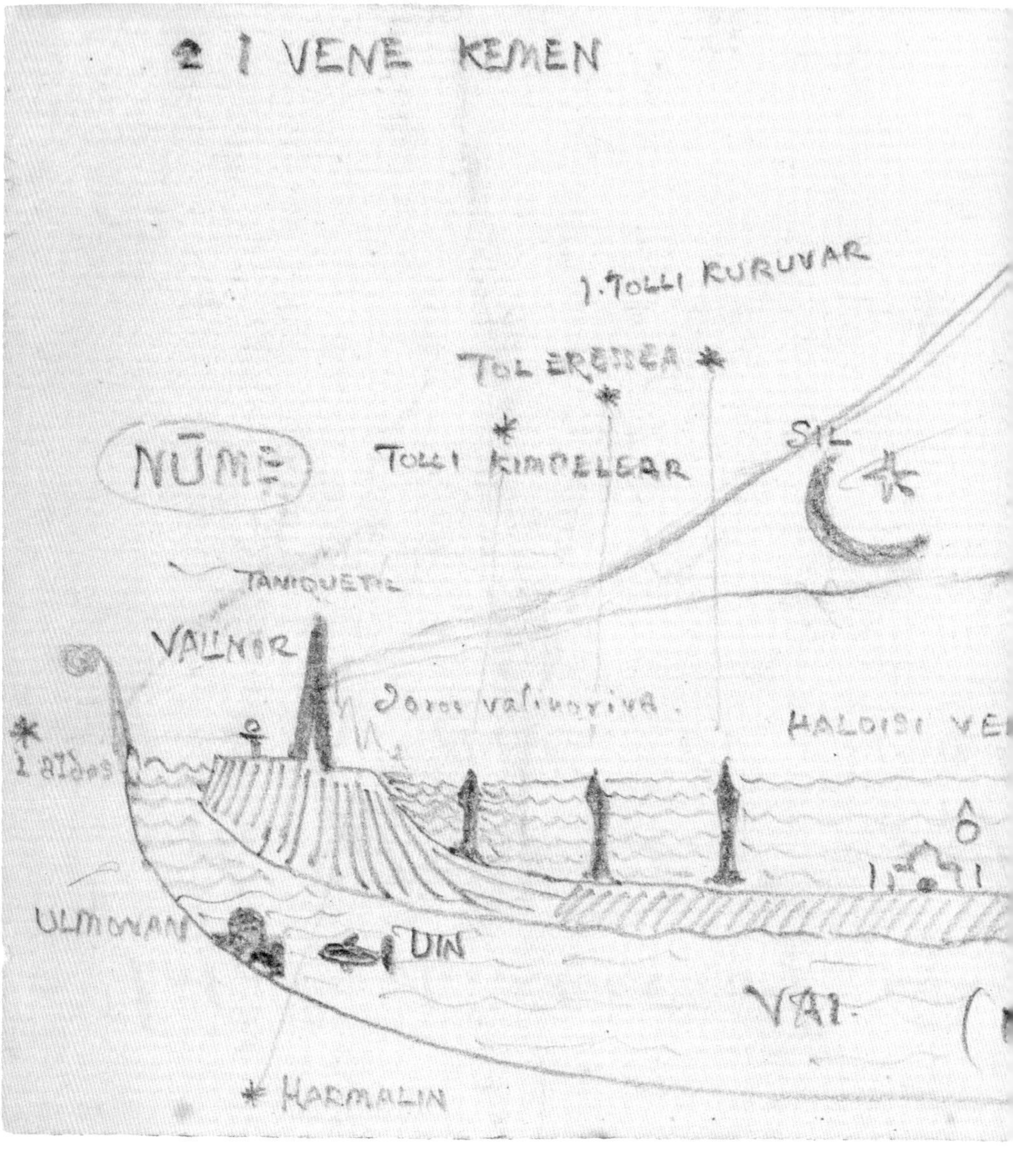

2 | VENE KEMEN

1. TOLLI KURUVAR

TOL EREMEA *

NŪMĒ

TOLLI KIMPELEAR *

SIL

TANIQUETIL

VALINOR

Joros valinoriva.

HALDISI VE

* 1 atdas

ULMONAN

DIN

VAI

* HARMALIN

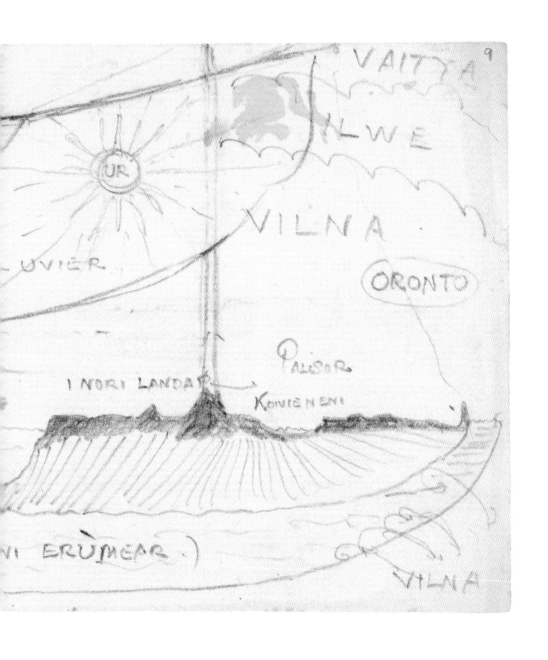

9

VAITYA

ILWE

VILNA

ORONTO

UR

UVIER

PALISOR

I NORI LANDA

KOIVIE NENI

VI ERUMEAR

VILNA

7.1 'I Vene Kemen', perhaps meaning 'Ship of the Earth', in the Elvish language, Qenya, c.1918-1919.
Oxford, Bodleian Library, MS. Tolkien S 2/III, fol. 9r

all afterwards.'[2] Tolkien also made eastward and westward extensions to the map, more roughly drawn and overlapping the primary sheet.

In the early 1930s he drew another small-scale map, developed from and replacing the first; this was the basis of Christopher Tolkien's *Map of Beleriand and the Lands to the North* in the published *Silmarillion*. The later map too was long used and reworked by its maker, becoming 'covered all over with alterations and additions of names and features, not a few of them so hastily or faintly pencilled as to be more or less obscure'.[3] Both of these maps, and extensions, include a grid by which Tolkien could estimate distance or extent; on the later map he gave the scale as 3.2 centimetres to 50 miles. Two statements in the 'Quenta Silmarillion' manuscript – the length of Dorthonion and the extent of West Beleriand at its widest – are incorrect according to the second map, and were corrected long after to harmonize with the cartography.

Neither of these two large maps extends to the west much beyond the coast of Beleriand – that is, beyond Middle-earth proper and into the wider world of which it is a part. When Tolkien came in the late 1930s and early 1940s to write about the star-shaped island Númenor, raised in the Great Sea between Valinor and Middle-earth, he seems again to have worked without a map to guide him. There are three renderings of Númenor among his papers, but they were made comparatively late, around 1960.

Contemporary with the later large 'Silmarillion' map, Tolkien wrote the *Ambarkanta* ('Of the Fashion of the World'), a description of the Earth (Ilu, later Arda), 'globed' within the 'Walls of the World' (Ilurambar). Upon all sides of the lands and inner waters is the 'Enfolding Ocean' (Vaiya), 'more like to sea below the Earth and more like to air [Vista and Ilmen] above the Earth'.[4] At this stage in his development of 'The Silmarillion', Tolkien regarded the Earth as cartographically (if not topographically) flat, although part of a 'globe' defined by encircling seas and airs. In relation to the *Ambarkanta* he drew five maps or diagrams, each of them circular or a modified oval, like medieval *mappaemundi*. Three of these illustrate the divisions of land, air and sea described in the text, recalling those medieval maps that

7.2 The first large 'Silmarillion' map which was Tolkien's working map for several years, c.1926.
Oxford, Bodleian Library, MS. Tolkien S 2/X, fol. 3r.

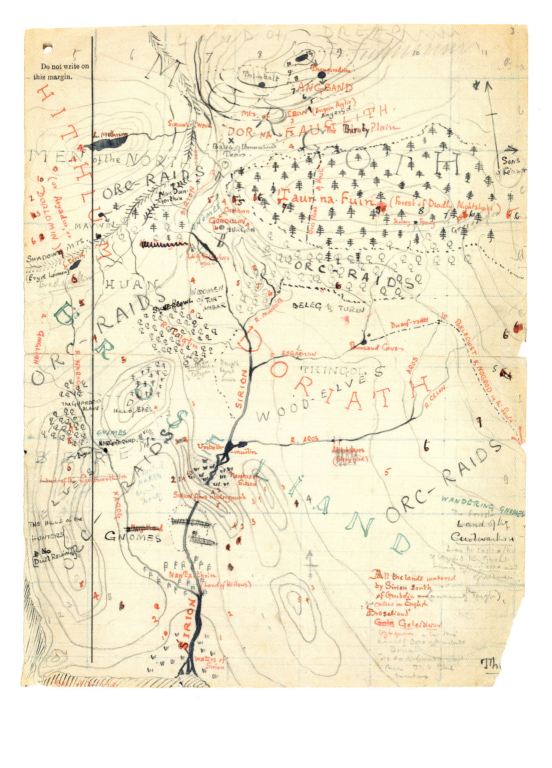

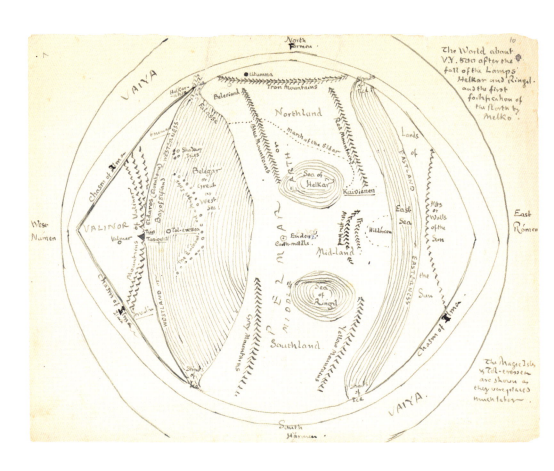

7.3 'The World about V.Y. 500 after the Fall of the Lamps Helkar and Ringil and the First Fortification of the North by Melko', map for the *Ambarkanta*, early 1930s. Oxford, Bodleian Library, MS. Tolkien S 2/III, fol. 7r.

depict zones of climate. The other two maps are more akin to complex *mappaemundi*, illustrating land masses and bodies of water.

One of the latter, *The World about V.Y. [Valian Year] 500 after the Fall of the Lamps Helkar and Ringil and the First Fortification of the North by Melko*, is a development of the *Book of Lost Tales* sketch-map, enlarged to west and east, with greater detail and notable differences, such as that the Sea of Helkar (once the site of the Southern Lamp) was now in the north, and that of Ringil (formerly the Northern Lamp) now in the south. The later map is remarkable also for its symmetry, as if the world were created by a thoughtful artist – as, indeed, it was in Tolkien's mythology, by divine art. The Mountains of Valinor in the west are echoed by the Walls of the Sun in the east, the West Sea by the East Sea, the Blue and Red Mountains of the north by the Grey and Yellow Mountains of the south. 'The chief departure from symmetry' in the map, as Christopher Tolkien writes, is 'the difference in shape of the great Seas, and this was due to the eastward thrusting or "crowding" of Middle-earth', as the land is here labelled for the first time (beneath the word *Pelmar*, 'The Enclosed Dwelling' or habitable surface), 'at the time of the making of Valinor and the raising of its protective mountain-chain'[5] – a marring or imperfection by the Valar (or 'gods') of their original design.

Mapping *The Hobbit*

Whether Tolkien conceived *The Hobbit* originally (by 1929) in connection with 'The Silmarillion', or joined it to his larger work only when he wrote *The Lord of the Rings* as a sequel to *The Hobbit* and consciously an extension of the mythology, the lands in which Bilbo Baggins has his adventures lie outside the parts of Middle-earth in which the 'Silmarillion' tales occur. The name 'Middle-earth' in fact is not found in *The Hobbit*, nor is 'the Shire' as the location of Hobbiton, Bilbo's home. At least as it came to be expressed in the nomenclature of *The Lord of the Rings*, the setting of *The Hobbit* stretches from Hobbiton in Eriador eastward across the Misty Mountains and through Mirkwood to the Lonely Mountain and the Iron Hills. Eriador is east of the Blue Mountains, which are at the eastern edge of the large 'Silmarillion' maps but became the westernmost mountains of Middle-earth at the cataclysmic end of the First Age, when many lands were destroyed. For *The Hobbit*, then, Tolkien imagined extensive new territory, which he depicted in new maps.

Some were mere sketches, made probably while he was working out details. Other maps are clearly finished: one of the Misty Mountains and the upper part of the Great River (the Anduin of *The Lord of the Rings*), one of the Lonely Mountain and surrounding lands, one of the Long Lake with a view of the Mountain, plans of the exterior of the Mountain, and a general map of 'Wilderland' from roughly the Ford of Rivendell in the west (the 'Edge of the Wild') to just beyond the Lonely Mountain in the east. Presumably most or all of these were part of the 'home manuscript' of *The Hobbit*, which Tolkien took pains to make presentable for lending to friends.

When *The Hobbit* came to the attention of George Allen & Unwin in 1936, its ten-year-old reader, Rayner Unwin, recommended that it be published 'with the help of maps',[6] then a common feature of children's books for convenience and added interest – for example, E.H. Shepard's map of the Hundred Acre Wood for *Winnie-the-Pooh* by A.A. Milne (1926) and Stephen Spurrier's 'pirate' map of Lakeland in *Swallows and Amazons* by Arthur Ransome (1930). Tolkien wanted five maps in the published *Hobbit*, but he drew them with shading and multiple colours, which were too expensive to print. Rather than redraw all five, he chose to include only two, *Wilderland*, which he remade with only black and blue inks, adding a notable amount of detail (especially hundreds of trees comprising Mirkwood, replacing contour lines), and *Thror's Map*, on which the story of *The Hobbit* turns.

Probably the first version of Thror's (originally Fimbulfambi's) map is sketched on a page of the earliest manuscript of *The Hobbit*. There it is said to show 'the Black [i.e. Lonely] Mountain and the surrounding country.... Over here is the Wild Wood and far beyond to the North, only the edge of it is on the map, is the Withered Heath where the Great Dragons used to live.' 'A picture of a dragon in red' is said to be drawn 'on the Mountain', though there is none in Tolkien's sketch, while a rune on the west side of the

7.4 The earliest version of Thror's map, drawn for *The Hobbit*, late 1920s. Marquette, MS. Tolkien Mss-1/1/1, fol. 1a.

WITHERED HEATH.

WILD WOOD

MOUNTAIN

Ruins of Dale Town

R. Running

Mountain marks a secret entrance and a sinister hand points towards it.[7] The most curious feature of the sketch-map is a pictographic compass rose, first interpreted by Douglas A. Anderson in *The Annotated Hobbit*: north, at the top, is denoted by the northern constellation Ursa Major, the Great Bear (it seems possible to identify this also with Ursa Minor, which contains the North Star) and south by a shining sun, but west is shown as three mountain peaks, perhaps the Mountains of Valinor, and east as a radiant archway, possibly the Gates of Morn, the latter two elements borrowed from 'The Silmarillion'.[8]

Tolkien later redrew this map more in keeping with the text (a dragon appears in red on the Mountain) and probably for the 'home manuscript'. Its title, *Thror's Map. Copied by B. Baggins*, suggests that he meant it to be a 'facsimile' of the hobbit's 'copy', and the 'copy' is thus implied to have been made from a still earlier map, to give verisimilitude to the story. Again oriented with north at the top, the directions in its compass rose are indicated by Anglo-Saxon runes. Tolkien wrote the hidden letters (which tell Bilbo and the dwarves how to find the secret door into the Mountain) on the other side of the sheet, directing 'For moon-runes hold up to a light', thus imitating as closely as possible the revealing of the letters by moonlight in the house of Elrond (Chapter 3). Tolkien wanted *Thror's Map* to be included in the published *Hobbit* in this form, but for the sake of economy Allen & Unwin insisted that it appear as an endpaper, with the 'hidden' runes shown on its face.

When redrawing the map yet again, for publication, with the red dragon above rather than 'on' the Lonely Mountain (though the latter reading remained in the text), Tolkien made it more elaborate and 'archaic' in appearance. Its stylized mountain and rivers now resembled details on medieval maps,[9] and there are references to 'the Great Worms' (dragons), spiders, Men and the Elvenking. Although it is focused on the Lonely Mountain and the Desolation of Smaug, it points in four directions to features not on the map – the Iron Hills, Esgaroth, Mirkwood, the Grey Mountains and the Withered Heath – locating its geography within a larger context, most of which is shown in *Wilderland*.

7.5 'Thror's Map Copied by B. Baggins', drawn for *The Hobbit*, c.1930. Oxford, Bodleian Library, MS. Tolkien Drawings 33r.

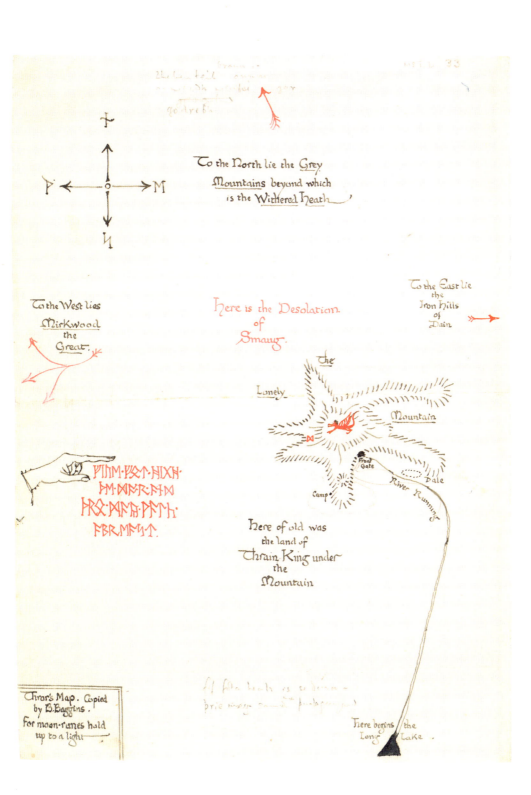

Unusually among his maps, Tolkien oriented the final *Thror's Map* with east at the top, probably because it now needed to be (as an endpaper spread) horizontal instead of vertical, rather than as a nod to the pre-fifteenth-century *mappamundi* tradition (in which east was most significant, as the location of the Earthly Paradise). In a prefatory note for the third (1966) edition of *The Hobbit*, Tolkien explained that eastward orientation was 'usual in dwarf-maps'.

The positions of the Front Gate to the Lonely Mountain and of the town of Dale, fixed in the final *Thror's Map*, led Tolkien to revise his text in proof, so that Thorin and company follow a correct geography relative to the map when moving from the Gate to a look-out post in Chapter 13. But he realized too late that there was a contradiction in the phrase 'Here of old was Thrain King under the Mountain', written on the map: if Thrain was the son of Thror, and Thror was the last King under the Mountain before the dwarves were driven away by the dragon, Thrain could not have been King under the Mountain, and therefore could not have been named in the inscription. Rather than change the map, which would have been more costly, Tolkien added an author's note to the second (1951) edition of *The Hobbit* stating that the Thrain referred to on the map was an earlier king of the same name; and later he emended the text of Chapter 1 to read that Thorin's grandfather (Thror) had given the map to his son (now Thrain II) for safety, and that the Lonely Mountain had been discovered by Thorin's 'far ancestor, Thrain the Old'.

Thror's Map points the way to 'long-forgotten gold', as the dwarves sing in the first chapter of *The Hobbit*. In this respect its most important literary precursor was the map of Treasure Island in Robert Louis Stevenson's book of that name (though the novel itself left Tolkien cool). Stevenson famously drew the map of an island from his imagination before he had any thought of a story: 'It was elaborately and (I thought) beautifully coloured; the shape of it took my fancy beyond expression; it contained harbours that pleased me like sonnets'.[10] From this, a tale took shape in which the map is an object of interest and a catalyst of events, while a physical map accompanying the text sets the scene and intrigues the reader. The latter also led Stevenson to introduce certain actions in the story, such as the wanderings of the *Hispaniola* because the map has two harbours. *The Hobbit* certainly did not itself begin with a map, but with words, as Tolkien variously recalled. A letter he wrote long after the fact suggests that he created Thror's map as a separate entity before proceeding with the text ('for some years [after writing the first words] I got no further than the production of Thror's Map'[11]); whether this was so or not – and the roughness of the sketch-map in the manuscript suggests that it was its first iteration – he invented the map very early on, necessarily together with its function in the story. Like Stevenson's map, it is integral with the plot.

Mapping *The Lord of the Rings*

Bilbo Baggins in *The Hobbit* 'loved maps, and in his hall there hung a large one of the Country Round with all his favourite walks marked on it in red ink' (revised text, Chapter 1). It would be interesting to know what other maps he might have seen, or could have seen given the insularity of his people as Tolkien would later describe them; that of the 'Country Round' defined his comfortable world before his journey in *The Hobbit* expanded his horizons. Respectable hobbits, we are led to understand in the early chapters of *The Lord of the Rings*, do not concern themselves with the world beyond their borders, indeed they are concerned to keep it out; therefore, it would stand to reason that few would have, or need to have, the skill to read a map with a larger scope, and the prospects of a wider world such a map represents might be daunting. Even Frodo, one of the most educated hobbits in *The Lord of the Rings*, makes only so much of the 'storied and figured [ornamented] maps' he is shown at Rivendell (Book II, Chapter 3), and is content to follow Aragorn and Gandalf. For Sam Gamgee, 'maps conveyed nothing to [his] mind, and all distances in these strange lands seemed so vast that he was quite out of his reckoning' (Book II, Chapter 3). Pippin looks at maps, but does not remember them; instead, it is level-headed Merry who spends his time most usefully at Rivendell, and later is able to put his study of Elrond's maps into practice.

Unlike *The Hobbit*, *The Lord of the Rings* contains no map upon which the story hinges. And yet the three maps published in the latter work are meant, like the endpaper maps in *The Hobbit* though more modern (or less 'medieval') in design, to have been drawn from books of lore: in his original (1954) foreword to *The Lord of the Rings*, Tolkien wrote that the Shire map was 'approved as reasonably correct by those Hobbits that still concern themselves with ancient history'. But apart from the internal workings of *The Lord of the Rings*, Tolkien was more practically concerned that maps be provided for readers' use in navigating his book's expansive setting. In April 1954 he apologized to the author Naomi Mitchison who had received, for review, page proofs of *The Fellowship of the Ring* and *The Two Towers* lacking maps (which were still being revised):

> I am sorry about the Geography [Mitchison had asked questions about the geography of the story]. It must have been dreadfully difficult without a map or maps. There will be in volume I [when published on 29 July] a map of part of the Shire, and a small-scale general map of the whole scene of action and reference (of which the map at the end of *The Hobbit* [*Wilderland*] is the N.E. [north-east] corner). These have been drawn from my less elegant maps by my son Christopher, who is learned in this lore.... I wisely started with a map, and made the story fit (generally with meticulous care for distances). The other way about lands one in confusions and impossibilities, and in any case it is weary work to compose a map from a story...[12]

Strictly speaking, the only maps with which Tolkien could have 'started' when he began to write *The Lord of the Rings* were those he had made for *The Hobbit*. But by the time he completed the initial text of his *Hobbit* sequel in 1949 he had made a variety of working maps, and in his letter to Mitchison was surely referring generally to his practice of using maps as aids to writing. He remarked several times on this process. He told Rayner Unwin, for example, that in a complicated story like *The Lord of the Rings* 'one cannot make a map for the narrative, but must first make a map and make the narrative agree'.[13] And he commented to interviewers Charlotte and Denis Plimmer that 'believable fairy-stories must be intensely practical. You must have a map, no matter how rough. Otherwise you wander all over the place. In the *Ring* I never made anyone go further than they could on a given day.'[14] Again, to calculate distances he overlaid measured grids on maps, or drew on graph paper. He was much more concerned with this when writing *The Lord of the Rings*, planned from the start for publication, than he was when creating *The Hobbit* for a private audience.

Even for his own purposes in *The Hobbit*, Tolkien made no maps of Hobbiton, or of the lands through which Bilbo and company pass to reach Rivendell. The *Wilderland* map merely points, beyond the 'Edge of the Wild', to 'Western Lands' and to Hobbiton. Nor does *Wilderland* encompass the whole of the north-east (upper right) corner of the *Lord of the Rings* general map as Tolkien remarked to Naomi Mitchison, but extends east only to the Lonely Mountain and the Desolation of Smaug, far short of distant Rhûn. Within this quadrant, however, Tolkien added details, such as the names of a watercourse, wood and marshy area west of the Anduin: the river Gladden and the Gladden Fields. Eventually the setting of *The Lord of the Rings* would reach many leagues west and south of the *Hobbit* maps, and Tolkien would invent a rich variety of new features.

The earliest of many small working maps, among them plans of Bree and of roads and rivers between Weathertop and the Ford of Bruinen, date from within a year or two of Tolkien beginning to write *The Lord of the Rings* in December 1937. He made the earliest map of the lands south of those shown in *Wilderland*, with the *Hobbit* map in hand, presumably in Autumn 1939, when writing Book II, Chapter 3 ('The Ring Goes South'). Probably in 1941, he began to create a much larger map of Middle-earth: ultimately measuring 45.5 × 49.2 centimetres at its furthest extent, it was continuously in development for about five years. Christopher Tolkien describes it as

> [made] with great care and delicacy until a late stage of correction, and it has an exceedingly 'Elvish' and archaic

air.... My father made a good deal of use of pencil and coloured chalks: mountain-chains are shaded in grey, rivers (for the most part) represented in blue chalk, marshland and woodland in shades of green (Mirkwood is conveyed by little curved marks in green chalk, suggestive of treetops).[15]

As he revised, Tolkien added sheets and panels, overlapping earlier workings, gluing the whole together so that the sections cannot now be separated. Possibly in connection with his new start on Book V in July 1946, the first map having become battered and no doubt too difficult to revise further, he made a replacement, and this in turn became his principal working map. Still other large maps, of the northern and southern parts of Middle-earth, would come later, as he completed Book VI in 1948, while always in conjunction with his small-scale maps he drew closer details of the geography of the story, such as a map of the White Mountains and the Stone of Erech as he considered the route of the Grey Company in Book V, Chapter 2.

Once George Allen & Unwin began physical production of *The Lord of the Rings* at the end of 1952, the question of maps to include in the book became urgent. On 8 August 1953, Tolkien apologized to his publisher that he had not yet made new drawings of those he thought essential.

> The minimum requirements are ... a larger scale map of the Shire; a small scale map of the whole country; and another map of the southern country (Gondor [and Mordor [and Rohan]).... If I draw them to scale, and see that the distances referred to in the text are observed with reasonable accuracy, will it be possible to have them re-drawn and made prettier? Or do you wish me to make them for reproduction in my amateurish way? I wish I had more skill – and more time![16]

Two months later, he was 'in a panic' about the maps:

> I have spent an enormous amount of time on them without profitable result. Lack of skill combined with being harried. Also the shape and proportions of 'The Shire' as described in the tale cannot (by me) be made to fit into [the] shape of

a page; nor at that size be contrived to be informative.… Even at a little cost there should be picturesque maps, providing more than a mere index to what is said in the text. I could do maps suitable to the text. It is the attempt to cut them down and omitting all their colour (verbal and other) to reduce them to black and white bareness, on a scale so small that hardly any names can appear, that has stumped me.[17]

Christopher Tolkien stepped into the breach, making a new version of the general map of Middle-earth and a smaller map, titled *A Part of the Shire*, to precede Book I. These were his second such maps, having drawn versions in 1943, to which his father referred together with his own maps as *The Lord of the Rings* progressed.

Tolkien was defeated again when he came to the remaining map, of Rohan, Gondor and Mordor, needed for the third volume of *The Lord of the Rings*. He wrote to his publisher in April 1955: 'The map is hell! I have not been as careful as I should in keeping track of distances. I think a large scale map simply reveals all the chinks in the armour – besides being obliged to differ somewhat from the printed small scale version [the general map], which was semi-pictorial.'[18] Again Christopher Tolkien made the published map – scaled five times larger than the general map – in the nick of time, by working continuously for twenty-four hours.

The finished *A Part of the Shire* followed a series of sketch-maps of the area. The earliest of these is a rough drawing, made by Tolkien perhaps in early 1938, but with few details north of Hobbiton and the East Road. All versions of the Shire map are limited in scope, as the title of the published map implies, just as the *Hobbit* maps had been limited. As in *Wilderland*, Tolkien indicates tantalizingly at each edge that further territory lies beyond: Oatbarton to the north, Longbottom to the south, Bree to the east, and Michel Delving on the White Downs to the west. Christopher Tolkien recalled that his father gave him 'some latitude of invention', so that he could fill in empty spaces in his Shire map of 1943, and this effort was repeated in the final map. Names such as Little Delving, Needlehole, Nobottle, Rushock

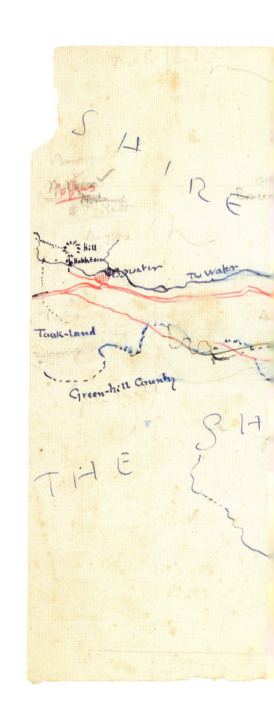

7.6 The earliest map of the Shire, drawn for *The Lord of the Rings*, c.1938.
Oxford, Bodleian Library, MS. Tolkien Drawings 104r.

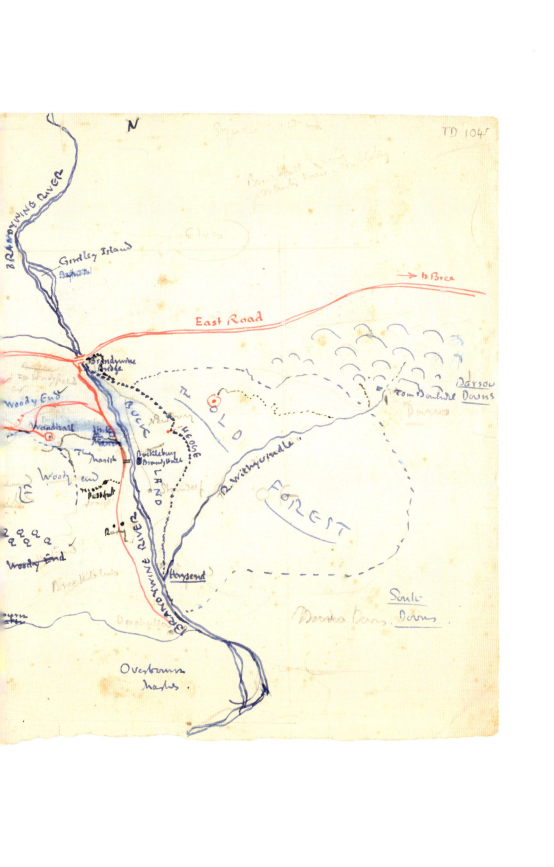

N

BRANDYWINE RIVER

Gridley Island
Bamfurl

→ to Bree

East Road

Elves

Brandywine Bridge

Woody End

Woodhall

BUCKLAND

The OLD FOREST

R. withywindle

Tom Bombadil Downs
Barrow Downs

Buckleberry
Brandyhall

The Marish

Woody End

Passfurd

Ring

BRANDYWINE RIVER

Haysend

South
Barrow Downs. Downs.

Woodyland

Deephallow

Overbourn
Marshes

Bog and Scary, among many others, were added, probably borrowed, Christopher thought, from his father's collection of books on English place names.[19] Some of the names that appear on the published map do not also appear in the text, or do not appear there in the same form.

Although he wrote of making a map for *The Lord of the Rings* and then making the story fit, one cannot say how often Tolkien altered his writing to suit his cartography while the work was in progress. For that matter, he also modified or replaced his working maps as needed. In October 1944, for instance, he struggled 'with the dislocated chronology of the Ring,' but solved the problem 'at last by small map alterations', as well as minor changes to the narrative.[20] A more dramatic example came late in the writing of Book V, when he introduced a sharp bend in the Anduin below Osgiliath, altering the course of the formerly straight river on the second large *Lord of the Rings* map and making large-scale drawings of the affected area in his manuscript, on a gridded sheet, and as an aerial view. At the same time, he changed the text of Book V, Chapter 1 ('Minas Tirith') so that the Anduin, flowing 'in a wide knee about the hills of Emyn Arnen in South Ithilien, bent sharply west, and the out-wall rose upon its very brink; and beneath it lay the quays and landings of the Harlond for craft that came upstream from the southern fiefs.' Christopher Tolkien had little doubt that his father made these changes so that the black fleet would not be seen from the Harlond until just before it was 'brought right under the wall of the Pelennor, and victory assured in the face of disaster by the exceedingly dramatic and utterly unlooked for arrival' of Aragorn and the other deliverers of Minas Tirith.[21]

Alterations to the text of *The Lord of the Rings* relative to its maps are more evident in its second edition, made after the passage of time had allowed errors or inconsistencies to be seen by the author or perceptive readers. To give only one instance, in the original text of Book I, Chapter 12 of *The Lord of the Rings*, the East Road between Weathertop and Rivendell runs alongside the Loudwater (Bruinen) 'for many leagues to the Ford', while the general map of Middle-earth shows it approaching the river at an acute angle; but in the

1965 revised text, 'the Road runs along the edge of the hills for many miles'. The published map was in error on this point, but Tolkien preferred to emend the description.

On 28 July 1965, he wrote to his American publisher, speaking of his work on the second edition: 'I ran into some difficulties with the maps. I have finally decided, where this is possible and does not damage the story, to take the *maps* as "correct" and adjust the narrative.' In the same letter, Tolkien remarked:

> [the Shire map] is most at fault and much needs correction (and some additions), and has caused a number of questions to be asked. The chief fault is that the Ferry at Bucklebury and so Brandy Hall and Crickhollow have shifted about 3 miles too far north (about 4 mm.). This cannot be altered at this time, but it is unfortunate that Brandy Hall clearly on the river-bank is placed so that the main road runs in front of it instead of behind. There is also no trace of the wood described at top of p. 99 [Book I, Chapter 4: 'Beyond that they came again to a belt of trees …']. I have had simply to disregard these map-errors.[22]

But he did not disregard all of them forever. In the Shire map first printed in the second Allen & Unwin edition (1966), the position of Brandy Hall was corrected relative to the ferry, the Yale (mentioned in Book I, Chapter 3) was added south of Whitfurrows and a connection drawn between the East Road and the road from Tuckborough to Stock was omitted, the latter perhaps because there was a confusion between the map and the roads or paths taken by the hobbits as they journey from Hobbiton to Crickhollow.

Cartography and story

Tolkien made maps for a variety of reasons. Some were aids to his writing; with these, he did not have to rely wholly on memory or scattered notes, and was better able to coordinate action. Small- and large-scale maps became essential as his invented world grew and changed, along with the complexity of his stories. When it came to the shared 'home manuscript' of *The Hobbit*, he provided maps so that readers could more comfortably trace the course of his story across its fictional geography. For this reason, too, maps were included in the published *Hobbit* and in *The Lord of the Rings*. But cartography was also another means for Tolkien to tell stories; maps expand and define the landscape of his tales, or serve as 'artefacts' which 'authenticate' his internal conceit that the stories of Middle-earth are accounts of actual events, found in manuscripts made in ages past. The latter is a device as old as the (comparatively simple) maps employed in Jonathan Swift's *Gulliver's Travels* (1726), and has never ceased to be effective in adding another dimension to a story.

Carl F. Hostetter

EDITING THE TOLKIENIAN MANUSCRIPT

8

S CANNING the spines of and paging through the more than twenty volumes of his father's writings that Christopher Tolkien edited (or co-edited), anyone can readily appreciate that he expended an immense amount of time and effort on them. Merely adding up the page-count – more than 8,000 (excluding the re-editions of the Three Great Tales[1]) – induces staggerment. But it is easy to fail fully to appreciate just how enormous an achievement that figure represents, for underlying those thousands of printed pages is a comparable number of mostly manuscript sides – and some typescripts, often bearing at least some manuscript revision – in his father's notoriously difficult handwriting. It is of course the editor's job to mediate the Tolkienian manuscript and its difficulties for the reader, a large part of which involves interpreting Tolkien's challenging and sometimes defeating handwriting, and otherwise turning what Tolkien has put on paper into a readable and neatly printed text.

To express and encourage further and fuller appreciation of Christopher's efforts and achievement as editor of his father's voluminous manuscript legacy, I offer here by way of practical example a little *vade mecum* of the task of editing the Tolkienian manuscript. To this end, and at the invitation of the Tolkien Archivist, I have selected four brief texts from the Bodleian's Tolkien archives, which I will refer to as Text 1, Text 2, and so on, none of them published before (though two are earlier drafts of texts that have been published), and all of them exhibiting challenging and illuminating aspects of the task.[2]

In order to present the manuscripts on pages facing my edition of each of them, I have kept those editions short enough to fit on a single page, by transposing what I would normally supply as a preceding introduction to each text – in which I discuss its probable date, context, and other relevant internal and external clues and characteristics – to the introductory paragraphs below, in the course of discussing the various challenging editorial aspects they present. I begin with a few words on what I take, following Christopher's own example, to be the principal goal and general approach in editing his father's manuscripts.

Goal and approach

One thing to note right away is that Christopher Tolkien never published what is known as a 'diplomatic edition' of any of his father's manuscripts: that is, an edition that attempts to reproduce every written feature of a manuscript – punctuation (or lack thereof), spelling, abbreviations, strike-throughs, insertions, underlines – as a sort of facsimile in type. To be sure, diplomatic editions have their place, particularly for collation and textual criticism of works that survive in numerous and competing manuscript versions; but that place is not here. Rather, what Christopher chiefly aimed for was clarity of the printed text, uncluttered by details and uninterrupted by distractions not bearing on the substance of a text or its revisions. Thus, he often acts silently – that is, without employing editorial square brackets or other indication of the editor's hand – to expand abbreviations and supply needed punctuation and 'minor' words (e.g. articles) that Tolkien would drop when writing hastily. Nor does he record deletions or Tolkien's alterations of wording or expression where these don't affect the substance of the text or otherwise add to our understanding of it or of the development of Tolkien's thought.

A good example of this can be seen here in Text 3.I (see p. 141), where Tolkien has, in the act of writing, partially struck through and altered a sentence that originally began 'Late on a misty day of October the sun was red as it sank in the' to instead begin 'On a misty day of October the western sky was red as the Sun sank into'. No doubt Tolkien noticed the redundancy of specifying that the sun was sinking late in the day, and simply acted on the spot to eliminate it. Reproducing this deletion and alteration in the body of the edited text would be both distracting and pointless. If the editor judges this alteration to be of sufficient stylistic interest, it can be noted in a footnote to the text at this point; but as this change in no way bears on the substance of Tolkien's text or its development, it is certainly not necessary to do so. Likewise, in Text 1 (see p. 136), where Tolkien vacillates between 'as' and 'like' at one point, and among 'yet', 'but', and 'still' at another, these might be judged worth remarking on in editorial notes, but do not need to be.

Handwriting

I have already touched on what is undoubtedly the most challenging aspect of editing Tolkien's manuscripts: his handwriting. When starting a new composition, and especially when recommencing a previous draft, Tolkien would not infrequently start with a careful and sometimes even calligraphic hand. But soon enough, as new ideas or better expressions arise, beauty of form gives way to rapidity of thought. Words and passages are struck out and replaced, sometimes in the act of writing, sometimes crammed between lines and in margins, and the page becomes more or less crowded with cancellations and revisions. Niceties like punctuation and prepositions start to disappear, as do clear distinctions between vowels. Eventually a sort of 'universal vowel' is adopted, in which – especially when Tolkien uses a hard pencil or (in later writings) ballpoint pen – just a gentle lift or swell in the line, if that, is all one has to judge which and how many vowels might be intended. At his most rapid, when hand and pen are struggling their hardest to keep up with thought, Tolkien employs too the 'universal consonant', where words are little more than gentle seismic squiggles whose trace is jostled by a descender here or jolted by a series of ascenders there.

Fortunately, since fluent readers of written languages don't typically have to work out each letter form to parse a word or sentence, but instead rely on overall word form, with practice word form and context will often more or less readily supply the correct reading even of Tolkien's more opaque renderings. But by the same token readers sometimes misinterpret word forms because they fail to distinguish among closely similar forms, or because contextual assumptions lead them to expect words not actually present.

Some of the more readily notable characteristic features, particularly of Tolkien's hastier handwriting, are: (1) a *b* and an *h* that look like *l*; (2) the letters *f, g, p, q* and *y*, all of which Tolkien routinely writes with deep and wide descenders, and (save in the case of *f*) the tops of which (i.e., the bowls of *g, p* and *q*, and the arms of *y*) are only cursorily rendered, such that *g, p, q* and *y* can be mistaken for each other; (3) the combination *th*, which frequently lacks the crossbar of the *t*, and often merges into an apparent single letter resembling an *h*, and hence a *the* that can look like nothing more than an elongated *b, h* or *l*; (4) a *t* that in other circumstances resembles a *b, h* or *l*; (5) an initial *s* that looks like a slightly curved undotted *i* or short *l*; (6) an adjacent or final *s* that resembles a horizontal loop or appended hook or even just a diagonal line or dip; (7) an *r* that looks like a reverse *c* or an *s*; (8) an *a* and an *o* that look like each other or like *u*; (9) an *a* and an *e* that look like each other and like *c*; (10) an *n* that looks like *u*; (11) a *v* that looks like *w* and vice versa; (12) combinations *by* and *ly* that look like single letters, each other, and one form of *g*; (13) a combination *ng* that looks like one form of *g* (and so like some forms of *p, q,* and *y*).

A familiarity with the idiosyncrasies of Tolkien's handwriting, of which Christopher Tolkien was unquestionably the master, can greatly facilitate interpretation of Tolkien's more hastily written manuscripts. To impart some of this familiarity, I give a tabulation, on the Elvish Linguistic Fellowship website, of the more idiosyncratic, difficult, or otherwise potentially misinterpreted or even opaque letter forms encountered in these texts.[3]

Dating and context

Tolkien's extant creative writings span seven decades. In that time, not only did his conceptions of his mythology change, sometimes radically, but so too did his literary style, his tone, his handwriting, and even his choice of writing implements – e.g. nib-pen versus pencil versus (from the 1950s on) ball-point pen – and his sources of paper. Only very rarely would Tolkien himself indicate when any given text or part thereof was written. It is important, therefore, both when first interpreting and when presenting a Tolkienian text, to bring as much information to bear as can be gleaned both from within the text and from its physical form and placement, in order to set each text in its conceptual and chronological context as precisely as possible. The four texts I've selected here each provide good examples of the sorts of contextual information that can be brought to bear. Christopher usually does this in an introduction preceding each text. This and other editorial matter is also usually set in type at a size smaller than that of the text itself, so as to make what is authorial more readily distinguishable from what is editorial. For reasons stated above, I will instead do so here, outside the editions proper, and in a freer fashion than usual.

Text 1: Unfinished alliterative English poem associated with 'Narqelion'

To those familiar with Tolkien's handwriting from the start of the legendarium around 1915 through to the end of his work on 'The Book of Lost Tales' around 1925, Text 1 is instantly seen to be quite early. This hand is characteristically more spacious and rounded than is typical of his later texts. Further, near the bottom of the page Tolkien has written the Qenya words *oïkta rāmavoite malinai*, a quote from the earliest extant Qenya poem, titled 'Narqelion', the manuscript of which Tolkien dated both 'Nov. 1915' and 'March 1916'. One might assume (as I first did) that this present text – which moreover starts out as an alliterative English rendering of the Qenya poem (though it quickly diverges) – likewise dates to as early as 1915.

Despite such strong internal and formal evidence, though, external evidence – namely, the nature of the paper used and the contents of its verso – shows that this date is too early by about three years. Tolkien has here, as so often throughout his life, made use of scrap paper: namely, a discarded slip from the compilation of what is now called the *Oxford English Dictionary*, the staff of which Tolkien joined in very late 1918.[4] The earliest date at which this text could have been written on this paper (the *terminus ad quem*, in technical parlance) is, therefore, very late 1918.

Text 2: 'The Fashion of the World'

The first and most obvious clue as to the date of this text is the paper on which it is written. As Christopher Tolkien explains, this is an example of the paper used for Oxford examinations, a supply of which his father obtained after becoming an external examiner at Oxford in 1924,[5] and would continue to refresh and employ throughout writing *The Lord of the Rings* and into the 1950s. The writing is, however, characteristic of Tolkien's hand rather later than the 1930s. Internal evidence further narrows the date. Notable is the presence of the name *Melkor* (as opposed to earlier *Melko*): while a single example of this form of the name is found in a *Quenta Silmarillion* text dating to 1937, it is not attested again until the versions of the 'Ainulindalë' ('Music of the Ainur') that, as Christopher explains in detail, Tolkien wrote in or before 1948.[6] Moreover, and I think determinatively, the reference to the 'Round World' and the presence of certain phrases and matters in the pencil text that Tolkien is seen to be working out here – for example, 'also their Music had been but the growth and flowering of the thought of the Ainur in the Timeless Halls'[7] – relate this text closely to the C and C* versions of around 1948, thus providing its probable date.[8] Indeed, noting that in this text Tolkien seemingly devises for the first time the name 'Timeless Halls', it appears that this text was drafted prior to the composition of 'Ainulindalë' C, in which that name appears *ab initio*.

Text 3: From a draft of 'The Disaster of the Gladden Fields'

Were this text not part of the draft of what became the text of 'The Disaster of the Gladden Fields' that Christopher Tolkien published in *Unfinished Tales*,[9] and were it not written on the verso of a printed Allen & Unwin notice – to large quantities of which Tolkien had ready access following the success of *The Lord of the Rings*, this particular example announcing the forthcoming publication of the book *Belief* by Prof. H.H. Price of Oxford, which was published in 1969 – I would still be able readily to date this as Christopher does to 'the final period of [Tolkien's] writing on Middle-earth'.[10] It is entirely characteristic of these final writings, most notably in exhibiting Tolkien's frequent use later in life of the ballpoint pen.

For editors of Tolkien's late manuscripts this was a nigh-on disastrous development, and it is easy to see why here. When using a broad-nib pen, as Tolkien does in Text 3.I, even when writing somewhat hastily, the variation in line thickness imparted by the nib provides additional clues as to the intended letter form. This information is completely lost in ballpoint, to the extent that Tolkien himself could not always read what he'd written, as Text 3.II shows: Tolkien has here written in red ballpoint his attempted interlinear decipherment of the earlier black ballpoint text; and as indicated by his own queries and lacunae, he doesn't always succeed.

Text 4: *Note on the languages spoken by Beren and Lúthien*
Similarly, this text is easily identifiable as being very late, by the handwriting and by the use of ballpoint pen. It too is draft material, related to the text Christopher published as 'The Problem of *Ros*' in *The Peoples of Middle-earth*.[11] And it too is written on printed stationery – a form reply bearing Tolkien's 76 Sandfield Road address – which in this case is less determinative of date than that of the previous text. The Tolkiens moved into that home in March 1953 and occupied it until July 1968, so this stationery could have been printed at any point in those fifteen years. However, the handwriting is unquestionably very late, and I am confident in dating it, as Christopher Tolkien does its later version, to 1968 or later.[12] Tolkien, an inveterate recycler of paper, likely retained a supply of these sheets after the move and continued to use them as scrap for some time.

8.1 & 8.2 Unfinished alliterative poem, associated with 'Narqelion', c.1918. Broad-nib pen and soft pencil on discarded *Oxford English Dictionary* slip.
Oxford, Bodleian Library, MS. Tolkien S 1/XIV, fols 45r & 45v.

Text 1: Unfinished alliterative English poem associated with 'Narqelion'

Text

> With leaping leaves   the lift is filled;   *lift* air
> The wind with wings   that whispering go
> Like fleet-winged flocks   a-wandering[i]
> Of birds with plumes   of palest gold.
> 5 These are the elm's children   that at chill winter's
> First bitter breath   abandon her arms.
> Where the beech burns[ii]   and the bloodred leaves
> Of the wallcreepers   in weeds of flame[iii]   *weeds* clothes
> Yet of glowing summer   a gleed lingers,[iv]   *gleed* glowing ember
> 10 [?&] the high housefold   [?&] the hoar gables[v]   *housefold* ?roof

> ∴ *oïkta rāmavoite malinai*[vi] ∴

NOTES

i. Line 3 replaces what began as two lines: 'As wandering flocks of fleet-wingéd / golden birds'. It is interesting to note that the first version alliterates on the 'fl' of 'flocks' and 'fleet-wingéd', while the final version alliterates on the 'w' of 'fleet-winged' and 'a-wandering'.

ii. Here 'burns' replaced earlier 'burneth' and is preceded by 'yet' emended to 'still', both later deleted.

iii. The two halves of this line were formed from parts of what were originally two lines: 'Of the wallcreepers [*struck through*: weave a robe / Of flaming fire] in weeds of flame'.

iv. The working-out of this line was done above what became line 7. It originally read 'But the flame of summer like fire lingers'. With various deletions and replacements this became 'While a gleed lingers of the glow of summer', and then 'Yet a gleed lingers of the glowing summer'. This was then copied below what became line 8, but was itself struck out in the act of writing and replaced with the final form.

v. 'Housefold' appears to be Tolkien's neologism – the *OED* knows nothing about it – likely formed with a sense of 'fold' provided by its Old Icelandic cognate *faldr*, 'hood'. Tolkien twice considered replacing 'hoar' with synonymous 'grey'.

vi. This phrase is part of line 4 of the late 1915 Qenya poem 'Narqelion', and probably means 'of birds having wings of yellow', thus echoing line 4 of the present poem. It should be noted, however, that this poem is not a translation of the Qenya poem, from which it departs markedly, though it is clearly associated with and inspired by it. See *Vinyar Tengwar*, 40, April 1999, for Christopher Gilson's full presentation and analysis of 'Narqelion'.

Text 2: 'The Fashion of the World'[i]
Text 2.I — Pencil layer

Round world.
The Valar can labour to build the world – since the Music
was incomplete – with the world [?encompassing] the solar
system or the universe.
The round world can be made to keep Morgoth out? and be
complete [?only] in time for the Elves to come [?into it].
It is said that in the beginning of the overlordship of the
Valar the world was dark and still unshapen, for though in
the Great Music its design had been foretold,[ii] that Music had
not itself been completed; whereas also their Music had been
but the growth and flowering of the thought of the Ainur
in the Timeless Halls (and other musics and other histories
there may have been, but only of that in which we are the
chords made visible do we know).[iii] But when Ilúvatar said
'let these things be' and set the flame imperishable of Being
in the void,[iv] then it became the task of those Ainur who
had taken part in the music by their labours to bring their
thought to fruition and shape the matter according to the
design of the Music which had arisen in their minds[, ?sung]
for Ilúvatar.
Now therefore the first of the labours of the Valar was to
make light to be in the visible world like to the motion of
thought had been to them, and to show forth all things.
And it is said that Varda made the stars, and there were 9
[?brethren] among the Ainur and [?to them have great]

Text 2.II — Ink layer

Varda came from far stars for she had made many of them,
especially the <u>Great Bear</u>. Nienna [?watched what she] did,
and was [?a recorder] and made little, but not bright or hot
things.[v]
The Fashion of the World. The Valar cannot throw Melkor
out. He stays in the North. The Valar make a land for
themselves in the midst of the Great Sea, and [in the] East
and North they make mountains so that only the sunset light
comes there, and beyond is alone sea.
Elves <u>not</u> gods should make language.

8.3 'The fashion of the world', c.1948. Broad-nib pen over soft pencil on Oxford examination paper.
Oxford, Bodleian Library,
MS. Tolkien B 40, fol. 129r.

i.   Note that the rough yet prominent map of Middle-earth (with Aman to the West) accompanying the ink text broadly resembles the European, African and Asian continents.

ii. As first written, this clause began 'for though its fate and for [?all time] the Great Music had'; this was mostly struck out, and altered to 'in the great music its form and fate had been', in which 'form and fate' were then also struck out and replaced with 'design', yielding the final version. A false start preceding this sentence reads 'In the beginning of the overlordship of the Valar they said that the world was dark and'.

iii. As originally written, the end of this clause read 'flowering of thought [*struck through*: beyond the circles of time] in the Timeless Halls where the'.

iv. As originally written, the text continued here with 'then those of the Ainur that entered in had most part in this music (and other musics and other flowers [?may] have later [?awoken]), by [?this]'.

v.   What is tentatively read as 'recorder' here in fact appears to end in 'ded'.

Text 3: From a draft of 'The Disaster of the Gladden Fields'[i]
Text 3.I — Broad-nib pen

There had been heavy rains for some days past and the river was swollen with swift water. So they [*above*: Isildur] had turned aside, and taken to the higher ground closer to the eaves of Greenwood, the southern part of which crowned long steep slopes, falling down to the great Anduin valley. On a misty day of October the western sky was red as the Sun sank into cloud above the peak of the distant mountains. The Dúnedain had that day [?passed] the Gladden Fields, far away to their left. Some were singing, for the day's march was nearly at an end, and three parts of their long journey to the Pass of Rivendell were behind them. Suddenly, as cloud swallowed the sun, they heard the fell voices of Orks, and saw them charging down the slopes from the forest, yelling their war-cries. In the fading light they seemed a host beyond count, and no doubt they were 10 times the number of the Dúnedain.

Text 3.II — Ballpoint pen

Reasons for the legend
(a) The Ring was found in the <u>water</u> of the Gladden Fields.
(b) No trace of Isildur's body was found, though his [*deleted*: ?mail] [?cast aside was later retrieved] by Thranduil.[ii]

8.4 Draft of 'The disaster of the Gladden Fields', c.1968. Broad-nib and ballpoint pens on Allen & Unwin publication notice.
Oxford, Bodleian Library, MS. Tolkien B 42, fol. 77r.

(c) If Isildur had gained the far bank with the Ring he could not have been shot, and being a man of supreme hardihood would probably have come to help before he foundered (as did Ohtar).

(d) Now, it was known that Saruman had secretly dragged the waters [?above, below, and in] the Gladden Fields.[iii] Long after, when Orthanc was set in new order by King Elessar and all its secrets searched a small [?shapen] casket of gold on a [?lank] chain was found. It had no letter or sign upon it but with it was none other than the Elendilmir itself (long thought lost): the white star upon a silver fillet, of which all later Kings and chieftains of the North (= Arnor) had worn only a replica made by the Elves. Isildur had [?personally] only worn it when he assumed the lordship.

NOTES

i.   A deleted note in the top margin reads 'Paths made by the Silvan Elves'.
ii. 'Isildur's' is a correction and expansion of what Tolkien actually wrote here, namely 'E's', apparently for 'Elendil's'. In the next item, (c), Tolkien likewise originally wrote 'If Elend' before realizing his error and replacing it with 'If Is[ildur]'.
iii. What is tentatively read 'below' here in fact appears to end in 'ng'.

Text 4: Note on the languages spoken by Beren and Lúthien

Beren spoke in Bëorian to Lúthien. It was his halting use of Sindarin that amongst other things displeased Thingol, at their first meeting. It was said that Lúthien learned Beren's tongue and spoke it always to him in private. When he asked her why, she fell silent and looked afar before she answered. 'Why? Because I must forsake thee or forsake my people and become one of the children of Men. Since I will not do the first, I will learn to speak the language of my new kin.'

So it may be assumed that Dior continued the custom and it was handed on to his sons and Elwing his daughter.

It was said by the loremasters that when Eärendil, who wedded Elwing, spoke the errand of the Elves and Men before the Valar he spoke in Quenyan, Sindarin, Hadorian, and Bëorian.

8.5 & 8.6 Notes on the languages spoken by Beren and Lúthien, c.1969. Ballpoint pen on printed form-reply stationery. Oxford, Bodleian Library, MS. Tolkien B 42, fols 217r & 217v.

Bëorian *ros* is [?usually] related to Hadorian *roth*
(*roþ*) 'foam [of] sea'.[i] *Rothinzil* to be Hadorian Adûnaic
translation of [Quenya] *Vingilótë*. [?This ? ?did] not
require *Wingi*.

This [i.e., *wingi*] does not appear to have been
Adûnaic and was possibly Nandorin.[ii] It is not at all like
an Adûnaic word in shape.

Dior was also proud of his descent from Elwë,
and the names of his 2 sons [i.e., Eluréd and Elurín]
(murdered by the sons of Fëanor) were [derived from]
<u>Elu</u>. But this he associated with *el* 'star'. Elwing used the
same element for her children [i.e., Elrond and Elros].

NOTES

i.   The gloss read here as 'sea' could also be read as 'ice', though the
      element *roth* nowhere else has that meaning.
ii.   Cf. J.R.R. Tolkien, *The Peoples of Middle-earth*, ed. Christopher
      Tolkien, HarperCollins, London, 1996, p. 365, n.55.

I am grateful to Christopher Tolkien for giving me the
opportunity to work with his father's manuscripts,
particularly his linguistic writings; and especially for the
many years of unfailing kindness, understanding, and
friendship he showed me in our long correspondence.

Stuart D. Lee

A MILESTONE IN BBC HISTORY? 9

THE 1955–56 RADIO DRAMATIZATION
OF *THE LORD OF THE RINGS*

T HE 1955–56 BBC radio dramatization of *The Lord
of the Rings* often receives only a minor mention
in studies around the adaptation of Tolkien's
works.[1] Series One, entitled *The Fellowship of the Ring*, was
broadcast in November and December 1955 and covered
the first volume. Series Two (November–December 1956, by
now entitled *The Lord of the Rings*), completed the story by
attempting all of *The Two Towers* and *The Return of the King*.
Both series consisted of six episodes (*c.* thirty minutes each).
Now overshadowed by the seminal BBC radio drama by Brian
Sibley and Michael Bakewell in 1981, and the films of the
books, this adaptation is often remembered only for Tolkien's
intense dislike of it.[2] Moreover, as no recordings survive, it
would seem there is little to discuss. This article will attempt
to redress this using the scripts of the original series, and
correspondence held in the BBC Written Archives.[3] This
dramatization was the first attempt to portray any of Tolkien's
fiction through mass media, and importantly it took place
during Tolkien's lifetime when the books were more or less
'hot off the shelf' (*The Fellowship of the Ring* published in July
1954, *The Two Towers* in November 1954 and *The Return of the
King* in October 1955).[4]

Series One
Tolkien had a long and strained relationship with the BBC
dating back to his first interaction with it in 1936 (when part
of his translation of *Pearl* was read on regional radio). The
late 1940s and 1950s saw failed projects (e.g. a broadcast on
Richard Rolle in 1949, or a biographical piece on Joseph
Wright in 1955) and successful ones (e.g. his translation of *Sir
Gawain and the Green Knight*, which aired on 6 December
1953, and *The Homecoming of Beorhtnoth Beorhthelm's Son*,

on 3 December 1954).[5] This level of activity alone would be sufficient to demonstrate an ongoing, if often frustrating relationship between the broadcaster and Tolkien. In the middle of this there was the first ever dramatization of *The Lord of the Rings*. The producer, Terence Tiller, may have first encountered Tolkien when he had been approached about producing *Homecoming* in 1954 (which he declined). However, what is clear is that by late 1954 (only a few months after the publication of *The Fellowship of the Ring* and *The Two Towers*) a successful pitch was made to dramatize *The Fellowship of the Ring*, because on 25 January 1955 Tiller was already engaging the services of E.H. Wakeham (BBC Rights Department) to negotiate the necessary approvals and fees.

Even at this stage Tolkien was voicing concerns about covering '390 pages' in under five hours' broadcast time but due to being 'bogged down in the business of term, and the labours of producing VOL III' he was unable to comment further (26 January 1955).[6] He did add that Rayner Unwin had given his approval. Tiller replied (2 February 1955) noting Tolkien's understandable request for more details before giving consent, explaining that 'the dialogue of the original book would be preserved as far as possible'. A Narrator would be used to link scenes,[7] assisted by newly commissioned music for background and leitmotifs, as well as sound effects.[8] Importantly, at this stage it was envisaged that each of the six episodes would last forty-five minutes (four and a half hours in total), but even so Tiller acknowledged this could cover only a third of *The Fellowship of the Ring*. Cutting would be necessary, especially for most of the songs, but he preferred this to excessive 'summarising'. Tiller promised not to alter the narrative except 'where the ear requires more information than the eye' and cited his previous radio adaptions of C.S. Lewis's *The Great Divorce* and *The Pilgrim's Regress* as examples.

Matters were seemingly resolved, permissions agreed, as well as a fee of £30 per performance (BBC memo, 1 March 1955). By June drafts were ready (Tiller to Tolkien, 1 June 1955) and both men met at the BBC Club to discuss progress (24 June 1955). Allen & Unwin also sent Tiller draft versions of the appendices and maps for *The Lord of the Rings* (acknowledged

29 July 1955, thus two to three months before publication of *The Return of the King*).

Importantly, in the correspondence we have two interesting examples of Tolkien's direct engagement with the script, giving further insights into his work. First, in a letter stamped '5 Feb 1955', having noted he will instruct Allen & Unwin to approve, Tolkien recognized the need to cut the songs, acknowledging they were 'seldom contributors to the action, but a means of depicting character or providing decorative background'.[9] He added that though the songs 'have no special music … one or two are written to "tunes"', giving two examples – Sam's 'Troll-song' which 'goes to the old tune assoc. with "The Fox went out on a Winter's night"', and the 'Elvish chant (p. 394) has in mind the tones used in the <u>Lamentatio</u> of Tenebrae'.[10] This indicates that when he wrote the 'verse' pieces scattered throughout *The Lord of the Rings*, most did not have a defined music to accompany them, but at least two did, drawing their inspiration from English folk-music and Catholic reciting tones.

The second example is a letter sent to Tiller (10 September 1955).[11] Tolkien is responding to a request about accents to help the actors.[12] Referencing 'Vol iii p 408 and 411' and 'characterization in my text', he observed 'the Hobbit "gentry" should <u>not</u> be made rustical in actual tones and accents', adding their 'divergence from High Speech is cast rather in forms of grammar and idiom: they just speak unstudied modern English'. Merry and Pippin ('two young hobbits of the highest birth in the land') should sound like Frodo (whose 'superior linguistic skill would be exhibited only in Elvish'), and he was vehemently against 'anything more than the merest tinge of "country" (if any) in their speech'. Comparing 'gentlehobbits' with 'the Great' the difference is more 'one of period … than dialect', with the Great using 'a more archaic language (when functioning as the Great)', and speaking 'with greater solemnity and precision', whereas hobbits 'just use our own rather slack colloquial'.[13]

Tolkien noted Sam and Butterbur ('Breelanders, Men and Hobbits, were in the same linguistic position') could be given 'a "country accent" of some kind – fairly but not too strongly marked', but was concerned at a mention of

76 SANDFIELD ROAD,
HEADINGTON,
OXFORD.

TELEPHONE: OXFORD 61639.

Your ref.
03/F/TT.

Dear Mr Tiller,

Thank you for your letter. I am most interested by your reply to mine. I may as well say at once that I will approve of the project, and am writing to Allen and Unwin to tell them to go ahead with the contract.

I shall, of course, be much interested to see what it comes out like in script and performance. I shall be happy (as they say, meaning only too ready) to offer any comments or provide any information. The time-factor alone would, I fear, cause most of the 'songs' to vanish. They would take a long time to sing, and are seldom contributors to the action, but a means of depicting character or providing decorative background. Still, I shall be glad if some

5 FEB 1955

survive. [Since I am not a musician, they have no special music, though naturally one or two are written to 'tunes'. Sam's Troll-song, for instance (p. 219) goes to the old time assoc. with "The fox went out on a winter's night"; and the Elvish chant (p. 394) has in mind the tones used in the *Lamentatio* of *Tenebrae*.]

I missed your adaptations of Lewis. I am sorry. As I assisted at the births of the books, I should have been deeply interested.

I hope to hear from you again in due course; and to meet you. I shall be freer when term is over (and Vol III put to bed).

Yours sincerely
JRR Tolkien.

9.1 & 9.2 Two page letter from Tolkien to Tiller in which he discusses the songs in *The Lord of the Rings*, received 5 February 1955.
BBC Written Archives Centre, R19/2194/2.

'West-Country' which, 'since Elizabethan days … seems to have been favoured as "stage dialect", though not often with any local or historical accuracy'. While he recognized the text purports to be a 'translation into modern terms of a vanished past', any 'accent' should be consistent and could be 'vaguely "countrified"', but at all costs it should be noted he had 'avoided making the dropping or misuse of h a feature of any kind of hobbit-speech', and wanted this observed. Moreover, Tolkien would 'passionately' not want any 'supposedly "Zummerzet" z/v for s/f'. To help, Tolkien suggested 'the pronunciation of r as a main characterizing detail', with 'Hobbit-gentry' speaking as we do 'at our most unstudied'; Sam, 'in addition to a rustic tone and vowel-colouring, should use the burred (or reverted) r'; the Great, and the Elves, 'should sound their rs as a trill (though not with a Scots extravagance) in all positions', which he observed was 'a great enhancement of English, as well as (now) having an archaic flavour'.

Tiller sent Tolkien the scripts (21 September 1955) with the news of further enforced compression, as each episode had now been reduced to thirty minutes. He expected shock 'at the extent of the cutting', and noted that 'inevitably a great deal of the flavour of your work has been lost'. Tiller had therefore 'telescope[d]' incidents and simplified 'geographical details and similar intricacies', concluding 'I hope that the main themes of your work have not been totally obscured or mutilated beyond reason.' Tolkien replied (27 September 1955), remarking that 'I do not think that with the time at your disposal you could have done any better.'[14] He admitted that 'a weakness of the books is the necessity of historical build-up concurrent with the tale of the events', and that this presents an even greater weakness in dramatic form. That said the script now read as 'much more of a "fairy-tale" in the ordinary sense', and the hobbits seemed 'sillier' and others 'more stilted'. As the author he now realized there were 'few, if any, unnecessary details in the long narrative', and their cutting deprived 'the story of significance at some later point'. While it couldn't 'be helped', Tolkien provided suggestions for the abridgements in episodes two and six.[15] In the archives the former survive, relating to the attack on Weathertop. 'Suggestion for alteration of Script' shows that Tolkien offered two solutions (A and B), with 'A' preferred 'because F.[rodo] was in no condition to give a detailed description, and because Narrator can do it better anyway'. Someone has written 'Please Type' across version A ('giving description of Wraiths to Narrator') and the revised script (note the director's timings) confirms that Tolkien's suggestions were used. A comparison with the original text in *The Fellowship of the Ring* (Book I, Chapter 11) shows that Tolkien also recognized the need, when dramatizing, to balance the narrator's voice with the dialogue, and to speed the action along.

Tiller replied (6 October 1955) relieved at Tolkien's 'tolerant and understanding letter', and agreed that nothing in the books was 'superfluous' and cutting had been 'painful'. Tiller hoped it would not come across as a 'mere "fairy-tale"' or 'empty fantasy', but with an odd disregard for Tolkien's letter of 10 September (above) suggested that Sam, Merry and Pippin would have strong 'West-country accents'.

Scripts were then sent out to the actors, studios booked, and the production was in full swing. Rehearsals were on the weekend of broadcast (Tolkien was invited to attend these but never did). Tiller clearly recognized the importance of the work, and writing to Frank Phillips (11 November 1955) he remarked, 'The implications of *The Lord of the Rings* are far deeper than those of a fairy-tale. The trilogy has created a totally new mythology, with great relevance to the contemporary spiritual situation.'

Series One: episode summaries

The following presents a brief description of and commentary on each episode. The timings are from the paper scripts assumed to be the director's (as they contain notes such as 'check pronunciation of Gloin' [*sic*]). Numbers in parenthesis are the script page numbers – each page would have taken on average around ninety seconds to read. Italics indicate dialogue not in the original text.

1 'The Meaning of the Ring'. The Narrator introduces 'Hobbits', cutting to Bilbo (2–3) who summarizes *The Hobbit*

following page, left
9.3 Tolkien's 'Suggestion for alteration of Script', after the length of each episode was reduced from 45 to 30 minutes, September 1955.
BBC Written Archives Centre, R19/2194/2.

following page, right
9.4 Part of the Director's script showing that Tolkien's revised script (version A) was used, October 1955.
BBC Written Archives Centre, R71/289.

Suggestions for alteration of Script. Part III pp. 19–20.

Version A. (giving all description of Wraiths to Narration).

1. p.19. after "forefinger of his left hand", continue Narrator —

: At once the shapes became terribly clear. He could see under their black mantles. In their white faces burned merciless eyes. They had long grey robes; on their grey hairs were helmets of silver, and in their haggard hands were swords of steel. Their keen eyes pierced him as they rushed towards him. The tallest was crowned like a king. He gleamed with a pale light, and in his left hand he held a long pale knife. He strode up and towered above Frodo.

2. Frodo. O Elbereth! Gilthoniel! ....

3. Frodo. What has happened? Where's the pale King?

4. Sam. We lost you, Mr. Frodo. When did you get to?

5. Frodo. Didn't you see them? —— the wraiths, and the King?

6. Aragorn. No, only their shadows. And now they are gone again. I wonder what it means. There was a King, you say? Tell us more!

7. Frodo. No! Oh, his cold eyes and cold knife! I struck at him, and called out; but there came a pain like poisoned ice in my shoulder and ... I fell into darkness. Strider! I am sorry. I shouldn't have put it on [the Ring;] but I did take it off again. Or, I think so. Oh, the cold knife!

Aragorn. Ah. And here it is — the accursed knife. ✗✗

PLEASE TYPE!

Version B. (with description given to Frodo.)

1 p.19 (as script.)

2, 3, 4, 5. 6 as above.

7. Frodo. I ... I put the Ring on. Then the shapes became terribly clear, and I could see under their black cloaks. Their faces were white with cruel bright eyes; but they were all in grey: with silver helmets on their grey hair, and they had grey hands with swords of steel. Their eyes pinned me down, as they rushed at me; but one was very tall, and he gleamed with a pale light. He had a crown on like a king's, and in one hand he had a long knife. I struck at him .... (continue as above, but omit [the Ring]).

very?

I prefer A. Both because F. was in no condition to give a detailed description, and because Narrator can do it better anyway.

PART THREE

I. NARRATOR: Over the lip of the dell rose four tall shadows,
seeming black holes in the deep shade behind them.
Frodo thought he heard a faint hiss as of venomous
breath, and felt a thin piercing chill.   The shapes
advanced .... Pippin and Merry threw themselves flat
on the ground.   Sam shrank to Frodo's side.   Frodo
was quaking as if he were bitter cold, but his terror
was swallowed-up in a sudden temptation to put on
the Ring, disregarding all warnings.   Resistance
became unbearable.   He slowly drew out the chain,
and slipped the Ring on the forefinger of his left
hand.   *music*   At once the shapes became terribly clear.
He could see under their black mantles.   In their
white faces burned merciless eyes.   They had long
grey robes; on their grey hairs were helmets of
silver, and in their haggard hands were swords of
steel.   Their keen eyes pierced him as they rushed
towards him.   The tallest was crowned like a King.
He gleamed with a pale light, and in his left hand
he held a long pale knife.   He strode up and
towered above Frodo.

(MUSIC SURGES TO ATTACK.   CRY FROM FRODO.
SHRILL CRY FROM ONE BLACK RIDER)

2. FRODO: O Elbereth!   Gilthoniel!

(FADING.   MUSIC COLLAPSES - FADE OUT.   PAUSE.
KEUNEXEXEX   FADE BACK SOUND OF FIRE)

3. FRODO: What has happened?   Where is the pale King?

4. SAM: We lost you, Mr. Frodo.   Where did you get to?

5. FRODO: Didn't you see them? ------ the wraiths, and the King?

6. ARAGORN: No, only their shadows.   And now they are gone again.
I wonder what it means.   There was a King, you say?
Tell me more!

7. FRODO: But   Oh, his cold eyes and cold knife!   I struck
at him, and called out; but there came a pain like
poisoned ice in my shoulder and ... I fell into

cont.over...

and the episode with Gollum. Bilbo invites Frodo to stay (3–4) and we move quickly to the birthday party. The Narrator explains Bilbo's vanishing (4–6), Bilbo discusses his plans with Gandalf, departs, and Gandalf meets Frodo (7–9). The Narrator is used to summarize Frodo's time in the Shire, and then introduces 'strange happenings' linked to 'Mordor'. Gandalf comments 'Mordor. There it was said, the Dark Tower had been rebuilt ...', he returns and discusses the Ring with Frodo (11–19, *c.* 14 minutes). Sam is discovered eavesdropping, and Frodo resolves to go to Rivendell.

2 'Black Riders and Others'. The Narrator describes the selling of Bag End, and the hobbits' departure from the Shire. They hide from the Nazgûl (2–3) and the action is conveyed through dialogue:

Pippin: *That's not Gandalf! Look at Him.*
Sam: *Not in that black hood. You can't see his face, even; only his boots.*
Pippin: *He's not looking for us – he's – smelling for us. Sniffing ...*
Frodo: *Don't let him see us. Don't breathe.*

Gildor and the Elves arrive (3–5), the hobbits then meet Farmer Maggot (6), and then Merry at the river-ferry (8). They discuss plans (9–11) and set off into the Old Forest. They encounter Old Man Willow (13), are saved by Tom Bombadil and taken to his house to meet Goldberry (13–16). They spend time with Tom (*c.* 6 minutes).

3 'Aragorn'. The hobbits leave Tom but fall asleep on the Downs. Frodo gets lost, wakes in a Barrow (2), and a Wight calls to him. The Narrator provides the description (drawn from *The Fellowship of the Ring*, Book I, Chapter 8):

A tall figure ... like a shadow against the stars. He [Frodo] thought there were two eyes, very cold though lit with a pale light that seemed to come from some remote distance.

Frodo sees the other hobbits asleep. The directions note this should be accompanied by a song 'immeasurably sad and dreary, cold and miserable and horrible, sometimes high in the air and thin, sometimes like a low moan from the ground'. The Barrow-wight sings: 'Cold be hand and heart and bone …' (*The Fellowship of the Ring*, Book I, Chapter 8), and Frodo sees the moving dismembered arm (4) and strikes it. Frodo (clumsily) remarks '*Oh dear! I still haven't killed the Barrow-Wight …*'. He summons Tom, who arrives ('Frodo: *Daylight! And the barrow has fallen wide open! And here's Tom Bombadil himself!*'). Tom dismisses the Wight, frees the hobbits, and gives them daggers from the hoard. The hobbits leave (7) and arrive at The Prancing Pony (8) where they meet Aragorn (8–15), ending with Merry saying he has seen the Black Riders. They leave Bree after the attack by the Nazgûl and arrive at Weathertop. The fight on Weathertop is described by the Narrator (19 – see above). They fly to Rivendell, meet Glorfindel, and Frodo encounters the Nazgûl at the ford (24).

4 **'Many Meetings'.** Frodo wakes and discusses events with Gandalf (*c.* 7 minutes). He meets Sam, Glóin and Bilbo (5–9) and the rest of the episode covers the Council of Elrond (see below). Characters such as Galdor and Glorfindel are given speaking parts, and the episode ends with Frodo volunteering to take the Ring.

5 **'The Moria Gate'.** The Fellowship forms and departs Rivendell (1–4). They journey to Caradhras, are attacked by Wargs (5–7), then go to Moria (9) and are attacked by the lake creature before entering the gates (11). The remainder of the episode is the journey through Moria but the whole Chamber of Mazarbul scene is omitted. They arrive at the bridge of Khazad-dûm, Gandalf fights the Balrog, and the remnants of the Fellowship escape.

6 **'The Breaking of the Fellowship'.** The Fellowship arrives at Lórien (1), they meet Haldir (1–5), and then Galadriel and Celeborn. The scenes of the Mirror of Galadriel (6–7), Galadriel's gift-giving (9), and the departure (10) are covered. Legolas shoots at the Winged Beast (11), and then the

Fellowship rests. Boromir attempts to take the Ring (13), but Frodo escapes and he departs with Sam. The episode ends with the Narrator saying:

> So Frodo and Sam set off on the last stage of the Quest together; and the River bore them swiftly away. At length they came to the southern slope of the dividing mountains. They drew their boat out, shouldered their burdens, and set off – down into the Land of Shadow.

Directions indicate 'Ring music' at the close, which changes to 'Mordor music' but ends on 'hopeful fade'.

Series Two

The idea of commissioning a dramatization of the remaining two volumes appeared relatively early on. In a note from Tiller to the composer Smith-Masters (11 January 1956) he observed 'Tolkien was not wildly enthusiastic about the programmes, but he is at least willing to let me adapt Volumes 2 and 3 ... so he can't have been really displeased.' A week later C. Holme (Chief Assistant, Third Programme) wrote to Tiller, commenting on the success of Series One (though he noted he was 'the only enthusiast over here for Tolkien's book'), but that the chances of securing another twelve programmes were slim. Holme asked if 'the rest cannot be done in six of 30 minutes each', observing that 'Volume 2 is more homogeneous than Volume 1, and could therefore be represented by fewer episodes, whereas Volume 3 is not only shorter in itself than the other two, but could be shorter still in adaptation by ending it with the victory and restoration of Gondor ...'.[16] He suggested the return to the Shire and final departure to the West could be treated as an epilogue, omitted altogether, or 'disposed of in a few lines of narration'.

Tiller (25 January 1956) was 'appalled at the cutting that would be necessary', but agreed six programmes would be better than leaving the whole thing unfinished. Approval was gained in March, but in the archives all that then survives is a letter from Tiller to Tolkien (17 September 1956) where the former admits 'cuts would have to be more drastic'. The first three scripts were sent to Tolkien (1 November 1956) with Tiller noting the task had been 'formidable', as he felt he could not simply concentrate on Frodo and Sam, and he was therefore forced to 'script-in' his own narration more than in the first series. Tiller concluded by asking about the accents of the Rohirrim, Orcs and the people of Minas Tirith. Tolkien replied on the matter of the accents the next day, and on 6 November he followed up with comments on the three scripts.[17] Tolkien resignedly accepted that Tiller had done his best but asked '*why* this sort of treatment was allowed', as he felt the text now came across as 'simple-minded' and would be confusing (exactly the reaction recorded by listeners – see below). While he admitted he lacked experience 'in the medium', he felt more could be made of the Narrator through the reading of longer descriptive passages. Clearly Tolkien was having second thoughts as to whether the books could be dramatized at all – even though he had been reasonably complementary about Series One to Tiller. The epic scale of the text suggested to him that it could not, but he concluded by noting Tiller 'had a very hard task'.

Series Two: episode summaries
In contrast to Series One, the scripts for Series Two survive only on microfilm.

1 'Fangorn'. The Narrator summarizes Series One and then cuts to Boromir's death (who dies without speaking to Aragorn). The hunt for Merry and Pippin is described in a single paragraph. The Riders of Rohan soon appear (3) followed by a conversation with Éomer. Pippin and Merry are held by the Orcs until the attack by the Riders (7–8). The hobbits escape and meet Treebeard, followed swiftly by the Moot (9–14). The episode closes with Aragorn, Legolas and Gimli meeting Gandalf, who describes his fight with the Balrog.

2 'Rohan and Isengard'. The Narrator describes the approach to Edoras, and the meeting with Théoden and Wormtongue (1–3). Within two pages (4–5) Théoden has escaped his bewitchment, the Rohirrim have ridden to Helm's Deep, and the battle is waged and completed. The ride to Isengard, the meeting with Merry and Pippin, and the exchanges with Saruman (6–13). The company return to Helm's Deep and Pippin looks into the palantír (14–15). Aragorn takes the palantír and a winged Nazgûl is sighted.

3 'Into the Dark'. The Narrator begins by describing Frodo and Sam 'on the brink of a tall cliff'. Sam remarks (1), 'What a fix! That's the one place, in all the lands we've heard of, that we don't want to see any closer; and that's the one place we're trying to get to' (*The Two Towers*, Book IV, Chapter 1), with Frodo supplying 'Mordor!' They meet Gollum and then journey (4–5) to Cirith Gorgor where Gollum reveals there is 'another way'. The Narrator quickly covers the journey and adds bluntly 'And there they were captured by a band of tall men.' Faramir, Mablung and Frodo talk (7–10) and Gollum is discovered at the waterfall. The hobbits depart, fight Shelob (12–16), and Frodo is taken by Gorbag and Shagrat (17). The episode ends with Sam beating at the doors (in effect the end of *The Two Towers*) and the Narrator saying, 'Frodo was alive but taken by the Enemy.'

4 'The Siege of Gondor'. Gandalf and Pippin ride to Minas Tirith, meet Denethor, and Pippin swears his oath of allegiance (2). Pippin meets Beregond (3), and plays with Bergil (4–5). The Narrator cuts back to the Rohirrim, where the troops meet Halbarad and the Rangers who remind Aragorn 'If thou art in haste, remember the Paths of the Dead.' They ride to Dunharrow and enter the Paths of the Dead (7–8). The Narrator describes Théoden meeting Hirgon, the messenger from Minas Tirith with the Red Arrow, and Éowyn/Dernhelm equips Merry (10). In Gondor Pippin and Beregond see the Nazgûl (11), there is Faramir's flight and Gandalf's intervention (described by the Narrator). Faramir, Gandalf and Denethor meet, with the latter becoming more sinister ('witless halfling'). The Narrator says that 'battle was joined beneath the walls of the City itself', and Faramir is wounded (13). Denethor builds his pyre, and the Lord of the Nazgûl enters the city, at which point Rohan arrives (14–16).

5 'Minas Tirith & Mount Doom'. The Narrator summarizes the action so far, followed by the dramatized death of Théoden, and a narrated end of the battle. We move to the Houses of Healing (4–5), and Gimli and Legolas tell Merry and Pippin of their journey. The Council (in effect a short speech by Gandalf) meets and then the Narrator describes the approach to the Gates of Mordor (6), the Mouth of Sauron (7), followed by a description of the battle and Pippin's fight with the Troll. We return to Sam (8), and the action in the tower and discovery of Frodo (9–11). The two dress as Orcs with a suggestion that Frodo and Sam hear the death of the Witch King (11–12). They arrive at Mount Doom and the Ring is destroyed (13–14); the whole action with Gollum is covered in less than a minute. The episode concludes with Frodo's 'Here at the end of all things.'

6 'Many Partings'. The Narrator describes the end of the battle and the fall of Sauron (2). Sam wakes to find Gandalf and Frodo (2). Aragorn is crowned at the Field of Cormallen (3–4); then Aragorn and Arwen, and Éowyn and Faramir, are married (narrated). This is followed by the departure of the company for Isengard where they meet Treebeard (5). Aragorn, Galadriel and Celeborn depart (6) and the remainder arrive at Rivendell. They head for Bree and meet Butterbur (7); and then we have the Scouring of the Shire and death of Saruman (8–13). The Narrator describes the rebuilding process, the marriage of Sam and Rosie, and Frodo asking Sam to join him (14). They journey to the Grey Havens, Frodo departs (15–16), and Sam returns to the Shire. The episode closes with Sam's 'Well, I'm back.'

Reception

The broadcast of the two series was without publicity (certainly compared with 1981).[18] The *Radio Times* ran no feature, and the shows were simply listed with a tagline and credits. Both series also suffered from inconsistent broadcast times and were up against stiff competition – Series One went out at the same time as *Quatermass II* and *What's My Line?* on television, and *The Archers* and other shows on radio; while Series Two coincided with the opening of the Melbourne Olympics.

But how were they received by critics, Tolkien and listeners? Paul Ferris of *The Observer* described the 1955 broadcasts as 'the best light listening for the next five weeks', having the 'pure quality of fairy-tale ... charming without being slight'.[19] A reviewer in *The Times* ('The Meaning of the Ring', 15 November 1955) noted that Tolkien's 'relaxed, vivid, and masculine style with its rich coinages in the names of the creatures' adapted naturally to radio and his 'power of unfolding the matter holds the attention even when he is being expository'.

Tolkien himself appeared balanced in his views (at least to Tiller). In a letter (8 December 1955) he observed *The Times* 'was appreciative', but he was angered by the BBC show *The Critics* ('they were intolerable with a superiority that only ignorance can maintain').[20] He noted he had received many letters expressing enjoyment of the production and that 'non-readers got a great deal out of it'. It had gone down especially well with older children, with the only complaint being the late time of broadcast.[21] Tolkien thought most of the criticism he had seen was 'silly' (especially that the hobbits should 'pipe and squeak', asking rhetorically 'Why should tones rise with fall in stature?'). He felt the Elves were 'managed excellently', as was the Council of Elrond ('masterly'), but criticized Bilbo (he sounded 'bored'), and the announcer's mistake in stating Goldberry was Tom's daughter and that Old Man Willow was an ally of Mordor.[22] He liked Glóin's accent but added it was 'a bit heavily laid on', noting 'dwarves spoke the Common Tongue natively, like Jews, but they had a uvular back R'. He pondered about another series suggesting 'Vol ii might go even better in this form.'

Tiller replied (12 December 1955) taking full responsibility for the announcer's mistake over Goldberry's relationship with Tom Bombadil, but he noted it was never fully explained in the book, asking, 'Who is she?'. Tiller also agreed that the reaction 'without the BBC' had been very positive and he would submit a proposal for 'Volume Two'. Tolkien replied (15 December 1955) acknowledging 'that not all is in the "book"', and that he had quite forgotten 'that Bombadil's adventures as set out in the Oxford Magazine of 1934 (!) were not included' (in effect excusing Tiller of the Goldberry mistake).

He added that 'Gimli was v. good, and C.S. Lewis who heard the last "fit" agreed.' Again, positively, he concluded he would 'like to have the thing continued – if you are the producer'. This balanced praise does seem at odds, however, with Tolkien's more private criticisms in his letters noted earlier.

When it comes to the reaction of listeners there are full reports attached to the scripts – results of surveys by the BBC's Audience Research Department. Four survive for Series One (episodes 1, 2, 3 and 6) and two for Series Two (episodes 1 and 6). These list audience size, an 'appreciation index', and a summary description complete with anonymized feedback. For both series it was estimated that 0.1% of the adult population heard them, and the appreciation index for Series One began at 56 rising to 64 by episode six (against an average for a Third Programme drama of 65), but Series Two never rose above 59.

Considering the direct feedback recorded there is a clear difference between Series One and Two. With Series One, while compression was criticized (especially in terms of reducing the atmosphere) it is notable how positive most comments were, especially around the performances. One reader, in a direct letter to Tiller, described it as '"The Archers" of the Third Programme, a milestone in BBC history'. Some expected the hobbits to have 'high pitch voices' (see Tolkien's comments on this above) and a few objected to Victor Platt's Sam (with his 'BBC Mummersetshire' accent). Most interesting was the clear divide the programme engendered. There were those who simply objected to time wasted on a 'children's story' ('if we must occupy the Third Programme with fairy tales then let us have Enid Blyton' – 'Chemical Manager'). Then there were the comments from listeners who were frustrated because they simply did not 'get it'. Was it an allegory, for example? 'One expected satire, or recognisable symbolism', complained a 'Lecturer in English' and a 'Clerk in Holy Orders' found it without 'mythological overtones, or anything, so far as I could see'. As the series closed it was noted as a 'brave effort', with some listeners having now found 'a pertinent allegorical meaning' (good versus evil) and wanting more ('You just can't leave it at this point!'). But again there were criticisms. The summary reports some listeners disliking 'the naive acceptance of witchcraft and the convenient intervention of various "Dei ex machine" at crucial points', and, as they saw it, 'stereotyped characters of the conventional fairy-story'.

Series Two was criticized much more. Added to those who saw it as childish were non-readers of the book who were just confused, or fans of Tolkien who described it as an 'absolute ruin', 'a farce', with 'ignominious' compression that resulted in a 'juvenile adventure story'. As one reader (a 'Civil Servant') commented, 'The result was the conversion of a glorious, rich, detailed, and self-consistent narrative into a footling and ridiculous sounding adventure story of the "with one bound Jack was free" type.'

1981 and all that

Is it possible to compare the 1955–56 dramatization with Sibley and Bakewell's or, indeed, with the films of Peter Jackson? Due to the lack of recordings this may seem pointless at first – outside the reader reports we have no way to compare Ian Holm's 1981 Frodo, for example, with that of Oliver Burt; or Ian McKellen's Gandalf with Norman Shelley's. Furthermore, the enforced compression of Series Two that so enraged listeners would suggest any comparison would be aligning apples with pears. However, considering Series One alongside the equivalent episodes from 1981 and the 2001 film is more fruitful. In terms of running time the six episodes in 1955 equated to just under three hours in total before Frodo and Sam's departure at the end of the first volume. In 1981, 'The Breaking of the Fellowship' was the tenth episode (of twenty-six 30 minute broadcasts, or in the one-hour episode versions the sixth episode of thirteen). So 1981 allotted five hours to what was covered in three hours in 1955. Interestingly, Jackson covered the same in two hours and fifty-eight minutes in 2001 (cinema version).

As noted above, Tolkien singled out for praise the 1955 dramatization of the Council of Elrond, which in the book is heavily reliant on dialogue and reads more like a play. In the dramatization this begins in effect with the Narrator stating 'Next morning, the Council of Elrond assembled', at just around sixteen minutes in, and ended twelve minutes and fifteen seconds later with Sam's 'A nice little pickle we have landed ourselves in, Mr Frodo!' In 1981 the 'Council' began with Elrond's 'Welcome, welcome …' and again ran until Sam's comment (total length sixteen minutes fourteen seconds). In the film, however, the scene only runs for six minutes thirty seconds (although some of the back-story of the Ring covered during the Council in the book had appeared in earlier scenes).

As a rule of thumb, then, Series One in the 1955 dramatization was compressed by about two-thirds compared with 1981 but tended to match the filmed version in length (though extensive descriptions of landscape and action can, of course, be dispensed with through images and pan shots). Notably, though, 1955 did include the dramatization of Tom Bombadil and the Barrow-wights which, despite Tolkien's criticism of Shelley's performance, still reads reasonably well (but, as a consequence, gave even less time for the rest of the book). Bombadil was cut in the 2001 film, and also in 1981 (though Sibley did offer a dramatization in *Tales from the Perilous Realm* for Radio 4 in 1992). Sibley has noted that Bombadil had been omitted partly out of necessity (he felt to do it properly would have required one hour), partly because it was possible to do so without affecting the narrative, but most importantly because from the point where the Black Riders appear in the Shire the 'story is set and running', and there is a 'sense of chase', up to Rivendell.[23] Bombadil would have felt like a lull in this. Moreover, with the thirty-minute episode format each one required a cliffhanger ending and it was not clear how to do this while incorporating Bombadil.

In summary, 1955–56 should certainly be seen as a first 'brave attempt' (noted by a listener) but also a lost opportunity. The performances, on the whole, were well received and the script (apart from a few clumsy interventions) showed signs of promise, dashed mainly by the need for compression. Had the books been out longer and become more established then perhaps the BBC senior managers would have agreed to each episode lasting forty-five minutes, and even running to three series. This in turn may have encouraged Tolkien to be more engaged with the process and to have led to more insights from him on the adaptation;

but alas, it was not to be. Even then Tolkien, despite some obvious reservations, found Series One well done in places. One can only imagine the delight he would have had in hearing the 1981 version with its much longer running time, better writing, and better production quality.

Programme details

CAST LIST

John Baker	Orc
Nicolette Bernard	Galadriel, additional voices
Oliver Burt	Frodo
Michael Collins	Merry
Frank Duncan	Halbarad, Legolas, additional voices
Valentine Dyall	Théoden, Treebeard, Orc
Robert Farquharson	Denethor, Saruman
Felix Felton	Bilbo, the Black Captain, the Voice of Sauron, Orc, additional voices
Garard Green	Celeborn, Elrond, additional voices
Olive Gregg	Éowyn
Derek Hart	Narrator
David Hemmings	Bergil
Noel Johnson	Éomer
Basil Jones	Pippin
Annette Kelly	additional voices
Godfrey Kenton	Aragorn, Mablung, additional voices
Eric Lugg	Gimli, additional voices
Victor Platt	Sam
Derek Prentice	Beregond, Boromir, Faramir, Orc, additional voices
Molly Rankin	additional voices
Bernard Rebel	Wormtongue
Prunella Scales	Ioreth
Gerik Schjelderup	Gollum, Orc
Norman Shelley	Bombadil, Gandalf, old man, additional voices
Roger Snowdon	Orc

First Series (1955)
Broadcast BBC Third Programme: 14/11, 21/11, 29/11, 4/12,
11/12, 18/12 (10.10pm, 9.50pm, 7.10pm, 9.30pm, 8.00pm, 7.20pm;
repeated 15/11, 23/11, 30/11, 5/12, 12/12, 21/12 (6.40pm, 7.00pm,
9.40pm, 6.35pm, 6.20pm, 7.20pm)

Second Series
(cast as First Series but with additions) (1956)
Broadcast BBC Third Programme: 19/11, 26/11, 2/12, 9/12, 16/12,
23/12 (10.30pm, 10.40pm, 8.45pm, 8.05pm, 5.25pm, 10.05pm);
repeated 22/11, 29/11, 7/12, 12/12, 18/12, 27/12 (7.50pm, 6.45pm,
7.20pm, 6.15pm, 7.10pm, 6.00pm).

10

Tom Shippey

'KING SHEAVE'
AND 'THE LOST ROAD'

J.R.R. TOLKIEN may well be the most fully documented author of all time. There are several reasons for this eminence: his public career as a Leeds and then an Oxford professor; the fact that he became popular well before his death in 1973, so that interviews and memories of him were well recorded; while for the same reason, not only were his manuscripts preserved, but the books he owned and signed were likewise eagerly collected.[1] The major reason, however, must be the devoted editorial work of Christopher Tolkien, at once personal and scholarly, which has led to the publication of a quite extraordinary *Nachlass* of more than twenty volumes, culminating (if one may state a personal preference) in the three great editions of *The Children of Húrin* (2007), *Beren and Lúthien* (2017) and *The Fall of Gondolin* (2018). It may be said without any qualification at all that no author has ever enjoyed a better or better-qualified literary executor than Tolkien found in his son Christopher, to whom his father's many millions of readers owe an immense debt of gratitude.

The conception of 'the Lost Road'
In Tolkien's literary life, however, there remains one unanswered and indeed unanswerable question: what was in his mind in his attempts to write a sequence of stories on the theme of 'the Lost Road'? This was clearly of great importance to him. His first attempt, later published in *The Lost Road and Other Writings* (1987), the fifth volume of *The History of Middle-earth*, occupied a good deal of his time between 1936 and 1937, months in which Tolkien was also very busy with the maps and proofs of *The Hobbit*, which might have been expected to take all the attention he could spare from his professional duties.[2] Even more surprisingly, between 1944 and 1946, when Tolkien was well advanced with the composition of *The Lord of the Rings*, and under pressure

from his friends and his publisher to finish the work, he broke off to make a second attempt at the 'Lost Road' sequence, eventually published as 'The Notion Club Papers' in *Sauron Defeated* (1992), the ninth volume of *The History of Middle-earth*. Christopher Tolkien indeed comments that while his father wrote to his publisher on 21 July 1946 explaining that the 'Papers' had been written 'in a fortnight of comparative leisure', they seem in fact, very surprisingly, to have usurped the completion of *The Lord of the Rings* for anything up to a year and a half.[3]

Nevertheless, neither 'The Lost Road' nor 'The Notion Club Papers' ever achieved what one might call escape velocity. Tolkien remained stalled on (especially) the issue of transmission: he worked on the frame of his narratives rather than the narratives themselves. He did however give two accounts of his overall plan for the projected book. His idea was to write a collection of some ten stories from very different periods, extending from the present day back through Anglo-Saxon history and the Ice Age to the far and fictional prehistory of Númenor. The connecting thread would be 'the occurrence time and again in human families … of a father and son called by names that could be interpreted as Bliss-friend and Elf-friend' (in modern English, Edwin and Alwin, in Anglo-Saxon, Eadwine and Ælfwine, in Lombardic legend, Audoin and Alboin, in Númenor, Herendil and Elendil).[4] Significantly, Tolkien made limited progress only with the four stories to which names could be attached. One might well suggest – though this is pure speculation – that Tolkien's original inspiration was the realization that the Lombardic legend of Audoin and Alboin contained names which were, allowing for the problems writers in Latin always faced in recording Germanic names, the exact philological equivalents of Anglo-Saxon Eadwine and Ælfwine. (Exact philological equivalence was a matter of great importance to both J.R.R. and Christopher Tolkien, because of their professional training.) The recurrence of the names furthermore showed that the idea of an 'elf-friend' was common to Germanic tribes, even if it was not clear what such a person might be.

One further purely speculative suggestion is that Tolkien's model for his project was the story collection *The Path of the King*, published in 1921 by John Buchan. This is a collection of fourteen stories which traces the descendants of a Viking king through to Abraham Lincoln, connected by an heirloom in the shape of a ring – in the end lost by young Abe while fishing. 'Don't you worry about the ring, dearie,' says his dying mother. 'It ain't needed no more.' The prophecy made to his Viking ancestor a thousand years before, 'A great kingdom waits, not for you, but for the seed of your loins', is about to be fulfilled. We know that Tolkien had a high opinion of Buchan as a writer.[5] He would moreover have appreciated Buchan's theme of buried continuity. A speaker in the Prologue to *The Path of the King* declares, 'The spark once transmitted may smoulder for generations under ashes, but the appointed time will come': to which we might compare Legolas, 'seldom do [the things that Men begin] fail of their seed … And that will lie in the dust and rot to spring up again in times and places unlooked-for.'[6]

The origin of 'King Sheave'

Such speculations apart, one has to admit that Tolkien made almost no progress with the actual stories he intended to tell, except for the story of Herendil and Elendil, which became part of his mythology of 'The Fall of Númenor'. The modern story of Oswin, Alboin and Audoin (the latter two names knowingly anachronistic in twentieth-century England, and the first paralleled by Númenórean Valandil) might have developed into a story of rediscovering 'the Lost Straight Road': as is further hinted in 'The Notion Club Papers', where we learn that Alwin Arundel Lowdham's father Edwin set sail in his boat *The Éarendel* and was never seen again. The Lombardic legend of Alboin and Audoin, names apart, can only be called unpromising from an elvish point of view: it shows a code of honour among Germanic tribes, along with behaviour which is frankly orcish.[7] The projected story of the Tuatha-de-Danaan finds a certain reflection in Tolkien's late poem 'Imram'. But the best, if inadequate, guide to what was in Tolkien's mind comes from the poem 'King Sheave', printed for us, with the prose version which might have formed part of a completed Anglo-Saxon story of Ælfwine, and with Christopher Tolkien's accompanying notes, in *The Lost Road*.[8]

The inspiration for this, as so often with Tolkien, is quite clearly a philological crux, or rather a whole string of such cruxes, in the opening section of the poem *Beowulf*. This describes the funeral of the Danish king Scyld, and what it says, using Tolkien's own translation (which I have very slightly modified here and there in the discussion that follows), is this:

> Oft Scyld Scefing robbed the hosts of foemen, many
> peoples, of the seats where they drank their mead, laid fear
> upon men, he who first was found forlorn … To him was
> an heir afterwards born, a young child in his courts whom
> God sent for the comfort of his people: perceiving the
> dire need which they long while endured aforetime being
> without a prince …

Scyld then died, was placed in a boat, and the boat was filled with treasures:

> With lesser gifts no whit did they adorn him, with treasures
> of that people, than did those that in the beginning sent him
> forth alone over the waves, a little child … [The mourners]
> gave him to the Ocean, let the sea bear him … None can
> report with truth, nor lords in their halls, nor mighty men
> beneath the sky, who received that load.[9]

Even this brief account raises a number of major difficulties, and some minor ones. An example of the latter is that in our single manuscript of the poem Scyld's heir is named as 'Beowulf', though he has no connection at all with the hero of the poem: almost all editors, and Tolkien also, have concluded this is a simple error by the scribe getting ahead of himself, and the child's proper name should have been 'Beow' (Anglo-Saxon for 'Barley'). Meanwhile the aforementioned major difficulties are:

– Is 'Scefing' a patronymic, 'the son of Scef'? Or a nickname, 'with a sheaf' (Anglo-Saxon *scēaf*)?
– What is meant by 'was found forlorn'?
– What is the 'dire need' which the Danes endured 'without a prince'?
– What explains this unique case of a ship-burial, with

treasure, in which the ship is pushed out to sea, but not set on fire? (Surely, in any real world, an irresistible temptation to not-quite-grave-robbing?)

– Who was expected to 'receive that load'?

– And, of course, who 'sent [Scyld] forth alone over the waves' in the first place? (Presumably, it was they who were expected to take him back again – with the Danish treasures as a thank-offering?)

It is all, as Tolkien said, 'a most astonishing tangle', only made worse by such analogues as scholars have been able to discover.[10]

Thus, in the late tenth century the *Chronicle* of Æthelweard lists in its genealogy of the English kings the names Beo, Scyld and Scef, and says of the last that 'he came in a swift boat, surrounded by arms, to an island of the ocean called Scani [as] a very young boy, and unknown to the people', who nevertheless chose him to be their king. In the twelfth century William of Malmesbury gives a similar genealogy, and says that Sceaf 'was brought in a boat without any oarsman to Scandza … He was asleep, and by his head was placed a handful of corn, on which account he was called "Sheaf".' He too became a king.[11]

So, just to add to our difficulties:

– Was it Scyld or Sceaf who came over the waves alone?

– And was he 'surrounded by arms' or with 'a handful of corn'?

– And is this a Danish legend, or an English one, or even a Lombard one, as another Anglo-Saxon poem insists 'Sheaf ruled the Lombards'? (Who in historical times were nowhere near Scani, or Scandza, or Scandinavia, but lived in Lombardy, in north Italy.)

Tolkien dealt with the 'tangle', both in his 'Commentary' on *Beowulf* and in his poem 'King Sheave', by cutting a series of Gordian knots.

He concluded, first, that the poet of *Beowulf* probably 'meant (Shield) Sheafing as a patronymic', though this in fact, as Tolkien noted, makes no sense. If Scyld was washed up as a foundling, how would anyone know his father's name? In any case, Tolkien asserted, there had never been any such person as Scyld, whatever Anglo-Saxon genealogists might

claim: he was a 'fiction', a back-formation from the names
the Danes chose to call themselves, the 'Shieldings' or 'men
of the shield', parallel to martial names in the poem like the
Helmings ('people of the helmet'), or the Brondings ('people
of the sword'). Despite *Beowulf*, then, but in line with both
Æthelweard and William of Malmesbury, the mysterious
child from the sea had to be Sceafa, or Sheave. He was,
moreover, like his son Beow or Barley, a mythical rather than
a historical figure. As for the 'dire need' of the Danes, this was
an interregnum caused by the deposition of the tyrant-king
Heremod, who is mentioned twice later on in *Beowulf*, and
figures also as an ancestor, one above Scyld, in Anglo-Saxon
genealogies.[12]

These decisions leave aside the major issue of who was
responsible for the sending of Sheave (as I shall name him
from now on). Tolkien in fact, and rather surprisingly, does
not comment on this, but it seems very likely that what caught
his attention was line 44b in the poem. The translation of

10.1 'The arrival of Scyld
Scefing' from Fredrik Sander's
edition of the Poetic Edda,
Edda Sämund den vises (1893)
[artist unidentified].
Oxford, Bodleian Library,
28865 c.1.

line 44 given above tells us, 'With lesser gifts no whit did [Scyld's mourners] adorn him, with treasures of that people, than did those that in the beginning sent him forth'. 'With lesser gifts no whit' means, allowing for Anglo-Saxon understatement, 'with far more gifts': though this was an easy bar to raise, given that the child was sent forth *fēasceaft*, 'forlorn', or more strictly, 'destitute, without any possessions at all', as the poem says a few lines earlier.

But the striking thing, which would certainly have been noticed by Tolkien, a strict metrist, is that line 44 is metrically unusual, though not irregular. The alliterating stress on the first syllable of *þēodgestrēona*, 'treasures of the people', is picked up in the second half-line by *þonne þā dydon*, 'than those did'. In Old English metre, stress regularly falls on words of high alliterative 'rank', nouns, adjectives, disyllabic adverbs, non-finite verbs, but much more rarely on other verbal classes including possessive or (as in this case) demonstrative pronouns. Nevertheless, since conjunctions such as *þonne* are prosodically weaker even than pronouns, in line 44 the vital stress has to fall on the word *þā*, 'those'. Giving the pronoun both stress and alliteration, and moreover having it alliterate in the vital non-optional third-stress position of the line, is the equivalent, in modern terms, of printing the word in capital letters: 'than THOSE did that in the beginning sent him forth …'

But who are the mysterious 'those'? The sending is clearly providential. God saw the 'dire need' of the people. But it was not He who sent the child: the senders are plural. So the senders are acting for God, but have supernatural powers themselves. Whatever the poet of *Beowulf* may have thought – and that is a serious puzzle – Tolkien surely concluded that the senders were something very like the Valar, in his own mythology the demiurges responsible to the One for the fate of Arda: demiurges, it might be thought, mistaken in heathen times for gods themselves, and worshipped as such. (Indeed, one might well think, given Tolkien's habit of deriving fictional inspiration from a philological crux, that it was this line which gave him the very idea of the Valar.)

Be that as it may, Tolkien, like C.S. Lewis, and indeed like the poet of *Beowulf*, surely wished to make an accommodation of some kind between pagan myth and Christian revelation. It is significant that the *Beowulf*-poet, while well aware of the condemnatory word *hǣþen*, 'heathen' – obvious mark of a Christian standpoint – uses it only to describe Grendel, or the dragon's ancient hoard, except for two occasions. One of these comes in a passage which Tolkien thought was a later addition by a less tolerant hand, arguing the point at such length as to show that it was of great importance to him. The other is generally regarded by scholars as a further scribal error (like writing 'Beowulf' for 'Beow'), and in his translation Tolkien likewise rendered the suspect word not as 'heathens' but as 'mighty men'.[13] It is unlikely to be coincidence that in the whole of *The Lord of the Rings* the word 'heathen' is similarly used only twice, once by Denethor, bent on suicide, and once by Gandalf, rebuking Denethor.

Both Tolkien and the poet of *Beowulf*, then, while well aware that their heroes lived before the time of Christ, and were in consequence inevitably 'heathens', were not going to call them that. Heathens, or pagans, and pagan mythology itself, were not *ipso facto* evil. The good in them, nevertheless, could only be partial.

The poem 'King Sheave'

Coming finally to Tolkien's poem 'King Sheave' itself, what does it tell us about Tolkien's views on mythology, and about where the 'Sheave' story, as told in King Alfred's hall by the singer Ælfwine, might have fitted in with Tolkien's plan for 'The Lost Road'?

It is clear that Tolkien thought of Sheave (and his son Barley) as a 'corn-god' or 'culture-hero' from pagan times.[14] Yet to Tolkien he was more than an analogue of 'John Barleycorn'. Sheave brought the Longobards (who in Tolkien's poem have replaced the Danes of *Beowulf*) more than agriculture, and rescued them from more than dearth and hunger. Before his arrival they were in a state of deep and one might say existential despair. In three passages Tolkien stresses their unhappy condition: in lines 15–18, 'laughter they knew not … shadow was upon them', in lines 43–49, 'bleak … drear … dim … no light seeing', in lines 78–85, once again, 'sad country … dark shadow … Dread was their master'. The darkness, the grief, the shadow and the dread are all dispersed by the coming of Sheave, who brings light and song, healing and riches.

At the heart of the poem, moreover, there is a moment of what one can only call 'eucatastrophe', a term Tolkien invented.[15] Sheave, still sleeping, is taken from his boat, carried to a hall, and left there. In the morning his finders go to check on him – and find the hall empty: 'The house was bare, hall deserted … Their guest was gone. Grief o'ercame them' (ll. 57, 61). But then sunrise shows them Sheave, standing on a hill, harp in hand, cornsheaf at his feet, singing in an unknown tongue – and for the Longobards, the world changes. This scene may well recall the coming of the Maries

to the tomb of Jesus in the Gospels, and finding it empty: the great moment, of course, of Christian 'eucatastrophe'.[16] I give a further reason for making this connection below.

A very clear indication of Tolkien's Christian intention is the length of his poem: 'King Sheave' is 153 lines long. Christopher Tolkien notes that it was originally 137, with his father adding sixteen lines, at first in pencil. There is no doubt about the Christian symbolism of the number 153. It is 'the Number of Salvation', and the reason for giving it that significance is the passage in the Gospel of John, chapter 21.[17] Here, after Christ's death and resurrection, his disciples are fishing and catching nothing. Then Christ, on the shore, tells them to cast their nets on the other side, and immediately

10.2 The empty tomb signifying the resurrection of Jesus, by Romolo Tavani.

they catch a number of great fishes, 'one hundred and fifty and three'. Since this scene is the one in which the disciples become 'fishers of men', their catch evidently symbolizes the souls they save. The conclusion one has to draw is that Sheave was, quite deliberately, presented as a forerunner of Christ, bringing hope, in advance of revelation, to a pagan world.

There is moreover an Anglo-Saxon poem, which Tolkien no doubt knew (he knew them all), which shows distinct similarities to 'King Sheave'.[18] Its modern title is 'The Descent into Hell', but this gives a false impression. It describes a *release* from Hell, when Christ, according to medieval legend, went down into Hell, in the days between his death and his resurrection, to release the souls of the Patriarchs and the Prophets, who lived before his time and therefore did not have the chance of salvation. The poem opens with the two Maries finding the empty tomb, described with a powerful sense of shock and joy, which amounts once again to 'eucatastrophe'. There is a clear thematic connection between the Anglo-Saxon poem and 'King Sheave', in that both describe the liberation from doom and despair of groups of pre-Christians, respectively the Patriarchs and Prophets, and the heathen Longobards. Furthermore, and curiously, if perhaps coincidentally, the Anglo-Saxon poem is 137 lines long – the same length as 'King Sheave', before Tolkien added the sixteen-line coda which brought it up to 153. There must be at least a possibility that Tolkien had the Anglo-Saxon poem in mind as a model, a mythological parallel.

Finally, the poem's sixteen-line coda declares that Sheave had seven sons, who founded kingdoms in the North 'before the change / in the Elder Years' (ll. 142–43). The list of seven ends with the Langobards, or Longobards (Tolkien uses both spellings in the poem), who made a mighty realm 'where Ælfwine Eadwine's heir / in Italy was king' (ll. 152–53). Christopher Tolkien notes with regard to these last lines that 'I am at a loss as to what is referred to in [lines 142–43]', and in particular (his italics and capitalization) *'before the change in the Elder Years'*.[19] The events described in the main story of *Beowulf* can be dated to the first half of the sixth century, so that Scyld himself (insofar as he ever existed) would be a character from the fifth century, while Sheave's sons (insofar as they ever existed, and insofar as they were his sons) would likewise have lived in the pagan era of the ancient North. I would suggest accordingly, in view of what has been said above, that 'the change in the Elder Years' must refer to the Great Change of the coming of Christianity to the Northern pagans, an event of unique importance to Tolkien.[20]

This is strongly implied by one further Christian connection hinted at, not in the poem, but in the prose account which may have been intended to follow the story of the Anglo-Saxon Ælfwine in 'The Lost Road'. This states that the rule of Sheave was afterwards called 'the golden years, while the great mill of Sheaf was guarded still in the island sanctuary of the North; and from the mill came golden grain, and there was no want in all the realms'. As Christopher Tolkien points out, this has been adapted from the story of 'the mill of Fróthi' in Snorri Sturluson's thirteenth-century *Prose Edda*.[21] Snorri declared that Fróthi was the grandson of Skjold (or Scyld), and that he became king at the time when Christ was born – when, as other legends have it, there was peace in all the world. By mentioning 'the great mill of Sheaf', Tolkien transferred the *Fróðafrið* or 'peace of Fróthi' to Sheave. In so doing he implicitly redated Sheave to make him a contemporary of Christ, and it is true that this was centuries earlier than the dates inferred just above for Sheave's sons. Tolkien might have argued, however, that we, like Snorri, are here in mythic time rather than in history. The connection with Fróthi makes Sheave not so much a forerunner of Christ as an echo, or analogue, bringing hope but not as yet revelation.

The links between Tolkien's mythology and Christian mythology are, then, evident: the empty hall/tomb, the Number of Salvation, the mention of a great Change, the implied contemporaneity of Christ and Sheave and Fróthi, the (possible) connection with 'The Descent into Hell'. There is a further link between 'King Sheave' and the idea of 'the Lost Road' in the mention of Langobardic Ælfwine and Eadwine (Alboin and Audoin) at the end of the poem. But the most important point, never expressed by Tolkien in so many words, is surely the explanation of the strange funeral of Scyld which opened this discussion.

10.3 'The Funerary Boat', by Sian James. An illustration of the funerary ship of Scyld Scefing, based on the Old English epic poem, *Beowulf* (ll. 32-52).

The funeral of Scyld, and its implications

Ship-burials in the pagan and early Christian North are well-known from archaeology, Sutton Hoo being the obvious English example of a king buried with his treasures in his ship. Also familiar, in Northern myth, is the idea of 'the Viking funeral', the chief or king laid in his ship and pushed out to sea, while the ship is set on fire – the classic example being the funeral of the god Balder, also described by Snorri Sturluson.[22] The *Beowulf* ritual, however – ship, treasures, pushed out to sea, but not set on fire – remains unique, and uniquely implausible.

Tolkien, one feels, must have thought, first, that the habit of boat-burial (often symbolic boat-burial, in a grave marked out by stones arranged in the shape of a ship) bore witness to a belief that the desired afterworld was across the western sea, as were the Undying Lands in Tolkien's own mythology.[23] Moreover, the peculiar nature of Scyld's burial testified to a belief that in certain cases, for certain people like Scyld himself, arriving from the western sea, it would be possible for their funeral-ship not to be intercepted and robbed by pirates or fishermen (as would almost certainly happen in the real world), but to find its own way to the Undying Lands and to the unknown powers who had sent them to Middle-earth. The poet of *Beowulf*, then, had what one can only call an inkling of Tolkien's own image of 'the Lost Straight Road'. A story derived from him would accordingly fit strikingly well into Tolkien's own conception.

Having said so much, one has to concede that Tolkien's major problem remained. *Beowulf*, and his deductions from it, gave him striking images, and mythical connections – but still no story, no human story. Links between Christian and pagan are there in *The Lord of the Rings* as well, notably Frodo (whose name is only the Anglicised form of Fróthi, Christ's contemporary), and the carefully flagged date of the destruction of the Ring (25 March, traditional date of the Crucifixion and so of salvation). But they are embedded, as the world knows, in compelling narrative. The idea of the Lost Road had great emotional significance to Tolkien – the yearning for it is evident in one of his poems after another[24] – but emotion does not translate automatically to narrative. In the poem of 'King Sheave', however, we have at least our own 'inkling' of what Tolkien might have wished to convey.

Brian Sibley

'DOWN FROM THE DOOR WHERE IT BEGAN ...'

PORTAL IMAGES IN *THE HOBBIT* AND *THE LORD OF THE RINGS*

11

T HE LONG, endlessly winding corridor of literature, ancient and modern, is edged with doorways: entrances and exits; extraordinary and everyday; offering enticements or escapes; frustratingly closed or alluringly open; welcoming, denying, excluding or imprisoning; portals to the past, the future or the exotic territories of the imagination with all their beauty, terror and wonderments.

There is an ancient jesting question which asks, 'When is a door not a door?' to which one answer – other than 'When it's a jar!' – could be: 'When it's a symbol.' Certainly, for centuries – as represented in art, literature, philosophy and religion – the door has been used as a representation of many things: hope, ambition, opportunity, chance, change, enlightenment and salvation; and the writings and drawings of J.R.R. Tolkien reference many doors – safe and dangerous – some of which may be judged as possessing their own distinctive symbolisms. But drawing parallels is, inevitably, a risky enterprise. Writing in his essay 'On Fairy-Stories', Tolkien commented that while a man might wander into the realm of Faërie it would be dangerous for him, while there, 'to ask too many questions, lest the gates should be shut and the keys lost'.[1]

The doors described in the Tolkien legendarium are diverse: from the Door of Night that the Valar caused to be built into the otherwise impenetrable Walls of the World, to the Elf-made Seven Gates that guarded the way to the Hidden City. However, in any consideration of the proliferation of doors described in the history of events in the 'Great Years' of 3018–19, there is only one place to begin and that is in the Shire and on the doorstep of Bag End, home of Mr Bilbo

Baggins. 'It had', the author of *The Hobbit* tells us, 'a perfectly round door like a porthole, painted green, with a shiny yellow brass knob in the exact middle.'[2]

From Bag End to beyond…

As a door, the entry to Bag End is both common and uncommon: an everyday access to a home noted for easy and comfortable living; and yet, as doors go, architecturally unconventional. Round doors (outside the Shire) are seldom found in either life or literature and, with the possible exception of the rolled-back stone door in the Resurrection narratives, the entrance to Bag End – itself a way into a labyrinth of more round doors – remains a unique and iconic example: suggesting, as it does, that it is a doorway into a place that is, simultaneously, reassuringly familiar and yet outside our experience.

Symmetrically pleasing in shape with its central, brightly polished doorknob, it is, we are told, painted green – and, as we later learn, freshly painted only a week before. Bilbo's choice of paint colour may have greater meaning than might, at first glance, be supposed. Although green is the colour to which in normal light the human eye is most sensitive, it is not a primary colour (being made by mixing blue and yellow) but has, nevertheless, assumed the significance of one, with 20 per cent of people choosing it as their favourite colour.[3] Testament to its popularity can be found in the use of green baize as a covering for writing desks and card, gaming and billiard tables, while a green baize door in a certain stratum of society signifies the immutable frontier between the domain of the family and that of the domestic staff.

There are many and various connotations associated with the colour green, some less than pleasant such as envy, jealousy and sickness, or with unsettling ambiguities of interpretation, as represented by the green-hued antagonist in the fourteenth-century poem *Sir Gawain and the Green Knight* that was the subject of special interest to Tolkien, whose translation of the chivalric romance was originally broadcast by the BBC and posthumously published. Other significations given to the colour tend to be mostly positive, such as the obvious associations with nature and fertility

11.1 'The Hill: Hobbiton-across-the Water', watercolour for *The Hobbit*, 1937. This detail shows Bilbo's freshly-painted, round front door.
Oxford, Bodleian Library, MS. Tolkien Drawings 26.

– concepts valued by Tolkien and many of the races of Middle-earth – and which can be traced from the ancient symbolism of the foliage-featured 'Green Man' (likenesses of which proliferate among the decorations of historic buildings in Oxford) through to the twentieth-century enlistment of the word 'green' by those pursuing the politics of environmentalism.

On a more speculative level, there is no shortage of popular theories to explain the 'meaning' behind some people's preference for a green front door. A random search for 'green front door' on the internet will result in a variety of websites purporting to reveal the popularity and meaning of this choice. For example, does the choice of green indicate a perceived status as a worthy and dependable member of society with an adherence to traditional, conservative values? Certainly, that might serve as a description of Mr Baggins at the beginning of *The Hobbit*. Other interpretations associate the colour green with a process of change, growth or development and with the acquisition of wealth which also, as it happens, are outcomes of Bilbo's journey 'there and back again'.

Bag End was, however, certainly not the first literary residence to have a green door. For example, the title character in L. Frank Baum's *The Wonderful Wizard of Oz* (1900) lives in the Emerald City with its green, gem-studded gates; green is also the colour of Christopher Robin's tree home in the Hundred Acre Wood described in A.A. Milne's *Winnie-the-Pooh* (1926), while the same author's earlier story *The Green Door* (1925) is a disquieting fantasy about a door that, despite its mundane ordinariness, provides the route by which the hero discovers unexpected truths about himself and his world. Another green door that is similarly hazardous – indeed, mortally so – features in H.G. Wells' short story 'The Door in the Wall' (1911); while the door in O. Henry's 'The Green Door' (1906) is a threshold between chance and destiny that may only be crossed by one with the pure spirit of true adventure.

Bilbo's round green door, unlike many of the doors encountered in fantasy fiction, myths, legends and fairy-tales, does not serve as a portal *in* to mysterious realms and unexpected adventures, but a way *out* to such experiences. The exploits that befall Bilbo have less to do with the opening of a door as with the closing of a door on all that is homely, familiar and secure in order to journey towards the unknown. As Frodo would later recall: 'Remember what Bilbo used to say: "It's a dangerous business, Frodo, going out your door. You step onto the road, and if you don't keep your feet, there's no knowing where you might be swept off to."'[4]

This door to Bag End provides the setting to the story's opening scene, with Bilbo sitting beside it and bantering with a wizard over a pipe of tobacco until the conversation turns alarmingly to the subject of adventures. And it is to that same door – now embellished with a curious sign scratched there by Gandalf – that thirteen Dwarves come calling on Mr Baggins to enlist his assistance in a daring escapade. With Bilbo's repeated trips to answer the door as a succession of visitors vigorously and noisily tug on the bell-pull, the door becomes a major, if inanimate, character in the opening chapter and is part of the idealized image of Bag End as the perfect home, repeatedly and fondly recalled during the hobbit's later exploits.

Thus the adventure begins and, at virtually every turn of the road that unwinds from the door at Bag End, Bilbo and his companions are faced with a succession of doors and gateways: visible or hidden, friendly or forbidding. There is the big stone door to the trolls' cave (accessible courtesy of Troll William's key, picked up by Bilbo during the campfire mêlée); Rivendell, the Last Homely House, where the doors are flung wide in welcome; the suddenly revealed crack-of-a-door that opens at the back of the cave in the Misty Mountains; the almost-closed Goblin Gate, through which Bilbo just manages to squeeze himself with no more damage than the loss of his brass buttons; the high thorn-hedge with a broad wooden gate that is the entrance to Beorn's garden and house; and the Forest Gate, beyond the Edge of the Wild, leading into the shadowed, spider-infested darkness of Mirkwood.

As seen in Tolkien's illustration to Chapter 9 of *The Hobbit*, an avenue of beech trees and a bridge crossing a dark, swift-flowing river lead to the Elvenking's Gate – through

11.2 'The Elvenking's Gate', pen-and-ink drawing for *The Hobbit*, 1936. There are seven earlier drawings of this gateway as Tolkien experimented with the style and shape before settling on this final version with its imposing fortified entrance. Oxford, Bodleian Library, MS. Tolkien Drawings 19.

The E

enKing's Gate.

which Bilbo's companions pass as prisoners ('There is no escape from my magic doors for those who are once brought inside') – and the trap-doors in the King's wine-cellars that provide their escape and enable their arrival before the open doors of the great hall of Lake-town.[5]

Bilbo's safe passage through all these doors could be viewed as a metaphor for the gradual process of transformation that overtakes – and takes over – an unadventurous homebody. With each successive entrance or exit, the personal journey of this hitherto parochially minded anti-hero leads him to an increasing understanding of the complexity of his world; to greater self-knowledge; to the acquisition of wit and wisdom and to unexpected displays of physical and moral courage. For Bilbo, the doors and gateways of Middle-earth become the checkpoints of change; and all of them are but a prelude to the arrival at the goal of his quest in the chapter significantly entitled 'On the Doorstep'.

The two doors of Erebor

The drama continues to unfold before the two doors of the Lonely Mountain. The first of these, overlooking the ruins of Dale, is the once noble Front Gate to the domain of the King under the Mountain which, when Bilbo first glimpses it, has been reduced to a ruined, cavernous opening in the base of the mountainside from which pour great clouds of steam and dragon smoke along with the cascading Running River.

Tolkien depicts in words and illustration the river swiftly springing from the doorway to noisily foam and splash its way down a boulder-strewn course, preventing further progress by Bilbo and the Dwarf scouting party. It is a passage that evokes the river Thund ('The Swollen' or 'The Roaring') surrounding the walls of Valhalla in the 'Eldar Edda', a text that had furnished Tolkien with various names for his story, including 'Gandalf' and 'Thorin'. In Henry Adams Bellows' 1923 translation, *The Poetic Edda*, the description reads:

11.3 'The Front Gate', pen-and-ink drawing for *The Hobbit*, 1936. Smoke curls ominously from the main entrance to the dwarven halls under the Lonely Mountain, signifying that the dragon lies in wait. Oxford, Bodleian Library, MS. Tolkien Drawings 24.

Loud roars Thund, |
…
Hard does it seem | to the host of the slain
To wade the torrent wild.

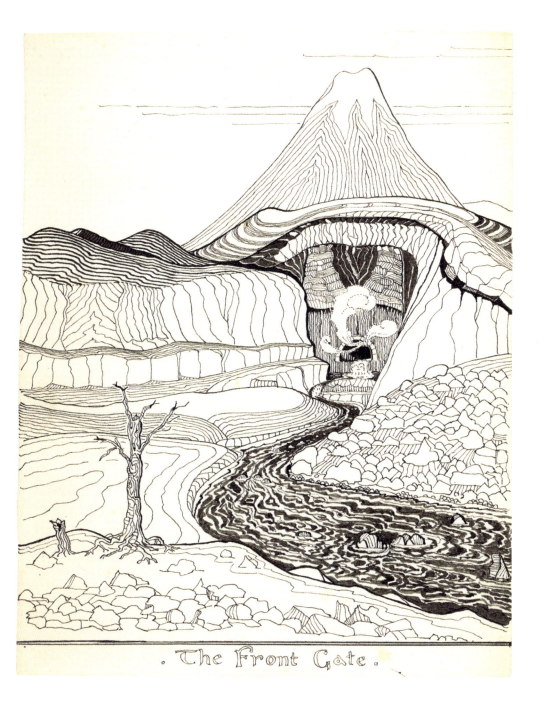

. The Front Gate .

The Dwarves, realizing the impossibility of entering the Lonely Mountain by the Front Gate, begin instead to search for another entrance – the secret door described in red runes on Thror's map: 'Five feet high the door and three may walk abreast.'[7] Allowing for the fact that *The Hobbit* was conceived as a story for children but that it went through various iterations before – and, indeed, after – it was published, it is possible that the runic inscription carries with it an allusion to another stanza in Bellows' translation of the 'Eldar Edda':

> Five hundred doors | and forty there are,
> I ween, in Valhall's walls;
> Eight hundred fighters | through one door fare
> When to war with the wolf they go.[8]

The location of the door having been reached, the company find only a flat wall of stone the smoothness of which is an indication of the work of masons, but without any of the usual appurtenances of a door: no threshold, doorposts, lintel nor any indication of lock or keyhole. The secret way into the Lonely Mountain is an enchanted and invisible door, subject to a date-and-time-specific magic – along with the convenient synchronicity of fiction.

Just as, during the visit to Rivendell, Elrond had discovered and revealed the hidden moon-letters on Thror's map by the light of a crescent moon such as had shone on the midsummer's eve when the silver-penned runes were written, so now the Dwarves and their hobbit burglar stand on the back doorstep at the very moment on the very day when the door divulges its secret existence, as foretold by Elrond: 'Stand by the grey stone when the thrush knocks ... and the setting sun with the last light of Durin's Day will shine upon the key-hole.'[9]

Despite the specificity of these instructions, Thorin and company bizarrely attempt a variety of ways to gain entrance, from pounding on the flat stone of the cliff wall, imploring it to yield and using odds and ends of half-remembered spells for opening, to an outright assault with picks and tools brought from Lake-town. As might be expected, none of these approaches are effective against potent magic. In the end, as foretold in the runes, it is the thrush (a crow in earlier drafts of the story) that indicates the moment of revelation – in a similar, though more portentous style, to the way in which the robin in Frances Hodgson Burnett's *The Secret Garden* (1910) leads Mary Lennox to the locked door in the garden wall.

The challenge of managing the business of doors, locks and keys is an ages-long trope of literature – consider the Winged Keys in *Harry Potter and the Philosopher's Stone* (1997) and, over a hundred years earlier, the trials and tribulations of the heroine of *Alice's Adventures in Wonderland* (1865), trapped in a long, low hall of locked doors with just 'a tiny golden key' that will only unlock the one door that is too small for Alice to pass through – and it is one that can be traced back to references in sacred texts and world mythologies including those of the Nordic tradition such as Valgrind, the Death-Gate standing before Valhalla, described in the edition of the *Poetic Edda* previously cited:

> There Valgrind stands, | the sacred gate,
> And behind are the holy doors;
> Old is the gate, | but few there are
> Who can tell how it tightly is locked.[10]

As John D. Rateliff has chronicled in his book *The History of The Hobbit*, the business of gaining access to the Lonely Mountain took some time to finesse as a plot point. So in one early version the key was acquired *en route* (on a bunch of curious keys found hanging on a nail in the trolls' cave) but in the final version Gandalf hands both map and key to Thorin in Bilbo's parlour at the outset of the story. However, during the process of writing and revision one significant inconsistency was overlooked when, with the magical appearance of the keyhole and the turning of the key, the door comes into view: 'Long straight cracks appeared and widened. A door five feet high and three broad was outlined and slowly, without a sound swung inward.'[11] It is a subtle distinction but, in terms of dwarf-widths, a door 'five feet high and three broad' is not necessarily the same thing as one that is 'five feet high … and three may walk abreast'.

With the enchanted door to the Lonely Mountain finally revealed and wedged open, burglar Baggins is sent upon his errand of reconnoitre that leads to his encounter and conversation with Smaug which, in turn, results in the destruction of the mountainside where the door once stood and the entrapment of the entire company. So it is that the company pass along passages and through doors – among them those to the once-great chamber of Thror, now half-burnt and hanging on twisted hinges – until they eventually approach, from within, the Front Gate of the Lonely Mountain, the great portal that, subsequently refortified by the Dwarves, provides the backdrop for the climactic Battle of the Five Armies and the heroic closing stages of the drama.

The Hobbit concludes with Bilbo and Gandalf arriving at the very place where the story began – on the doorstep of Bag End, although not quite as Mr Baggins might have expected to find it: 'There was a great commotion, and people of all sorts, respectable and unrespectable, were thick round the door, and many were going in and out – not even wiping their feet on the mat, as Bilbo noticed with annoyance.'[12]

With Bilbo being 'Presumed Dead' and the contents of his beloved home up for auction, this is hardly the comfortable refuge for which he had been longing during the wearisome return journey; but then – as Gandalf notes – Bilbo is no longer the hobbit he was when he set out a year before. It is as if a pale shadow of the disruption that his adventures imposed on his ordered life has followed him home and manifested itself in the very place that, hitherto, embodied the happiness of his settled existence. But then he is carrying with him Gollum's 'precious', the Ring, which – although he knows not its true significance – is so much more than meets the eye, being itself a portal (as round as the door to Bag End) offering a way into a parallel but invisible existence.

Nevertheless, order is restored and, as the book draws to its close, the reader finds Bilbo, seven years later, once again answering the doorbell and admitting Gandalf and Balin the Dwarf for a tranquil evening of tobacco and recollections. While the owner of Bag End will never be quite the same again, the home itself is restored to a safe haven.

The author's opening and closing illustrations to *The Hobbit* provide an intriguing juxtaposition, with the frontispiece depicting Bag End as viewed from the bottom of The Hill and the final picture showing the hobbit in tranquil mood, puffing on his pipe in the hall of Bag End with its celebrated round door open onto the world beyond – a visualization of the book's subtitle, 'There and Back Again'.

The road goes ever on…
A little over fifty years on, in the history of the Third Age, Tolkien takes up the narrative in the opening chapter of *The Fellowship of the Ring* when, once again, the door to Bag End opens onto more journeys, beginning with Bilbo, after his Long-Expected Party, crossing the threshold for the last time: 'He looked up, sniffing the air. "What fun! … This is what I have really been longing for, for years! Goodbye!" he said, looking at his old home and bowing to the door.'[13] It is a measure of the transformation that Bilbo's character has undergone that the hobbit who, years earlier, had found himself abandoning his second breakfast and running towards adventure without the remotest idea of what he was doing, is now calmly setting out from the same door with determination and pleasant expectations.

The years pass and it is Frodo who, shutting and locking the round door, turns his back on security and comfort and sets out not, as his uncle had originally done, on an adventure but on a quest of the greatest peril. With nothing but fear and uncertainty ahead, Frodo reflects on Bilbo's rhyme about the Road that goes ever on and the sense in which passing through the doorway of Bag End (or, indeed, any home) is always a step into the unknown: '[Bilbo] used often to say there was only one Road; that it was like a great river: its springs were at every doorstep, and every path was its tributary.'[14] Tolkien's simile underlies the unfolding action in *The Lord of the Rings*, as the pathways pursued by the Fellowship and their foes continually divide, cross and rejoin.

With the hobbits on the road – and with the sinister Black Riders at their backs – the ever-present sense of danger is, nevertheless, punctuated by reassuring interludes of rest and refreshment, all of which are found beyond hospitable doors:

11.4 'The Hall at Bag-End', pen-and-ink drawing for *The Hobbit*, 1937. This is the only image drawn by Tolkien which shows the view from inside a doorway looking out to the world beyond.
Oxford, Bodleian Library, MS. Tolkien Drawings 25.

Bag-End, Residence of
B. Baggins Esquire

firstly in the home of the doughty Farmer Maggot where the travellers are sustained with ale, mushrooms and sage advice, and then at Frodo's presumed new house in Crickhollow that, with its large round door and welcoming baths, is, however briefly, a home from home.

Tolkien's portrayals of warmth, light and cordiality as honest sentinels opposing coldness, darkness and hostility are described in simple, yet emblematic, language. On their arrival at Crickhollow, the windows are dark and shuttered and no light is visible – until, that is, Frodo knocks on the door and Fatty Bolger opens it, whereupon we read: 'A friendly light streamed out. They slipped in quickly and shut themselves and the light inside.'[15]

A similar, though more intense, mood is evoked when, after the horror of Merry and Pippin's encounter with Old Man Willow, Tom Bombadil comes to their rescue and issues an invitation to join him in his house:

> Down west sinks the Sun: soon you will be groping.
> When the night-shadows fall, then the door will open,
> Out of the window-panes light will twinkle yellow.[16]

Following Tom's sing-song voice the hobbits eventually see those twinkling lights and approach his house: 'Suddenly a wide yellow beam flowed out brightly from a door that was opened.'[17] Within, Goldberry hastens to shut out the night and the hobbits are greeted by a dazzlement of protecting light driving away the fears of darkness: 'The four hobbits stepped over the wide stone threshold, and stood still, blinking. They were in a long low room, filled with the light of lamps swinging from the beams of the roof; and on the table of dark polished wood stood many candles, tall and yellow, burning brightly.'[18] Tolkien had an understanding – historical, literary and spiritual – of the primitive, but enduringly powerful, symbolism of light as the repudiator of the terrors associated with darkness and death. In summoning those associations, he tapped into a millennia-old tradition rooted in numerous cultures and faith systems throughout the world.

In stark contrast to the almost divine radiance of Tom's house, Tolkien's narrative still allows for the menace that lurks in the shadows outside the walls of the sanctuary. Indeed, even within this safe-house, Frodo lies in 'a dream without light', haunted by fears and forebodings.[19] Proof of the transience of safety is almost immediately evidenced when, on leaving the warmth and security of Bombadil's home, the hobbits pass between the two huge standing stones 'like the pillars of a headless door' that is the portal to the deathly domain of the Barrow-wight.[20]

When, after another escape (courtesy of Tom Bombadil) the hobbits arrive in Bree 'desiring only to find a fire, and a door between them and the night', they learn that not all doors can be secured against the forces of evil intent.[21] While the familiar imagery is present in Tolkien's description of The Prancing Pony – 'the door was open and light streamed out of it' – the welcoming atmosphere of the four-square inn and its stout-hearted landlord prove no protection against the emissaries of the Dark Lord.[22] Respite is only gained – following three traumatic weeks of pursuit, attack and flight – within the halls of Rivendell, which is for the Fellowship, as it transpires, truly the Last Homely House.

There is a strikingly poignant moment when the Ring-bearer and his companions are about to set out from Rivendell on their perilous task. Having made their farewells, the Nine Walkers stand at the entrance to Elrond's great hall contemplating the quest ahead; a scene which Tolkien heightens by returning once again – and for a last time for many chapters – to his favoured image of shelter, harmony and well-being: 'A gleam of firelight came from the open doors, and soft lights were glowing in many windows.'[23]

The threshold of danger: the Doors of Durin
Following the Fellowship's abortive attempt to cross the Misty Mountains by the pass of Caradhras, they are confronted by a doorway of great antiquity, protected by a powerful form of enchantment. The Moria Gate, or the Doors of Durin, built into the western side of Celebdil, is associated with a tragic history and, at first, seems impregnable. The episode inevitably recalls the similarly mysterious Dwarf-built door on the back-doorstep of the Lonely Mountain chronicled in *The Hobbit*, and just as the rays of the setting sun had

revealed the keyhole to the hidden door, so at the Moria Gate, the light of the moon reveals the door's outline with the words and insignia inscribed on its surface, as depicted in the author's elaborate illustration.

Tolkien goes to considerable narrative pains to explain the nature of Dwarven doors and the various forms of magic spell by which they are secured. Gimli reveals: "'Dwarf-doors are not made to be seen when shut.... They are invisible, and their own makers cannot find them or open them, if their secret is forgotten.'"[24] To which Gandalf adds: "'Some dwarf-gates will open only at special times, or for particular persons; and some have locks and keys that are still needed when all necessary times and words are known'" – knowledge he, seemingly, lacked when he, Thorin and company were attempting to enter the realm of the King under the Mountain.[25]

In the case of Durin's doors, however, entry requires neither lock nor key and is gained solely by a spoken password. There is a correlation between this episode and a tradition of password-guarded doors found in a number of folk-tales, such as 'Ali Baba and the Forty Thieves' as anthologized in the collection of Middle Eastern stories gathered during the Islamic Golden Age and known, in translation, by such titles as *One Thousand and One Nights* and *Arabian Nights*. In the story, Ali Baba discovers, by chance, the magic words 'Open, Sesame!' that unlock a secret cavern where the Forty Thieves have hidden their plunder and then relieves them of part of their wealth. This is the beginning of a tortuously convoluted tale involving Ali Baba's avaricious brother, who misremembers the password as 'Open, Barley' and becomes the first victim in a series of unpleasant deaths before a happy ending is reached for Ali Baba and his household. From the nineteenth century the story of Ali Baba provided a popular subject for pantomimes and *opéras comiques* and Tolkien would have been familiar with this tale through Andrew Lang's 1898 edition of *The Arabian Nights Entertainment*s, a work referenced in his 1939 essay 'On Fairy-stories'.[26]

Parallel password tales feature in the folklore of various countries including the German story 'Simeliberg' ('Simeli Mountain'), found in the second volume of Jacob and Wilhelm Grimm's *Kinder-und Hausmärchen*. Reminiscent of the tale of

11.5 The Doors of Durin, printed galley for *The Lord of the Rings*, 1954. These dwarven doors will only open with the correct password which is hidden in plain sight, 'Speak Friend and Enter'. Oxford, Bodleian Library, MS. Tolkien Drawings 90, fol. 37r.

Here is written in the Feänorian characters according-
ing to the mode of Beleriand: Ennyn Durin Aran
Moria: pedo mellon a minno. Im Narvi hain ech-
ant: Celebrimbor o Eregion teithant i thiw hin.

Ali Baba – although considerably shorter – the story involves the password 'Semsi mountain, Semsi mountain, open!' leading to a familiar outcome of success and, for a forgetful brother, death. Tolkien was familiar with both the German and English editions of the Grimms' stories, and referred to them in 'On Fairy-stories'.[27]

Unlike these stories and others of their ilk, the password controlling the Doors of Durin is not one that the characters learn through eavesdropping but is hidden in plain sight within the inscription: 'Speak, friend, and enter.' The doors with their ancient emblems wrought in *ithildin* and illumined by the moonlight symbolize an age long past, now overshadowed by the events of evil days, and when Gandalf finally solves the riddle of the opening spell, speaks the word 'Friend', and the doors swing wide, the company are precipitously driven into the darkness and incarcerated by the Watcher in the Water.

From Aragorn's sinister forewarning – 'I say to you: if you pass the doors of Moria, beware' – and the lengthy preamble to the opening of the Moria Gate it seems reasonable to suppose that Tolkien was wanting to prepare the reader for the discovery that his characters are now standing on the threshold to a far more dangerous environment and one that is in stark contrast to their earlier experience of safety characterized by the light and warmth found behind the door to Bag End or in the houses of Tom Bombadil and Elrond Half-elven.[28] Certainly, the Fellowship have scarcely entered Moria before the doomful mood is established with Tolkien's description of Frodo's feelings as he sits watch while his companions sleep: 'As if it were a breath that came in through unseen doors out of deep places, dread came over him.'[29] It is a dread that becomes a reality as the stone door to the Chamber of Mazarbul crumbles under the assault of Orcs and cave-troll.

Together and divided, the Fellowship is now set upon paths where almost every door, gateway and entrance they confront threatens danger to themselves or their endeavour and even the doors of hoped-for allies are warily guarded: viewed with suspicion, even hostility, they are led blindfold into the heart of Lothlórien and the doors to Théoden's Golden Hall are initially barred to them; while defensive

Ch XXV

Minas Morgul must be made more horrible. The usual 'gobbin' stuff is not good enough here.

The Gate shaped like a gaping mouth with teeth and a window like an eye on each side. As S. passes through he feels a horrible shudder. There are two silent shapes sitting on either side as sentinels.

Substitute something for foll. out for p.

The main outer gates were now closed. But a small door in the middle of one was open. (It faced south.) The Gate-house was dark or night and the pale skylight showed up as a small patch at the end of the tunnel. As S. and F. crept closer they saw in the gloom the great ominous shapes of the Sentinels on either side: still sitting soundless and unmoved: yet from them there seemed to issue a threat nameless.

"Stay here!" whispered F. drawing S. into the shadow of a wall not far from the gate. "While I wear the R., I can understand much of the language of the enemies, or of the thought behind their speech: I don't know which. I will go forward, and try and find out something. If I can't, come at a run; and get through the door if you can."

"Nay!" said S. "That will not do. If we have a fight at the gate, we might as well or better stay inside. We'd have the whole wasps' nest, orcs and boggs and all, buzzing after us, before we'd gone a dozen yards: and they know these horrible mountains as well as I mind me of Bag-End. Swagger is the after-pay, Mr. F., begging your pardon."

"Very well," said F. "if you'd say so, my swagger!"

doors, such the Hornburg-gates and the Great Gate of Minas Tirith, though staunchly built and thought to be impregnable, prove ultimately fallible and succumb to the forces of the Enemy.

Still other doors and gates serve as either impenetrable barriers or thresholds to entrapment or mortal danger. Tolkien repeatedly endows Sauron's fortifications with human physical characteristics, portraying them as mocking the Fellowship through such expressions as 'the grinning gates of Minas Morgul'.[30] A manuscript page from the J.R.R. Tolkien Collection held at Marquette University, Wisconsin, has the author's notes for what was, at the time, designated Chapter 25. 'Minas Morgul', writes Tolkien, 'must be made more horrible. The usual "goblin" stuff is not good enough here.' With a small sketch as illustration, he notes 'The Gate shaped like a gaping mouth with teeth and a window like an eye on each side.' In the final text, Frodo views the scene: 'Across the narrow valley, now almost on a level with his eyes, the walls of the evil city stood, and its cavernous gate, shaped like an open mouth with gleaming teeth, was gaping wide.'[31] Later, when the forces of Gondor and Rohan await the final conflict, the author employs a similar anthropomorphic description: 'The two vast iron doors of the Black Gate under its frowning arch were fast closed.'[32]

Elsewhere Tolkien uses onomatopoeia to evoke not just the look but also the sound of doors. Early in the story, the author describes Old Man Willow's imprisoning of the two young hobbits as happening with 'a noise like the snick of a lock when a door quietly closes fast'; and, much later, in concluding Book IV of the second volume, he writes of the dramatic shutting of the Undergate of the Tower of Cirith Ungol: 'The great doors slammed to. Boom. The bars of iron fell into place inside. Clang. The gate was shut. Sam hurled himself against the bolted brazen plates and fell senseless to the ground.'[33] When Tolkien takes up the story of Sam and Frodo at the beginning of Book VI, it is with Sam boldly entering the main gate to Cirith Ungol and, in so doing, arousing the Two Watchers, the gargoyle-like stone sentinels with their 'dreadful spirit of evil vigilance'.[34] The imminent danger of having raised the alarm is intentionally and amusingly undercut by Sam's ironic trivialization of his actions: "'That's done it! … Now I've rung the front-door bell!'"[35]

By this point in the story, Tolkien's reader has already stood before or crossed other thresholds not only significant to the outcome of the War of the Ring but redolent with the ancient archetypal symbolism of death as a final door into the unknown. Aragorn, Legolas, Gimli and the Grey Company enter the Door of the Dead to ride to the Stone of Erech and rouse the Oathbreakers: 'the Dark Door gaped before them like the mouth of night. Signs and figures were carved above its wide arch too dim to read, and fear flowed from it like a grey vapour.'[36] Later, Gandalf and Pippin enter Fen Hollen, the 'Closed Door', which is the province of the dead in Minas Tirith where they drag the still-living Faramir from the funerary pyre and witness the tragedy of Denethor's self-immolation.

As the story thunders towards its apocalyptic denouement, the forces of good are ranged before Sauron's evil stronghold awaiting confrontation and Tolkien evokes the tension and the antagonism of the Enemy and the sudden release of his wrath: 'Drums rolled and fires leaped up. The great doors of the Black Gate swung back wide. Out of it streamed a great host as swiftly as swirling waters when a sluice is lifted.'[37] And as the two armies engage, Frodo alone – then followed by Sam and Gollum – comes to the most fearful of Tolkien's doorways, once again described as a 'gaping mouth', this time in the side of Orodruin: the dark door of the Sammath Naur leading to the Cracks of Doom and the final struggle.[38]

Return journeys…

Just as Bilbo's travels in *The Hobbit* ended back at the door where they began so, too, does the far longer and more terrible journeying of Frodo; but where Bilbo only returned to see Bag End in the hands of auctioneers, Frodo and his fellow hobbits return to the dreadful reality that their beloved Shire has been brought to wrack and ruin by forces of corruption only less malevolent in scale than those with which they had engaged on distant battlefields.

The cataclysmic events that simultaneously took place before the Black Gates and beyond the door to Sammath Naur are suddenly refocused onto the parochial but no less particular. On the doorstep of Bag End, the once-powerful Saruman, now Sharkey – an enfeebled and embittered version of his former greatness – is slain by Gríma Wormtongue in an act of long-delayed vengeance. Sam and Merry reflect that the moment marks the final end-point of the War. Frodo responds with a sigh: 'The very last stroke. But to think that it should fall here, at the very door of Bag End! Among all my hopes and fears at least I never expected that.'[39]

There is, of course, one final return to the round green door of Bag End when, following the healing of the Shire and the departure of Frodo and the other Ring-bearers into the West, Sam returns to the Hill from the Grey Havens and Tolkien offers his familiar metaphor for warmth and welcome, hearth and home:

> And he went on, and there was yellow light, and fire within; and the evening meal was ready, and he was expected....
> He drew a deep breath. 'Well, I'm back,' he said.[40]

There and back again; door to door; journey done.

Catherine McIlwaine
CHRISTOPHER TOLKIEN: BIBLIOGRAPHY

Books

'Heiðreks Saga', ed. with introduction, translation and commentary by C.J.R. Tolkien, 2 vols, B.Litt. thesis, University of Oxford, 1953.

Hervarar saga ok Heiðreks, notes and glossary by G. Turville-Petre, with introduction by Christopher Tolkien, Viking Society for Northern Research, University College London, 1956.

Geoffrey Chaucer, *The Pardoner's Tale*, ed. Nevill Coghill and Christopher Tolkien, Harrap, London, 1958.

Geoffrey Chaucer, *The Nun's Priest's Tale*, ed. Nevill Coghill and Christopher Tolkien, Harrap, London, 1959.

The Saga of King Heidrek the Wise, transl. and ed. Christopher Tolkien, Thomas Nelson and Sons, London, 1960.

Geoffrey Chaucer, *The Man of Law's Tale*, ed. Nevill Coghill and Christopher Tolkien, Harrap, London, 1969.

J.R.R. Tolkien, *Sir Gawain and the Green Knight, Pearl and Sir Orfeo*, ed. Christopher Tolkien, George Allen & Unwin, London, 1975.

J.R.R. Tolkien, *The Silmarillion*, ed. Christopher Tolkien, with foreword, pp. 7–9, and *Map of Beleriand*, George Allen & Unwin, London, 1977; 2nd ed., with preface by Christopher Tolkien, p. x, HarperCollins, London, 1999.

Pictures by J.R.R. Tolkien, foreword and notes by Christopher Tolkien, George Allen & Unwin, London, 1979; revised ed., HarperCollins, London, 1992.

J.R.R. Tolkien, *Unfinished Tales of Númenor and Middle-earth*, ed. Christopher Tolkien, George Allen & Unwin, London, 1980.

The Letters of J.R.R. Tolkien, ed. Humphrey Carpenter, with the assistance of Christopher Tolkien, George Allen & Unwin, London, 1981.

J.R.R. Tolkien, *The Monsters and the Critics and Other Essays*, ed. Christopher Tolkien, George Allen & Unwin, London, 1983.

J.R.R. Tolkien, *The Book of Lost Tales, Part I* (Vol. I of *The History of Middle-earth*), ed. Christopher Tolkien, George Allen & Unwin, London, 1983.

J.R.R. Tolkien, *The Book of Lost Tales, Part II* (Vol. II of *The History of Middle-earth*), ed. Christopher Tolkien, George Allen & Unwin, London, 1984.

J.R.R. Tolkien, *The Lays of Beleriand* (Vol. III of *The History of Middle-earth*), ed. Christopher Tolkien, George Allen & Unwin, London, 1985.

J.R.R. Tolkien, *The Shaping of Middle-earth: The Quenta, The Ambarkanta and The Annals together with the earliest 'Silmarillion' and the first Map* (Vol. IV of *The History of Middle-earth*), ed. Christopher Tolkien, George Allen & Unwin, London, 1986.

J.R.R. Tolkien, *The Lost Road and Other Writings: Language and Legend before 'The Lord of the Rings'* (Vol. V of *The History of Middle-earth*), ed. Christopher Tolkien, Unwin Hyman, London, 1987.

J.R.R. Tolkien, *The Return of the Shadow: The History of The Lord of the Rings, Part One* (Vol. VI of *The History of Middle-earth*), ed. Christopher Tolkien, Unwin Hyman, London, 1988.

J.R.R. Tolkien, *Tree and Leaf*, 2nd ed., including the poem 'Mythopoeia', with new preface by Christopher Tolkien, pp. 5–8, Unwin Hyman, London, 1988.

J.R.R. Tolkien, *The Treason of Isengard: The History of The Lord of the Rings, Part Two* (Vol. VII of *The History of Middle-earth*), ed. Christopher Tolkien, Unwin Hyman, London, 1989.

J.R.R. Tolkien, *The War of the Ring: The History of The Lord of the Rings, Part Three* (Vol. VIII of *The History of Middle-earth*), ed. Christopher Tolkien, Unwin Hyman, London, 1990.

J.R.R. Tolkien, *Sauron Defeated: The End of the Third Age (The History of The Lord of the Rings, Part Four), The Notion Club Papers and The Drowning of Anadûnè* (Vol. IX of *The History of Middle-earth*), ed. Christopher Tolkien, HarperCollins, London, 1992.

J.R.R. Tolkien, *Morgoth's Ring: The Later Silmarillion, Part One, The Legends of Aman* (Vol. X of *The History of Middle-earth*), ed. Christopher Tolkien, HarperCollins, London, 1993.

J.R.R. Tolkien, *The War of the Jewels: The Later Silmarillion, Part Two, The Legends of Beleriand* (Vol. XI of *The History of Middle-earth*), ed. Christopher Tolkien, HarperCollins, London, 1994.

J.R.R. Tolkien, *The Peoples of Middle-earth* (Vol. XII of *The History of Middle-earth*), ed. Christopher Tolkien, HarperCollins, London, 1996.

J.R.R. Tolkien, *Narn I Chîn Húrin: The Tale of the Children of Húrin*, ed. Christopher Tolkien, illustrated by Alan Lee, HarperCollins, London, 2007.

J.R.R. Tolkien, *The Legend of Sigurd and Gudrún*, ed. Christopher Tolkien, illustrated by Bill Sanderson, HarperCollins, London, 2009.

J.R.R. Tolkien, *The Fall of Arthur*, ed. Christopher Tolkien, illustrated by Bill Sanderson, HarperCollins, London, 2013.

J.R.R. Tolkien, *Beowulf: A Translation and Commentary together with Sellic Spell*, ed. Christopher Tolkien, HarperCollins, London, 2014.

J.R.R. Tolkien, *Beren and Lúthien*, ed. Christopher Tolkien, illustrated by Alan Lee, HarperCollins, London, 2017.

J.R.R. Tolkien, *The Fall of Gondolin*, ed. Christopher Tolkien, illustrated by Alan Lee, HarperCollins, London, 2018.

Articles, notes and interviews
Christopher Tolkien, 'The Battle of the Goths and the Huns', *Saga-Book of the Viking Society for Northern Research*, vol. 14, no. 3, University College London, 1955–56, pp. 141–63.

J.R.R. Tolkien, 'Guide to the Names in *The Lord of the Rings*', ed. Christopher Tolkien, in *A Tolkien Compass*, ed. Jared Lobdell, Open Court, La Salle, IL, 1975, pp. 153–201.

J.R.R. Tolkien, *Les aventures de Tom Bombadil*, transl. Dashiell Hédayat, with unattributed note by Christopher Tolkien dated March 1974, p. 3, Christian Bourgois, Paris, 1975.

The Lord of the Rings 1977 Calendar, with explanatory notes by Christopher Tolkien, George Allen & Unwin, London, 1976.

Bill Cater, 'The Filial Duty of Christopher Tolkien', interview with Christopher Tolkien, *Sunday Times Magazine*, 25 September 1977.

Christopher Tolkien, *The Silmarillion by J.R.R. Tolkien: A Brief Account of the Book and Its Making*, Houghton Mifflin, Boston, 1977.

J.R.R. Tolkien, *The Silmarillion: Of Beren and Lúthien*, sleeve notes by Christopher Tolkien, Caedmon Records, New York, 1977.

The Silmarillion Calendar 1978, with 'Notes on the Pictures' by Christopher Tolkien, George Allen & Unwin, London, 1977.

J.R.R. Tolkien, *Of the Darkening of Valinor and Of the Flight of the Noldor From The Silmarillion*, sleeve notes by Christopher Tolkien, Caedmon Records, New York, 1978.

J.R.R. Tolkien Calendar 1979, with explanatory notes by Christopher Tolkien, George Allen & Unwin, London, 1978.

Christopher Tolkien, 'The Tengwar Numerals', *Quettar* 13 (February 1982), pp. 8–9; *Quettar* 14 (May 1982), pp. 6–7.

Christopher Tolkien, 'Future Publishing', *Amon Hen* 63 (August 1983), p. 4.

Christopher Tolkien, 'Moria Gate … another look', *Amon Hen* 70 (November 1984), p. 3.

[Christopher Tolkien], 'Notes on the Differences in Editions of *The Hobbit* Cited by Mr. David Cofield', *Beyond Bree*, July 1986, pp. 1–3.

J.R.R. Tolkien, *The Hobbit*, 50th anniversary ed., with foreword by Christopher Tolkien, pp. i–xvi, Unwin Hyman, London, 1987.

CRT [Christopher Tolkien], 'A Note on the Maps', in J.R.R. Tolkien, *The Lord of the Rings*, HarperCollins, London, 1994, p. 1140.

Alison Flood, 'Christopher Tolkien Answers Questions about Sigurd and Gudrún', interview with Christopher Tolkien, *The Guardian*, 5 May 2009.

Raphaëlle Rérolle, 'Tolkien, l'anneau de la discorde', interview with Christopher Tolkien, *Le Monde*, 5 July 2012.

'L'efigie des Elfes = Fragments on Elvish reincarnation', ed. Michaël Devaux, with the assistance of Christopher Tolkien and Carl Hostetter, *La Feuille de la Compagnie*, 3 (2014), pp. 94–161.

Christopher Tolkien, '*The Legend of Sigurd and Gudrún*: a prose account of the story', Tolkien Estate website, 2015, www.tolkienestate.com.

Christopher Tolkien, 'Note on the Text' in J.R.R. Tolkien, *The Lay of Aotrou & Itroun*, ed. Verlyn Flieger, HarperCollins, London, 2016, pp. xi–xiii.

Maps
A Part of the Shire, in J.R.R. Tolkien, *The Fellowship of the Ring*, George Allen & Unwin, London, 1954, p. 25.

Map of the north-west of Middle-earth, in J.R.R. Tolkien, *The Fellowship of the Ring* and J.R.R. Tolkien, *The Two Towers*, George Allen & Unwin, London, 1954, fold-out map at the back of each book.

Map of Rohan, Gondor and Mordor, in J.R.R. Tolkien, *The Return of the King*, George Allen & Unwin, London, 1955, fold-out map at the back of the book.

Map of Beleriand and the Lands to the North, in J.R.R. Tolkien, *The Silmarillion*, ed. Christopher Tolkien, George Allen & Unwin, London, 1977, fold-out map at the back of the book.

The Realms of the Noldor and the Sindar, in Tolkien, *Silmarillion*, between pp. 120–21.

The West of Middle-earth at the End of the Third Age, in J.R.R. Tolkien, *Unfinished Tales of Númenor and Middle-earth*, ed. Christopher Tolkien, George Allen & Unwin, London, 1980, fold-out map at the back of the book.

Númenórë, in Tolkien, *Unfinished Tales*, between pp. 168–9.

Sketch map of Cabed-en-Aras, in Tolkien, *Unfinished Tales*, p. 149.

The Earliest Map, redrawing of map from 'The Theft of Melko and the Darkening of Valinor', in J.R.R. Tolkien, *The Book of Lost Tales, Part I*, ed. Christopher Tolkien, George Allen & Unwin, London, 1983, p. 81.

Two sketch maps showing the proximity of Hithlum to the Chasm of Ilmen in the *Ambarkanta* maps, in J.R.R. Tolkien, *The Lost Road and Other Writings,* ed. Christopher Tolkien, Unwin Hyman, London, 1987, pp. 270–71.

The Second Silmarillion Map, redrawing of map in its original state, in Tolkien, *Lost Road*, pp. 408–11.

Redrawing of two sketch maps showing the roads and rivers between the Shire and Rivendell, in J.R.R. Tolkien, *The Return of the Shadow*, ed. Christopher Tolkien, Unwin Hyman, London, 1988, p. 201.

The First Map of The Lord of the Rings, redrawings of each section, in J.R.R. Tolkien, *The Treason of Isengard*, ed. Christopher Tolkien, Unwin Hyman, London, 1989, pp. 295–323.

Frodo's Journey to the Morannon, redrawing of part of large-scale map of Gondor and Mordor, in J.R.R. Tolkien, *The War of the Ring*, ed. Christopher Tolkien, Unwin Hyman, London, 1990, p. 117.

The White Mountains and South Gondor, partial redrawing, in Tolkien, *War of the Ring*, p. 269.

The Second Map [of The Lord of the Rings], redrawing, in Tolkien, *War of the Ring*, pp. 434–5.

Redrawing of the second Silmarillion map to include all later amendments, in J.R.R. Tolkien, *The War of the Jewels*, ed. Christopher Tolkien, HarperCollins, London, 1994, pp. 182–5.

North-east (with additions), redrawing of an annotated copy of part of the second Silmarillion map, in Tolkien, *War of the Jewels*, p. 331.

Audio

J.R.R. Tolkien, *The Silmarillion: Of Beren and Lúthien*, read by Christopher Tolkien, Caedmon Records, New York, 1977.

J.R.R. Tolkien, *Of the Darkening of Valinor and Of the Flight of the Noldor From The Silmarillion*, read by Christopher Tolkien, Caedmon Records, New York, 1978.

J.R.R. Tolkien, *The Homecoming of Beorhtnoth*, read by J.R.R. Tolkien, with introductory and concluding essays by Christopher Tolkien, cassette tape, Grafton, 1992 [distributed only to the attendees of the Tolkien Centenary Conference, Keble College, Oxford, August 1992].

J.R.R. Tolkien, *The Children of Húrin*, preface and introduction read by Christopher Tolkien, story narrated by Christopher Lee, CD and download, HarperCollins, London, 2007.

Film

J.R.R.T.: A Portrait of John Ronald Reuel Tolkien 1892–1973, documentary featuring Christopher Tolkien, VHS, The Tolkien Partnership, London, 1992.

J.R.R.T.: A Film Portrait of J.R.R. Tolkien, extended edition, documentary featuring Christopher Tolkien, VHS, The Tolkien Partnership, London, 1996.

Christopher Tolkien, *Christopher Tolkien and 'Aubusson weaves Tolkien' Project*, 7 February 2019, www.youtube.com/watch?v=rQmh_Sfq88Y

NOTES

1 INTRODUCTION

1 J.R.R. Tolkien to Christopher Tolkien, 30 April 1944, *The Letters of J.R.R. Tolkien*, ed. Humphrey Carpenter, with the assistance of Christopher Tolkien, George Allen & Unwin, London, 1981, no. 64.

2 Christopher Tolkien in his introduction to *Hervarar saga ok Heiðreks*, ed. G. Turville-Petre, Viking Society for Northern Research, University College London, 1956.

3 Christopher Tolkien, *The Silmarillion by J.R.R. Tolkien: A Brief Account of the Book and Its Making*, Houghton Mifflin, Boston, MA, 1977.

4 Christopher Tolkien interviewed by Raphaëlle Rérolle, *Le Monde*, 5 July 2012.

5 Letter from J.R.R. Tolkien to Michael Tolkien, 28 September 1937, Tolkien family papers.

6 Letter from J.R.R. Tolkien to Christopher Tolkien, 5 November 1937, Tolkien family papers.

7 J.R.R. Tolkien to Charles Furth, 4 February 1938, *Letters*, no. 22.

8 Letter from J.R.R. Tolkien to Christopher Tolkien, 13 May 1950, Tolkien family papers.

9 Letter from J.R.R. Tolkien to Christopher Tolkien, 10 August 1936, Tolkien family papers.

10 J.R.R. Tolkien to Christopher Tolkien, 30 September 1944, *Letters*, no. 82.

11 Letter from J.R.R. Tolkien to Gwyn Jones, 24 January 1945, Tolkien family papers.

12 Letter from J.R.R. Tolkien to Christopher Tolkien, 17 February 1945, Tolkien family papers.

13 Letter from J.R.R. Tolkien to Gwyn Jones, late June 1945, Tolkien family papers.

14 Letter from J.R.R. Tolkien to Christopher Tolkien, 22 October 1945, Tolkien family papers.

15 Letter from J.R.R. Tolkien to Christopher Tolkien, 5 September 1945, referring to C.S. Lewis and his brother W.H. Lewis, known as Warnie, Tolkien family papers.

16 Letter from J.R.R. Tolkien to Christopher Tolkien, 9 October 1945, Tolkien family papers.

17 Letter from J.R.R. Tolkien to Simonne d'Ardenne, 24 August 1970, Tolkien family papers.

18 Letter from David Vaisey to Christopher Tolkien, 5 May 1976, Special Collections accession files.

19 Letter from Christopher Tolkien to David Vaisey, 18 June 1976, Special Collections accession files.

20 'Editor and scholar Christopher Tolkien awarded Bodley Medal', Bodleian Library & Radcliffe Camera, press release, 3 November 2016, https://web.archive.org/web/20161112114128/https://www.bodleian.ox.ac.uk/bodley/news/2016/nov-03.

21 Letter from Christopher Tolkien to Richard Ovenden, 14 October 2016, Bodleian Library records.

22 J.R.R. Tolkien, *The Fall of Gondolin*, ed. Christopher Tolkien, HarperCollins, London, 2018, preface, p. 11.

23 Letter from Christopher Tolkien to David Vaisey, 18 June 1976, Special Collections accessions files.

24 Christopher Tolkien interviewed by Alison Flood, *The Guardian*, April 2009.

25 J.R.R. Tolkien, *The Hobbit*, George Allen & Unwin, London, 1937, ch. 3.

26 J.R.R. Tolkien, *The Lord of the Rings*, George Allen & Unwin, London, 1954, Book II, ch. 2.

27 Ibid., Book II, ch. 4.

28 Ibid., Book II, ch. 7.

29 Ibid., appendix A.I.

30 J.R.R. Tolkien to Christopher Tolkien, 30 January 1945, *Letters*, no. 96.

31 C. McIlwaine, *Tolkien: Maker of Middle-earth*, Bodleian Library, Oxford, 2018, p. 327; Rayner Unwin, 'Early Days of Elder Days', *Tolkien's Legendarium*, Westport, CT and Greenwood Press, London, 2000.

32 J.R.R. Tolkien, *The Lord of the Rings*, Book IV, ch. 8.

3 A PERSONAL MEMORY

1 Christopher received the telescope in November 1938 for his fourteenth birthday. At that time he had been off school for almost a year due to ill-health.

2 The Whitley bomber crashed on Linton Road, 4 May 1941, killing all three crew members and a local resident, Mrs Frances Hitchcox.

3 The journey took much longer than usual due to continuous evasive action taken by the boat, heavily laden with troops and refugees, in order to avoid enemy U-boats.

4 The family had been notified in advance of the date and approximate time of his return.

5 The British people suffered many privations during the war. Meat, eggs, cheese, butter, milk, sugar and tea were all rationed at this time. Christopher was able to bring home a large quantity of sugar, marmalade and jam on his return from South Africa, where these foodstuffs were widely available.

4 THE SON BEHIND THE FATHER

1 J.R.R. Tolkien, *The Peoples of Middle-earth*, ed. Christopher Tolkien, HarperCollins, London, 1996, p. 158 (quotation from the *Akallabêth*, manuscript A).

2 The impulse of this essay was derived from repeated discussions that I have had the pleasure to have with Christopher Tolkien at his home for fifteen years. My gratitude goes to his family, Mrs Baillie Tolkien,

Adam Tolkien and Rachel Tolkien; to Richard Ovenden and Catherine McIlwaine, for their invitation and their kind patience; and to Vivien Stocker, John Rateliff and Douglas A. Anderson for their help.

3 Gérard Genette, *Fiction and Diction* [1991], transl. Catherine Porter, Cornell University Press, Ithaca, NY, 1993.

4 J.R.R. Tolkien, *The Fall of Gondolin*, ed. Christopher Tolkien, HarperCollins, London, 2018, preface, p. 12.

5 In this essay, it is not possible to focus on *The Children of Húrin* or *Unfinished Tales*, which will merely be mentioned in passing.

6 Randel Helms, *Tolkien and the Silmarils*, Thames and Hudson, London, 1981, p. 93.

7 J.R.R. Tolkien, *The Silmarillion*, ed. Christopher Tolkien, George Allen & Unwin, London, 1977, foreword, pp. 7–8. This crucial quotation is discussed in detail on p. 68.

8 J.R.R. Tolkien, *The Book of Lost Tales, Part I*, ed. Christopher Tolkien, George Allen & Unwin, London, 1983, foreword, p. 7.

9 Ibid., pp. 1–6.

10 Ibid., p. 7.

11 Christopher Tolkien, quoted in 'L'anneau de la discorde. Christopher Tolkien, le fils conducteur', *Le Monde*, 7 July 2012, p. 6. There is no official English translation of this article, originally designed as an interview, which I had the great pleasure to prepare with Raphaëlle Rérolle, for the cultural supplement of *Le Monde*. I quote here (with a minor correction) from https://worldcrunch.com/culture-society/my-father39s-eviscerated-work-son-of-hobbit-scribe-jrr-tolkien-finally-speaks-out (accessed 25 April 2020).

12 Helms, *Tolkien and the Silmarils*, p. 94; J.R.R. Tolkien, *Narn I Chîn Húrin: The Tale of the Children of Húrin*, ed. Christopher Tolkien, HarperCollins, London, 2007, pp. 283–84.

13 Tolkien, *Peoples of Middle-earth*, pp. 140–65.

14 Ibid., p. 158 (line numbers and breaks added).

15 Tolkien, *Silmarillion*, p. 337.

16 Following his remarks on 'Past and Present Tense in Chapter 1' of the *Quenta Silmarillion* (in J.R.R. Tolkien, *The Lost Road and Other Writings*, ed. Christopher Tolkien, George Allen & Unwin, London, 1987, p. 208), see his later comment about the *Valaquenta* in J.R.R. Tolkien, *Morgoth's Ring*, ed. Christopher Tolkien, HarperCollins, London, 1993, p. 204.

17 See his comment on § 57 *ff.* of the *Akallabêth* in *Peoples of Middle-earth*, p. 156.

18 See www.tolkienestate.com (accessed 16 May 2020).

19 Tolkien, *Silmarillion*, foreword, p. 7.

20 Tolkien, *Book of Lost Tales, Part I*, foreword, p. 7.

21 Paul Zumthor, *Toward a Medieval Poetics*, transl. Philip Bennett, University of Minnesota Press, Minneapolis, MN, 1992.

22 J.R.R. Tolkien, *Unfinished Tales of Númenor and Middle-earth*, ed. Christopher Tolkien, George Allen & Unwin, London, 1980, introduction, p. 3.

23 J.R.R. Tolkien, *Beren and Lúthien*, ed. Christopher Tolkien, HarperCollins, London, 2017, preface, p. 14.

24 Tolkien, *Lost Road*, p. 202.

25 Tolkien, *Morgoth's Ring*, p. 199 *ff.*

26 Jason Fisher, 'From Mythopoeia to Mythography: Tolkien, Lönnrot, and Jerome', in Allan Turner (ed.), *The Silmarillion: Thirty Years On*, Walking Tree, Zurich, 2007, p. 130.

27 Tolkien, *Silmarillion*, foreword, p. 8.

28 The inclusion appears in keeping with '[his] father's expressed intention' but it remains Christopher Tolkien's decision. See Tolkien, *Silmarillion*, foreword, p. 8, and Christopher Tolkien, *The Silmarillion by J.R.R. Tolkien: A Brief Account of the Book and Its Making*, Houghton Mifflin, Boston, 1977, § 26. I quote here the version prepared by Adam Tolkien for the official Tolkien Estate website, www.tolkienestate.com.

29 J.R.R. Tolkien to Colonel Worksett, 20 September 1963, *The Letters of J.R.R. Tolkien*, ed. Humphrey Carpenter, with the assistance of Christopher Tolkien, George Allen & Unwin, London, 1981, no. 247.

30 Tolkien, *Unfinished Tales*, introduction, p. 1; Tolkien, *Silmarillion*, foreword, p. 9.

31 Genette, *Fiction and Diction*, p. 168; see Käte Hamburger, *The Logic of Literature* [*Die Logik der Dichtung*, 1957], transl. Marilynn J. Rose, Indiana University Press, Bloomington, IN, 1973.

32 Tolkien, *Letters*, no. 247; Tolkien, *Beren and Lúthien*, preface, p. 11.

33 Tolkien, *Beren and Lúthien*, preface, p. 10.

34 Ibid., p. 12.

35 For commentary on previous texts see, for instance, *Beren and Lúthien*, p. 29 and *passim*; for the foreword to *Book of Lost Tales, Part I*, see *Beren and Lúthien*, preface, p. 13.

36 Tolkien, *Fall of Gondolin*, preface, p. 13.

37 J.R.R. Tolkien, *The War of the Jewels*, ed. Christopher Tolkien, HarperCollins, London, 1994, foreword, p. x.

38 David Bratman, 'The Literary Value of *The History of Middle-earth*' in V. Flieger and C. Hostetter (eds), *Tolkien's Legendarium: Essays on The History of Middle-earth*, Greenwood Press, Westport, CT, 2000, pp. 69–91.

39 On the proximity between letters and essays (a literary genre to which critical discourses such as commentaries and introductions by Christopher Tolkien mentioned here belong) see, among numerous other references, G. Lukács, 'On the Nature and Form of the Essay' in *Soul & Form* [1910], ed. John T. Sanders and Katie Terezakis, transl. Anna Bostock, Columbia University Press, New York, NY, 2010, p. 20 *ff.*

40 William Fliss, 'In Memoriam: Marquette Memories of Christopher Tolkien', *Mythlore*, vol. 38, no. 2, 2020, pp. 123–25; John Rateliff, 'In Memoriam: The Last Inkling', ibid., pp. 125–27.

41 Tom Shippey, *The Road to Middle-earth*, Allen & Unwin, London, 1982, pp. 15, 17.

42 Tolkien, *Beren and Lúthien*, preface, p. 10.

43 Clyde S. Kilby, *Tolkien and The Silmarillion*, Harold Shaw, Wheaton, IL, 1976, p. 6.

44 Tolkien, *War of the Jewels*, foreword, p. x.

45 Tolkien, *Fall of Gondolin*, preface, p. 11.

46 Christopher Tolkien, *A Brief Account of the Book and Its Making*, § 24. The (original) private status of this text has been confirmed by Douglas A. Anderson: '[it] was taken out of a letter from Christopher to Austin Olney of Houghton Mifflin and distributed as a pamphlet at a booksellers's convention' (private email, May 2020).

47 Verlyn Flieger, *There Would Always Be a Fairy Tale: More Essays on Tolkien*, The Kent State University Press, Kent, OH, 2017, p. xiv.

48 Tolkien, *Unfinished Tales*, introduction, p. 3.

49 I quote here his remark in *War of the Jewels*, p. 356.

50 See *The Poetics of Aristotle*, transl. and commentary by Stephen Halliwell, University of North Carolina Press, Chapel Hill, NC, 1987, p. 72, on 'the fictional status of works of mimesis: their concern with images, representations, simulations of enactments of human life'. For modern readings in literary studies, see Hamburger, *Logic of Literature*, and Genette (*Fiction and Diction*, p. 21): 'The literature of fiction is literature that imposes itself essentially through the imaginary character of its objects'.

51 Aristotle, *Poetics*, transl. with an introduction and notes by Anthony Kenny, Oxford University Press, Oxford, 2013, p. 29.

52 Christopher Tolkien, *A Brief Account of the Book and Its Making*, § 25 (the full paragraph is quoted on p. 68).

53 Tolkien, *Silmarillion*, foreword, p. 8.

54 Tolkien, *Silmarillion*, p. 280.

55 Shippey, *Road to Middle-earth*, p. 200.

56 Tolkien, *War of the Jewels*, p. 260.

57 Douglas Charles Kane, *Arda Reconstructed: The Creation of the Published* Silmarillion, Lehigh University Press, Bethlehem, PA, 2011, pp. 214–15.

58 Ibid., p. 215.

59 Tolkien, *War of the Jewels*, p. 354.

60 Ibid., p. 355.

61 Ibid., p. 356.

62 'It seemed at that time that there were elements inherent in the story of the Ruin of Doriath as it stood that were radically incompatible with "The Silmarillion" as projected, and that there was here an inescapable choice: either to abandon that conception, or else to alter the story. I think now that this was a mistaken view, and that the undoubted difficulties could have been, and should have been, surmounted without so far overstepping the bounds of the editorial function.' Ibid, p. 356.

63 To be accurate, there is no such thing as 'editorial inventions' (Kane), which is an oxymoron, in this Chapter 22. I would like to thank J. Rateliff for discussing this whole point.

64 Tolkien, *Children of Húrin*, appendix, p. 288.

65 Ibid., appendix, p. 288.

66 Bratman, 'The Literary Value of *The History of Middle-earth*', p. 68.

67 Turner (ed.), *Thirty Years On*.

68 Helms, *Tolkien and the Silmarils*, p. 94.

69 Tolkien, *Children of Húrin*, appendix, p. 289.

70 Ibid. According to the *OED*, these terms (used by him to describe *The Silmarillion*) are exact synonyms, as someone like Christopher Tolkien perfectly knew.

71 Tolkien to Milton Waldman, 1951, *Letters*, no. 131.

72 Carl Hostetter in a post on a social network (22 January 2020) – quoted here with his permission: https://www.facebook.com/235455793222722/posts/tolkien-scholar-carl-f-hostetter-has-written-poignant-words-on-the-passing-of-ch/2345781618856785.

73 Elstir, the painter, is presented as bolder in his paintings than in his artistic theories, in Marcel Proust, *In Search of Lost Time* (1913–1927).

74 Douglas A. Anderson, private correspondence (May 2020).

75 Christopher Tolkien, *A Brief Account of the Book and Its Making*, §§ 24–25. Extracts from these two paragraphs have been previously discussed.

76 Referring to the action of combining, the construction, the arrangement, and the practice of literary production.

77 Tolkien, *War of the Jewels*, p. 356.

5 LISTENING TO THE MUSIC

1 J.R.R. Tolkien to Stanley Unwin, 24 February 1950, *The Letters of J.R.R. Tolkien*, ed. Humphrey Carpenter, with the assistance of Christopher Tolkien, George Allen & Unwin, London, 1981, no. 124.

2 J.R.R. Tolkien to Milton Waldman, [1951], *Letters*, no. 131.

3 J.R.R. Tolkien to Milton Waldman, 10 March 1950, *Letters*, no. 126.

4 J.R.R. Tolkien to Stanley Unwin, 24 February 1950, *Letters*, no. 124.

5 J.R.R. Tolkien to Stanley Unwin, 10 March 1950, *Letters*, no. 125.

6 J.R.R. Tolkien to Amy Ronald, 15 December 1956, *Letters*, no. 195.

7 C.S. Lewis, 'The Gods Return to Earth', *Time & Tide*, 14 August 1954; Edmund Wilson, 'Oo! Those Awful Orcs', *The Nation*, 14 April 1956; Edwin Muir, 'A Boy's World', *The Observer*, 27 November 1955.

8 Douglass Parker, 'Hwaet We Holbytla', *Hudson Review*, vol. IX, no. 4, Winter 1956–57, p. 602.

9 Ibid., p. 609.

10 J.R.R. Tolkien, 'On Fairy-Stories', in *The Monsters and the Critics and Other Essays*, ed. Christopher Tolkien, George Allen & Unwin, London, 1983, p. 153.

11 J.R.R. Tolkien to Joanna de Bertodano, [April 1956], *Letters*, no. 186.

12 J.R.R. Tolkien to Christopher Tolkien, 11 July 1972, *Letters*, no. 340.

13 J.R.R. Tolkien, *The Book of Lost Tales, Part II*, ed. Christopher Tolkien, George Allen & Unwin, London, 1984, p. 170.

14 See John Garth's essay in this volume which proposes an earlier date of composition, pp. 88–105.

15 J.R.R. Tolkien, *The Silmarillion*, ed. Christopher Tolkien, George Allen & Unwin, London, 1977, pp. 16–17.

16 J.R.R. Tolkien, *The Lord of the Rings*, Houghton Mifflin, Boston, 1965, p. 5.

17 J.R.R. Tolkien, *Sauron Defeated*, ed. Christopher Tolkien, HarperCollins, London, 1992, p. 119.

18 Ibid.

19 J.R.R. Tolkien to Katherine Farrer, 24 October 1955, *Letters*, no. 173.

20 Tolkien, *Lord of the Rings*, Book VI, ch. 9.

21 Tolkien, *Silmarillion*, p. 19.

22 Ibid., p. 19.

23 J.R.R. Tolkien, '*Beowulf*: The Monsters and the Critics', in *The Monsters and the Critics*, p. 20.

24 Ibid., p. 21.

25 Ibid., p. 24.

26 Tolkien, *Lord of the Rings*, Book VI, ch. 9.

27 Ibid., Book V, ch. 6.

6 THE CHRONOLOGY OF CREATION

1 J.R.R. Tolkien, *The Book of Lost Tales, Part I*, ed. Christopher Tolkien, George Allen & Unwin, London, 1983, p. 247.

2 Letter to Carl F. Hostetter, quoted in Hostetter, 'The Last Inhabitant of Middle-earth', Tolkien Collector's Guide, 22 January 2020, www.tolkienguide.com/modules/newbb/viewtopic.php?post_id=23977.

3 J.R.R. Tolkien to Christopher Bretherton, 16 July 1964, *The Letters of J.R.R. Tolkien*, ed. Humphrey Carpenter, with the assistance of Christopher Tolkien, George Allen & Unwin, London, 1981, no. 257. Tolkien began work for the *OED* by 24 December 1918; Rachel A. Fletcher, 'Tolkien's Work on the *Oxford English Dictionary*: Some New Evidence from Quotation Slips', *Journal of Tolkien Research*, vol. 10, no. 2, 2020, pp. 13–16.

4 Tolkien, *Book of Lost Tales, Part I*, p. 45.

5 Ibid., p. 61.

6 Cf. Tolkien, *Book of Lost Tales, Part II*, p. 202.

7 Ibid., p. 200; Tolkien, *Book of Lost Tales, Part I*, p. 22.

8 Tolkien, *Book of Lost Tales, Part II*, p. 163.

9 Ibid., p. 146.

10 J.R.R. Tolkien, 'Qenya Lexicon (Qenyaqetsa)', *Parma Eldalamberon*, no. 12, 1988, ed. Christopher Gilson, Carl F. Hostetter, Patrick H. Wynne and Arden R. Smith, pp. 85, 42, 97, 58, 86.

11 J.R.R. Tolkien, 'Gnomish Lexicon (I·Lam na·Ngoldathon)', *Parma Eldalamberon*, no. 11, 1995, ed. Christopher Gilson, Patrick Wynne, Arden R. Smith and Carl F. Hostetter, pp. 3–4.

12 Ibid., no. 11, pp. 50, 73, 43.

13 J.R.R. Tolkien, 'The Official Name List', *Parma Eldalamberon*, no. 13, 2001, ed. Christopher Gilson, Bill Welden, Carl F. Hostetter and Patrick Wynne, pp. 100–5.

14 J.R.R. Tolkien, 'Name-list to The Fall of Gondolin', *Parma Eldalamberon*, no. 15, 2004, ed. Christopher Gilson and Patrick H. Wynne, p. 20, s.v. *Ainon*.

15 Tolkien, *Book of Lost Tales, Part I*, pp. 45*ff*.

16 Tolkien, *Book of Lost Tales, Part II*, p. 202; Tolkien, *Parma Eldalamberon*, no. 11, p. 50; no. 13, p. 101; and no. 15, p. 21.

17 Tolkien, *Parma Eldalamberon*, no. 15, p. 23; no. 11, p. 32.

18 Fol. 1 is the exercise book cover. The sheets using the lion-and-unicorn paper are fols 2 and 3, folded, and fols 4 and 6, torn; the crest itself appears on fols 2v and 4v. Fols 5, 6 and 8 are on 'Superior Invader' paper.

19 C. McIlwaine, *Tolkien: Maker of Middle-earth*, Bodleian Library, Oxford, 2018, p. 208.

20 J.R.R. Tolkien, *The Lost Road and Other Writings*, ed. Christopher Tolkien, Unwin Hyman, London, 1987, pp. 8–10.

21 J.R.R. Tolkien, *The Lord of the Rings*, 50th anniversary edition, HarperCollins, London, 2004, p. xxiii; J.R.R. Tolkien, *The War of the Ring*, ed. Christopher Tolkien, Unwin Hyman, London, 1990, p. 234.

22 Tolkien, *Lost Road*, p. 155.

23 I described the date evidence from Wiseman's letters more briefly in 'Ilu's Music: The Creation of Tolkien's Creation Myth', in *Sub-creating Arda: World-building in J.R.R. Tolkien's Work, Its Precursors, and Its Legacies*, ed. Dimitra Fimi and Thomas Honegger, Walking Tree, Zürich and Jena, 2019, pp. 118–19.

24 Tolkien had also written to Wiseman after a 23 January medical board, but evidently did not respond there to the comment about starting 'the epic'.

25 J.R.R. Tolkien to W.H. Auden, 7 June 1955, *Letters*, no. 163; to Houghton Mifflin Co., 30 June 1955, no. 165; to Christopher Bretherton, 16 July 1964, no. 257.

26 Ellen Parton, email to the author, 6 March 2020.

27 Garth, 'Ilu's Music', p. 120.

28 Tolkien, *Book of Lost Tales, Part II*, p. 268.

29 Tolkien to Auden, *Letters*, no 163.

30 Tolkien, *Book of Lost Tales, Part I*, p. 81.

7 'I WISELY STARTED WITH A MAP'

1 For example, the world map in British Library Royal MS. 14C.xii, fol. 9v. The *Polychronicon* was a popular Latin history of the fourteenth and fifteenth centuries, edited by Ranulf Higden, a Benedictine monk. See David Woodward, 'Medieval *Mappaemundi*', in *The History of Cartography*, vol. 1, *Cartography in Prehistoric, Ancient, and Medieval Europe and the Mediterranean*, ed. J.B. Harley and David Woodward, University of Chicago Press, Chicago, IL, 1987, pp. 312–14.

2 Christopher Tolkien (ed.), in J.R.R. Tolkien, *The Shaping of Middle-earth*, George Allen & Unwin, London, 1986, p. 219.

3 Christopher Tolkien (ed.), in J.R.R. Tolkien, *The Lost Road and Other Writings*, Unwin Hyman, London, 1987, p. 407.

4 Christopher Tolkien, in Tolkien, *Shaping of Middle-earth*, pp. 235–36.

5 Ibid., p. 255.

6 Rayner Unwin, quoted in Christina Scull and Wayne G. Hammond, *The J.R.R. Tolkien Companion and Guide*, HarperCollins, London, 2017, *Reader's Guide*, vol. 1, p. 522.

7 J.R.R. Tolkien, quoted in John D. Rateliff, *The History of The Hobbit*, HarperCollins, London, 2007, p. 9.

8 J.R.R. Tolkien, *The Annotated Hobbit*, annotated by Douglas A. Anderson, Houghton Mifflin, Boston, MA, 2002, pp. 10–11.

9 Conventions of drawing mountains, rivers, etc. on early maps are discussed by David Woodward in 'Medieval *Mappaemundi*', pp. 286–370. Stylization in medieval cartography is perhaps best known from printed Ptolemaic atlases of the fifteenth century, notably the Ulm woodcut edition of 1482.

10 Robert Louis Stevenson, 'My First Book: "Treasure Island"' (1894), quoted in Jerry Brotton, Nick Millea and Benjamin Hennig, *Talking Maps*, Bodleian Library, Oxford, 2019, pp. 143–44. When Stevenson sent his map to his publisher to include in the first book version of *Treasure Island*, it never arrived. He was forced to draw it again, with lettering in 'different hands' by his father, but never felt that it was as 'right' as the original made in the midst of first invention. He reflected: 'It is one thing to draw a map at random, set a scale in one corner of it at a venture, and write up a story to the measurements. It is quite another to have to examine a whole book, make an inventory of all the allusions contained in it, and, with a pair of compasses, painfully design a map to suit the data' (p. 144). His thoughts are of a piece with Tolkien's contention that one must fit a narrative to a map, rather than a map to a narrative.

11 J.R.R. Tolkien to W.H. Auden, 7 June 1955, *The Letters of J.R.R. Tolkien*, ed. Humphrey Carpenter, with the assistance of Christopher Tolkien, George Allen & Unwin, London, 1981, no. 163.

12 J.R.R. Tolkien to Naomi Mitchison, 25 April 1954, *Letters*, no. 144.

13 J.R.R. Tolkien to Rayner Unwin, 11 April 1953, *Letters*, no. 137.

14 Charlotte Plimmer and Denis Plimmer, 'The Man Who Understands Hobbits', *Daily Telegraph Magazine*, 22 March 1968, p. 32.

15 Christopher Tolkien (ed.), in J.R.R. Tolkien, *The Treason of Isengard*, Unwin Hyman, London, 1989, pp. 299–300.

16 J.R.R. Tolkien to Rayner Unwin, quoted in Scull and Hammond, *The J.R.R. Tolkien Companion and Guide*, *Chronology*, p. 427.

17 J.R.R. Tolkien to W.N. Beard, 9 October 1953, quoted in Scull and Hammond, *Chronology*, p. 435.

18 J.R.R. Tolkien to Rayner Unwin, 14 April 1955, *Letters*, no. 161.

19 Christopher Tolkien, private correspondence with the authors, quoted in Wayne G. Hammond and Christina Scull, *The Lord of the Rings: A Reader's Companion*, HarperCollins, London, 2014, p. lvi.

20 J.R.R. Tolkien to Christopher Tolkien, 16 October 1944, *Letters*, no. 85.

21 Christopher Tolkien (ed.), in J.R.R. Tolkien, *The War of the Ring*, Unwin Hyman, London, 1990, p. 438.

22 J.R.R. Tolkien to Austin Olney, Houghton Mifflin Company, quoted in Hammond and Scull, *Reader's Companion*, p. lxi.

8 EDITING THE TOLKIENIAN MANUSCRIPT

1 *The Children of Húrin* (2007), *Beren and Lúthien* (2017) and *The Fall of Gondolin* (2018).

2 I thank as always my fellow editors of Tolkien's linguistic papers, Christopher Gilson, Arden Smith and Patrick Wynne, both for their particular assistance with readings in these texts and for the opportunity to learn from their own editorial work. Thanks are also due to the Bodleian Library and the Tolkien Estate, in particular Tolkien Archivist Catherine McIlwaine for the former and solicitor Cathleen Blackburn for the latter, for permission to work with Tolkien's papers in conjunction with the opening of the exhibit *Tolkien: Maker of Middle-earth* in 2018, during which I collected the texts edited here, and for permission to publish them here.

3 https://elvish.org/articles/Tolkien_handwriting_
   guide.pdf.
4 As Peter Gilliver, Executive Editor at the *OED*, has
   informed me.
5 J.R.R. Tolkien, *The Lays of Beleriand*, ed. Christopher
   Tolkien, George Allen & Unwin, London, 1985, p. 81.
6 J.R.R. Tolkien, *The Lost Road and Other Writings*, ed.
   Christopher Tolkien, Unwin Hyman, London, 1988,
   p. 338; J.R.R. Tolkien, *Morgoth's Ring*, ed. Christopher
   Tolkien, HarperCollins, London, 1993, pp. 4–8.
7 Tolkien, *Morgoth's Ring*, p. 14 §22.
8 C and C* are variant texts so described by
   Christopher Tolkien in *Morgoth's Ring*, p. 6.
9 J.R.R. Tolkien, *Unfinished Tales*, ed. Christopher
   Tolkien, George Allen & Unwin, 1980, especially
   pp. 272, 275–77.
10 Ibid., p.10.
11 J.R.R. Tolkien, *The Peoples of Middle-earth*, ed.
   Christopher Tolkien, HarperCollins, London, 1996,
   especially pp. 368–70.
12 Ibid., p. 367.

9 A MILESTONE IN BBC HISTORY?

1 The notable exception being C. Scull and W.G.
   Hammond, *The J.R.R. Tolkien Companion and Guide*,
   HarperCollins, London, 2017, 3 vols, *Chronology* and
   Reader's Guide (*Reader's Guide*, pp. 11–17).
2 See his letter to Molly Waldron, 30 November
   1955 (*The Letters of J.R.R. Tolkien*, ed. Humphrey
   Carpenter, with the assistance of Christopher
   Tolkien, George Allen & Unwin, London, 1981,
   no. 175) where he wrote he had not enjoyed the
   broadcasts, describing Norman Shelley's Bombadil as
   'dreadful' and a mistaken description of Goldberry
   and Willowman as 'worse still'. See also letter
   to Naomi Mitchison, 8 December 1955 (*Letters*,
   no. 176), plus the comment in June 1957, letter to
   Rayner Unwin (*Letters*, no. 198) describing the BBC's
   'sillification'.
3 Scripts for Series One survive on paper (R71/289) and
   microfilm (R. P. Nos. TLO 16820, -822, -821, TLO
   17626, -643, 18653), with correspondence (R19/2194/2)
   at the BBC Written Archives, Caversham. I am
   extremely grateful to Samantha Blake, BBC
   Archivist, for her assistance.
4 Strictly speaking the first adaptation of *The
   Return of the King* was by Silvia Goodall, *School
   Scripts: Adventures in English* (BBC Home Service,
   19 January–22 March 1956). This consisted of ten
   episodes: 'The Hobbits'; 'The Old Forest'; 'Strider';
   'The Ring Goes South'; 'Treebeard the Ent'; 'Riders
   of Rohan'; 'The Way to Mordor'; 'The Siege of Minas
   Tirith'; 'The Last Battle'; 'Mount Doom'.
5 The latter was not liked by Tolkien: see letter to
   Rayner Heppenstall, 22 September 1954 (*Letters*,
   no. 152).

6 Quoted in Scull and Hammond, *Reader's Guide*,
   p. 12.
7 Brian Sibley explained that while the 'Narrator' has
   gone out of fashion in radio dramatizations, he also
   used one in 1981 (Gerard Murphy) as it allowed him
   to 'capture the authorial voice of the book', convey a
   sense of place and passing of time, move the listener
   across scenes (especially useful when the Fellowship
   splits up), and give a sense of the vastness of Middle-
   earth (Brian Sibley, telephone interview with Stuart
   Lee, 6 September 2019).
8 The composer Anthony Smith-Masters of
   Marlborough College was engaged. Some of
   this music still survives and can be heard in
   'Tolkien: The Lost Recordings', *Archive on 4*, BBC
   Radio 4, 2016.
9 See Scull and Hammond, *Chronology*, p. 473.
10 A traditional English folk song also called 'The
   fox went out on a chilly night', which has a
   structure very similar to Sam's with the refrain
   'town-o, town-o' (see, for example, Dimitra Fimi's
   paper, 'Tolkien, Folklore and Foxes', delivered at
   'Tolkien 2019' in Birmingham, www.youtube.com/
   watch?v=rAAYOnkVnwk with the song at 9 mins 30
   sec); 'Tenebrae' is the service of darkness leading up
   to Easter – a Gregorian reciting tone is traditionally
   used that conjures up a feeling of sadness.
11 See Scull and Hammond, *Reader's Guide*, pp. 12–13.
12 See Scull and Hammond, *Chronology*, p. 500.
   Tolkien obviously had an ear for such things – see
   his comments on the dialect tones in *Homecoming*
   in the letter to Rayner Heppenstall (22 September
   1954, *Letters*, no. 152), and also his 'parlour game'
   recorded in A. Quirke, 'The Wizard of Oxford', *New
   Statesman*, 145 (5327), 12–18 August 2016, p. 55.
13 Presumably Tolkien is using 'Great' here to refer to
   status rather than size, as in the phrase, 'the great
   and the good' meaning ' distinguished and worthy
   people' (*OED*).
14 See Scull and Hammond, *Reader's Guide*, pp. 13–14.
15 See also Scull and Hammond, *Chronology*, p. 501.
16 See Scull and Hammond, *Reader's Guide*, pp. 15–16.
   It is worth noting that this is the ending, in a sense,
   that Peter Jackson also chose, i.e. omitting the
   Scouring of the Shire.
17 *Letters*, no. 193, and Scull and Hammond, *Reader's
   Guide*, pp. 16–17; *Letters*, no. 194, and Scull and
   Hammond, *Reader's Guide*, p. 17.
18 See, for example, Eric Fraser's specially designed
   cover for the *Radio Times*, www.bbc.co.uk/
   programmes/p01h96nf/p01gz0qt.
19 Paul Ferris, *Observer*, 20 November 1955, p. 10.
20 *The Critics* seemingly discussed the dramatization (20
   November 1955) but no recording survives. See also
   Tolkien's letter to Rayner Unwin, 8 December 1955
   (*Letters*, no. 177), in which he agreed with their view of

the dramatization (but with no indication of whether this was positive or negative) but was annoyed when they admitted they had not read the book.

21 Other correspondence to Tiller from listeners make the same complaint. For timings see 'Programme details' below.

22 The offending lines were 'Opening Announcement: … He [Sauron] has other allies too, from one of which the hobbits have been rescued by the strange and ancient power of Tom Bombadil. With Bombadil and his daughter Goldberry, the hobbits find temporary shelter.'

23 Brian Sibley, telephone interview with Stuart Lee, 6 September 2019.

10 'KING SHEAVE' AND 'THE LOST ROAD'

1 Books Tolkien is known to have owned or referred to, as well as others he is thought to have used, are scrupulously catalogued and annotated by Oronzo Cilli, *Tolkien's Library: An Annotated Checklist*, Luna Press, Edinburgh, 2019.

2 See J.R.R. Tolkien, *The Lost Road and Other Writings*, ed. Christopher Tolkien, Unwin Hyman, London, 1987, pp. 7–10, and further John D. Rateliff, 'The Lost Road, The Dark Tower, and The Notion Club Papers': Tolkien and Lewis's Time Travel Triad', in *Tolkien's Legendarium: Essays on* 'The History of Middle-earth', ed. Verlyn Flieger and Carl F. Hostetter, Greenwood Press, Westport, CT, 2000, pp. 199–218 (202–6).

3 See J.R.R. Tolkien, *Sauron Defeated*, ed. Christopher Tolkien, HarperCollins, London, 1992, pp. 145–48, and further Rateliff, 'The Lost Road', pp. 212–13.

4 For the two accounts, see Tolkien, *Lost Road*, pp. 7–8 and 77–80. The quotation comes from p. 7.

5 The two quotations come from John Buchan, *The Path of the King* (1921), here Thomas Nelson, London and Edinburgh, 1923, pp. 301–2, 21. For Tolkien's liking for Buchan, see Humphrey Carpenter, *J.R.R. Tolkien: A Biography*, George Allen & Unwin, London, 1977, p. 165, and further my entry on John Buchan in *The Tolkien Encyclopedia*, ed. Michael C. Drout, Routledge, London and New York, 2007, pp. 77–79.

6 Respectively, Buchan, *Path of the King*, p. 10; and J.R.R. Tolkien, *The Lord of the Rings*, George Allen & Unwin, London, 1955, Book V, ch. 9.

7 The story is summarized by Christopher Tolkien in Tolkien, *Lost Road*, pp. 53–54.

8 Tolkien, *Lost Road*, pp. 85–98.

9 J.R.R. Tolkien, *Beowulf: A Translation and Commentary*, ed. Christopher Tolkien, HarperCollins, London, 2014, pp. 13–14.

10 Tolkien, *Lost Road*, p. 93.

11 Both analogues are given by Christopher Tolkien, in translation, in Tolkien, *Lost Road*, p. 92. His father would certainly have been familiar with both, as they are printed and discussed at length by R.W. Chambers, *Beowulf: An Introduction to the Study of the Poem*, Cambridge University Press, Cambridge, 1921, a book Tolkien owned and cited; see Cilli, *Tolkien's Library*, p. 43.

12 For the 'patronymic', see Tolkien, *Beowulf*, p. 138; for the 'Shieldings', p. 137; for the 'dire need', p. 143.

13 For the two rejections of 'heathen', see respectively Tolkien, *Beowulf*, pp. 169–78, 71.

14 Tolkien, *Beowulf*, p. 138.

15 He introduces it near the end of his essay 'On Fairy-Stories'; see J.R.R. Tolkien, *The Monsters and the Critics and Other Essays*, ed. Christopher Tolkien, George Allen & Unwin, London, 1983, pp. 109–61, by happy coincidence (see below) on p. 153.

16 In the essay just cited (p. 156), Tolkien remarks: 'the Birth of Christ is the eucatastrophe of Man's history. The Resurrection is the eucatastrophe of the story of the Incarnation.' Both events have analogues in the poem of 'King Sheave' (the Resurrection) or the associated prose account (the Nativity).

17 See further T.A. Shippey, 'Chaucer's Arithmetical Mentality and *The Book of the Duchess*', *Chaucer Review*, 31, 1996, pp. 184–200, readily accessible (and there correctly formatted) under my name at www.academia.edu. Tolkien was not the first English poet to use this number symbolism.

18 It is edited and translated in T.A. Shippey, *Poems of Wisdom and Learning in Old English*, D.S. Brewer, Cambridge, 1976, pp. 112–19.

19 Tolkien, *Lost Road*, p. 91.

20 See the very full discussion in Claudio Testi, *Pagan Saints in Middle-earth*, Walking Tree, Zurich and Jena, 2018.

21 Tolkien, *Lost Road*, pp. 86, 96–97.

22 See Snorri, *Edda*, transl. Anthony Faulkes, J.M. Dent, London, 1995, p. 49.

23 Tolkien's interest in specifically Celtic ideas of the Otherworld in the West is discussed in Dimitra Fimi, 'Tolkien's "Celtic" Type of Legends: Merging Traditions', *Tolkien Studies* 4, 2007, pp. 51–71, especially pp. 54–57. Tolkien may well have felt that their evidence and that of *Beowulf* corroborated each other, bearing witness to a widespread belief in pre-Christian north-west Europe, both Celtic and Germanic (and perhaps to an underlying if mythic reality).

24 For instance, in order of publication: 'The Happy Mariners' (1920, 1923), 'The Nameless Land' (1927, reprinted in three versions in *Lost Road*, pp. 98–103), 'Firiel' (1934), 'Looney' (1934). Revised versions of the last two appeared in Tolkien, *The Adventures of Tom Bombadil* (1962); see the very full edition of that work by Christina Scull and Wayne G. Hammond, HarperCollins, London, 2014.

11 'DOWN FROM THE DOOR WHERE IT BEGAN'

1 J.R.R. Tolkien, *Tree and Leaf*, Allen and Unwin, London, 1964, p. 11.

2 J.R.R. Tolkien, *The Hobbit*, George Allen and Unwin, London, 1937, ch. 1.

3 'The Human Eye's Response to Light', www.nde-ed. org/EducationResources/CommunityCollege/ PenetrantTest/Introduction/lightresponse.htm; David Scott Kastan, *On Color*, Yale University Press, New Haven, CT, 2018, p. 83.

4 J.R.R. Tolkien, *The Lord of the Rings*, George Allen and Unwin, London, 1954–5, Book I, ch. 3.

5 Tolkien, *Hobbit*, ch. 4.

6 *The Poetic Edda, A complete metrical version of the Poetic or Elder Edda, including the Lays of the Gods and the Lays of the Heroes*, transl. Henry Adams Bellows, The American Scandinavian Foundation, New York, 1923, p. 93, 'Grimnismol, The Ballad of Grimnir', stanza 21.

7 Tolkien, *Hobbit*, ch. 1.

8 *Poetic Edda*, 'The Ballad of Grimnir', stanza 23.

9 Tolkien, *Hobbit*, ch. 3.

10 *Poetic Edda*, 'The Ballad of Grimnir', stanza 22.

11 Tolkien, *Hobbit*, ch. 11.

12 Ibid., ch. 19.

13 Tolkien, *Lord of the Rings*, Book I, ch. 1.

14 Ibid., Book I, ch. 3.

15 Ibid., Book I, ch. 5.

16 Ibid., Book I, ch. 6.

17 Ibid.

18 Ibid., Book I, ch. 7.

19 Ibid.

20 Ibid., Book I, ch. 8.

21 Ibid., Book I, ch. 9.

22 Ibid.

23 Ibid., Book II, ch. 3.

24 Ibid., Book II, ch. 4.

25 Ibid.

26 J.R.R. Tolkien, *On Fairy-stories*, ed. Verlyn Flieger and Douglas A. Anderson, HarperCollins, London, 2008, p. 308.

27 Oronzo Cilli, *Tolkien's Library: An Annotated Checklist*, Luna Press, Edinburgh, 2019, p. 108, entries 877–78, 881–82.

28 Tolkien, *Lord of the Rings*, Book II, ch. 4.

29 Ibid., Book II, ch. 4.

30 Ibid., Book II, ch. 10.

31 Ibid., Book IV, ch. 8.

32 Ibid., Book V, ch. 10.

33 Ibid., Book I, ch. 6; Book IV, ch. 10.

34 Ibid., Book VI, ch. 1.

35 Ibid.

36 Ibid., Book V, ch. 2.

37 Ibid., Book V, ch. 10.

38 Ibid., Book VI, ch. 3.

39 Ibid., Book VI, ch. 8.

40 Ibid., Book VI, ch. 9.

ABOUT THE CONTRIBUTORS

Vincent Ferré is Professor in Comparative Literature, University Paris-Est Créteil; director of the research group 'Literature, Ideas, Knowledge'; and vice-president of the 'Modernités Médiévales' society. His scholarship centres on the European and American novel, especially on Proust, Broch and Dos Passos; and on medievalism, in particular on Tolkien. He has published *Tolkien: Sur les rivages de la Terre du Milieu* (2001) and *Lire J.R.R. Tolkien* (2014). He has edited *Tolkien, trente ans après* (2004), *Dictionnaire Tolkien* (2nd ed., 2019) and *Tolkien. Voyage en Terre du Milieu* (2019); and co-edited *Tolkien aujourd'hui* (2011) and *Tolkien. La fabrique d'un monde* (2013).

Verlyn Flieger is Professor Emerita in the Department of English at the University of Maryland, where for thirty-six years she taught courses in Tolkien, medieval literature and comparative mythology. She is the author of five critical books on the work of J.R.R. Tolkien, *Splintered Light* (2nd ed., 2002), *A Question of Time* (1997), *Interrupted Music* (2005), *Green Suns and Faërie* (2012) and *There Would Always Be a Fairy Tale* (2017). She edited the extended edition of Tolkien's *Smith of Wootton Major* (2005). With Carl Hostetter she edited *Tolkien's Legendarium* (2000), and with Douglas A. Anderson the expanded edition of *Tolkien On Fairy-Stories* (2008). With Michael Drout and David Bratman she is a co-editor of the yearly journal *Tolkien Studies*.

John Garth won the Mythopoeic Award for Scholarship for *Tolkien and the Great War* (2003). He is also the author of *Tolkien at Exeter College* (2014) and most recently *The Worlds of J.R.R. Tolkien* (2020), arising from research during nine months as a fellow of the Black Mountain Institute in Nevada. He received the Tolkien Society's Outstanding Contribution Award in 2017 for his contribution to Tolkien studies. Garth read English at St Anne's College, Oxford; spent more than two decades in news media, mostly as a sub-editor on the London *Evening Standard*; and is now a freelance writer, editor and speaker.

Wayne G. Hammond is Chapin Librarian, emeritus, at Williams College in Massachusetts, where he was a specialist in rare books and manuscripts for more than forty-five years. His descriptive bibliographies of J.R.R. Tolkien (1993) and Arthur Ransome (2000) are standard references. **Christina Scull** was the Librarian of Sir John Soane's Museum, London, for over two decades, where she wrote *The Soane Hogarths* (1991). Together they have edited Tolkien's *Roverandom* (1998), *Farmer Giles of Ham* (1999), *The Lord of the Rings* (2004) and *The Adventures of Tom Bombadil and Other Verses from the Red Book* (2014), and their essential works about Tolkien include *J.R.R. Tolkien: Artist and Illustrator* (1995), *The Art of The Hobbit* (2011), *The Lord of the Rings: A Reader's Companion* (3rd ed., 2014), *The Art of The Lord of the Rings* (2015) and *The J.R.R. Tolkien Companion and Guide* (2nd ed., 2017).

Carl F. Hostetter is a member of the team selected by Christopher Tolkien to edit and publish Tolkien's writings on the languages of Middle-earth. He is also the editor of *Vinyar Tengwar*, a journal of Tolkienian linguistics, and has published numerous articles on Tolkien's invented languages and related topics. His recent work, *The Nature of Middle-earth* (2021), comprises his editions of numerous late and previously unpublished essays by Tolkien on both the physical and metaphysical nature of his invented world and its inhabitants.

Stuart Lee is a Reader at the University of Oxford and a member of the Faculty of English. He has lectured and tutored on Old English, the poetry of the First World War, fantasy literature with a specific focus on Tolkien, and digital humanities. He has published extensively on Tolkien, notably *The Keys of Middle-earth* (2nd ed. with E. Solopova, 2015) and *A Companion to J.R.R. Tolkien* (2nd ed., 2021); and edited the four-volume *Critical Assessments of Major Writers: J.R.R. Tolkien* (2017). He also led the creation of 'The First World War Poetry Digital Archive', ww1lit.nsms.ox.ac.uk/ww1lit, and several other online collections.

Catherine McIlwaine is the Tolkien Archivist at the Bodleian Library, Oxford, where she has worked on the Tolkien archive since 2003. She is the author of *Tolkien: Maker of Middle-earth* (2018), which won the Tolkien Society's Best Book Award 2019, and curated the Bodleian's summer exhibition of the same name in 2018. She has also written *Tolkien: Treasures* (2018), winner of the ACE Best General Publication Award 2019.

Richard Ovenden has been Bodley's Librarian since 2014. Prior to that he held positions at Durham University Library, the House of Lords Library, the National Library of Scotland, and the University of Edinburgh. He moved to the Bodleian in 2003 as Keeper of Special Collections, becoming Deputy Librarian in 2011. He was educated at the University of Durham and University College London, and holds a Professorial Fellowship at Balliol College, Oxford, and is a Fellow of the Society of Antiquaries, the Royal Society of Arts, the Royal Historical Society and a Member of the American Philosophical Society. He was made OBE in the Queen's Birthday Honours 2019, and received the Premio Acqui Storia, 'Testimone del tempo' award in October 2021. He is the author of *John Thomson (1837–1921): Photographer* (1997) and *Burning the Books: A History of Knowledge Under Attack* (2020), which was BBC Radio 4's Book of the Week in September 2020 and was shortlisted for the Wolfson History Prize in 2021.

Maxime Hortense Pascal is a writer and poet, living in the South of France. Her production covers a spectrum from poetry to novel, from verse to more rugged forms. Her collaboration with choreographers, musicians and contemporary artists (installations, dramaturgy) enlightens her writing by deepening its margins. She gives public readings and performances. She has a profoundly poetic appreciation of the works of Tolkien and has been a close friend of Christopher, Baillie, Adam and Rachel for over thirty years.

Tom Shippey has taught at several universities, including Oxford and Harvard, and held Tolkien's old Chair at Leeds for fourteen years. He has lectured and published on Tolkien for more than fifty years. His works include *The Road to Middle-earth* (3rd ed., 2003), *Tolkien: Author of the Century* (2000) and *Roots and Branches: Selected Papers on Tolkien* (2007). He has also published widely on medieval topics and his most recent book is *Laughing Shall I Die: Lives and Deaths of the Great Vikings* (2018).

Brian Sibley is a writer and broadcaster with an interest in the literature of fantasy and children's fiction. As a dramatist, he was co-responsible for the BBC's 1981 radio serialization of *The Lord of the Rings* and, later, dramatized some of Tolkien's short fiction as *Tales from the Perilous Realm*. Associated writings include books based on Tolkien's maps of Middle-earth, with artist John Howe, his biography of filmmaker Peter Jackson and his 'making of' volumes devoted to Jackson's *Rings* and *Hobbit* film trilogies. He is also known for biographies and critical studies of writers C.S. Lewis, A.A. Milne, Rev. W. Awdry, Lewis Carroll and Tove Jansson, as well as books on Walt Disney, cinema and popular culture.

Baillie Tolkien (née Klass) met Christopher Tolkien in 1964 when she was reading English at St. Hilda's College, Oxford. They were married in 1967. She has a BA from the University of Manitoba, Canada, and an MA from Oxford. After her studies she was employed as personal assistant and secretary, first by J.R.R. Tolkien, and then by Sir Isaiah Berlin. The letters "from Father Christmas" that Tolkien wrote to his children from 1920 to 1943 were found among his papers after his death, and previous editorial experience led to Baillie being assigned to edit them for publication in book form. After their move to France in 1975, Christopher worked at home and Baillie was associated with his activities as his father's literary executor. She is a director of the Tolkien Estate, and a trustee of the registered charity The Tolkien Trust, as well as Christopher's literary executor and trustee of his Estate.

Priscilla Tolkien (1929–2022) was the fourth child and only daughter of J.R.R. Tolkien and his wife Edith. She was born and brought up in Oxford, and studied English at Lady Margaret Hall, University of Oxford. After working as a secretary for several years, she did professional training in social work and became a probation officer. She later became a social work tutor and then a tutor in A-Level English in a sixth form college. Subsequently, she ran book discussion groups at home. She continued to be involved in the work of the Tolkien Estate and was a trustee of the registered charity, The Tolkien Trust, until her death.

FURTHER READING

Arduini, R., and C.A. Testi (eds), *The Broken Scythe: Death and Immortality in the Works of J.R.R. Tolkien*, Walking Tree, Zurich and Jena, 2012.

Aristotle, *Poetics*, transl. with an introduction and notes by Anthony Kenny, Oxford University Press, Oxford, 2013.

Bellows, H.A., *The Poetic Edda, A complete metrical version of the Poetic or Elder Edda, including the Lays of the Gods and the Lays of the Heroes*, transl. from the Icelandic by Henry Adams Bellows, The American Scandinavian Foundation, New York, 1923.

Brotton, J., N. Millea and B. Hennig, *Talking Maps*, Bodleian Library, Oxford, 2019.

Bushell, S., 'Paratext or Imagetext?: Interpreting the Fictional Map', *Word & Image*, vol. 32, no. 2, 2016, pp. 181–94.

Cilli, O., *Tolkien's Library: An Annotated Checklist*, Luna Press, Edinburgh, 2019.

Eilmann, J., and A. Turner (eds), *Tolkien's Poetry*, Walking Tree, Zurich and Jena, 2013.

Ekman, S., *Here Be Dragons: Exploring Fantasy Maps and Settings*, Wesleyan University Press, Middletown, CT, 2013.

Fimi, D., 'Tolkien's "Celtic" Type of Legends: Merging Traditions', *Tolkien Studies*, 4, 2007, pp. 51–71.

Flieger, V., *A Question of Time: J.R.R. Tolkien's Road to Faerie*, The Kent State University Press, Kent, OH, 1997.

—, *Splintered Light: Logos and Language in Tolkien's World*, rev. ed., The Kent State University Press, Kent, OH, 2007.

—, *Green Suns and Faerie: Essays on J.R.R. Tolkien*, The Kent State University Press, Kent, OH, 2012.

—, *There Would Always Be a Fairy Tale: More Essays on Tolkien*, The Kent State University Press, Kent, OH, 2017.

Fonstad, K.W., *The Atlas of Middle-earth*, Houghton Mifflin, Boston, MA, 1991.

Garth, J., *Tolkien and the Great War: The Threshold of Middle-earth*, HarperCollins, London, 2003.

—, 'Ilu's Music: The Creation of Tolkien's Creation Myth', in *Sub-creating Arda: World-building in J.R.R. Tolkien's Work, Its Precursors, and Its Legacies*, ed. Dimitra Fimi and Thomas Honegger, Walking Tree, Zurich and Jena, 2019, pp. 117–51.

Genette, G., *Fiction and Diction* [1991], transl. Catherine Porter, Cornell University Press, Ithaca, NY, 1993.

Glyer, D.P., *The Company They Keep: C.S. Lewis and J.R.R. Tolkien as Writers in Community*, The Kent State University Press, Kent, OH 2007.

Hammond, W.G., and C. Scull, *The Art of The Hobbit by J.R.R. Tolkien*, HarperCollins, London, 2011.

—, *The Lord of the Rings: A Reader's Companion*, HarperCollins, London, 2014.

—, *The Art of The Lord of the Rings by J.R.R. Tolkien*, HarperCollins, London, 2015.

Harmon, K., *You Are Here: Personal Geographies and Other Maps of the Imagination*, Princeton Architectural Press, New York, NY, 2004.

Helms, R., *Tolkien and the Silmarils*, Thames & Hudson, London, 1981.

Kastan, D.S., *On Color*, Yale University Press, New Haven, CT, 2018.

Lewis-Jones, H. (ed.), *The Writer's Map: An Atlas of Imaginary Lands*, Thames & Hudson, London, 2018.

Lukács, G., 'On the Nature and Form of the Essay', in *Soul & Form* [1910], transl. Anna Bostock, ed. John T. Sanders and Katie Terezakis, introduction by Judith Butler, Columbia University Press, New York, NY, 2010.

McIlwaine, C., *Tolkien: Maker of Middle-earth*, Bodleian Library, Oxford, 2018.

Moorman, C., *Editing the Middle English Manuscript*, University Press of Mississippi, Jackson, MS, 1975.

Pastoureau, M., *Green: The History of a Color*, Princeton University Press, Princeton, NJ, 2014.

Priestman, J., *J.R.R. Tolkien: Life and Legend*, Bodleian Library, Oxford, 1992.

Quirke, A., 'The Wizard of Oxford', *New Statesman*, 145 (5327), 12–18 August 2016, p. 55.

Rateliff, J.D., *The History of The Hobbit*, 2 vols, HarperCollins, London, 2007.

Scull, C., and W.G. Hammond, *The J.R.R. Tolkien Companion and Guide*, rev. ed., 3 vols, HarperCollins, London, 2017.

Shippey, T., *The Road to Middle-earth: How J.R.R. Tolkien Created a New Mythology*, revised & expanded edition, HarperCollins, London, 2005, pp. 351–61.

St Clair, K., *The Secret Lives of Colour*, John Murray, London, 2016.

Strachey, B., *Journeys of Frodo: An Atlas of J.R.R. Tolkien's The Lord of the Rings*, George Allen & Unwin, London, 1981.

Tolkien, C., *The Silmarillion by J.R.R. Tolkien: A Brief Account of the Book and Its Making*, Houghton Mifflin, Boston, 1977.

Tolkien, J.R.R., *The Silmarillion*, ed. Christopher Tolkien, George Allen & Unwin, London, 1977.

—, *Unfinished Tales of Númenor and Middle-earth*, ed. Christopher Tolkien, George Allen & Unwin, London, 1980.

—, *The Letters of J.R.R. Tolkien*, ed. Humphrey Carpenter, with the assistance of Christopher Tolkien, George Allen & Unwin, London, 1981.

—, *The Book of Lost Tales, Part I*, ed. Christopher Tolkien, George Allen & Unwin, London, 1983.

—, *The Book of Lost Tales, Part II*, ed. Christopher Tolkien, George Allen & Unwin, London, 1984.

—, *The Lays of Beleriand*, ed. Christopher Tolkien, George Allen & Unwin, London, 1985.

—, *The Shaping of Middle-earth: The Quenta, The Ambarkanta and The Annals together with the earliest 'Silmarillion' and the first Map*, ed. Christopher Tolkien, George Allen & Unwin, London, 1986.

—, *The Lost Road and Other Writings*, ed. Christopher Tolkien, Unwin Hyman, London, 1987.

—, *The Return of the Shadow: The History of The Lord of the Rings, Part One*, ed. Christopher Tolkien, Unwin Hyman, London, 1988.

—, *The Treason of Isengard: The History of The Lord of the Rings, Part Two*, ed. Christopher Tolkien, Unwin Hyman, London, 1989.

—, *The War of the Ring*, ed. Christopher Tolkien, Unwin Hyman, London, 1990.

—, *Sauron Defeated: The End of the Third Age (The History of The Lord of the Rings, Part Four); The Notion Club Papers and The Drowning of Anadûnê*, ed. Christopher Tolkien, HarperCollins, London, 1992.

—, *Morgoth's Ring: The Later Silmarillion, Part One, The Legends of Aman*, ed. Christopher Tolkien, HarperCollins, London, 1993.

—, *The War of the Jewels: The Later Silmarillion, Part Two, The Legends of Beleriand*, ed. Christopher Tolkien, HarperCollins, London, 1994.

—, 'I·Lam na·Ngoldathon: The Grammar and Lexicon of the Gnomish Tongue', *Parma Eldalamberon*, no. 11, 1995, ed. Christopher Gilson, Patrick Wynne, Arden R. Smith and Carl F. Hostetter.

—, *The Peoples of Middle-earth*, ed. Christopher Tolkien, HarperCollins, London, 1996.

—, 'Qenyaqetsa: The Qenya Phonology and Lexicon' including 'The Poetic and Mythologic Words of Eldarissa', *Parma Eldalamberon*, no. 12, ed. Christopher Gilson, Carl F. Hostetter, Patrick H. Wynne and Arden R. Smith, 1998.

—, 'Early Chart of Names' and 'Official Name List', *Parma Eldalamberon*, no. 13, 2001, ed. Christopher Gilson, Bill Welden, Carl F. Hostetter and Patrick Wynne, pp. 98–105.

—, *The Annotated Hobbit*, annotated by Douglas A. Anderson, Houghton Mifflin, Boston, MA, 2002.

—, early name list for *The Cottage of Lost Play*, selectively quoted in 'Names and Required Alterations', *Parma Eldalamberon*, no. 15, 2004, ed. Christopher Gilson and Patrick H. Wynne, pp. 5–11.

—, 'Name-list to The Fall of Gondolin', *Parma Eldalamberon*, ed. Christopher Gilson and Patrick H. Wynne, no. 15, 2004, pp. 19–28.

—, *The Tale of the Children of Húrin*, ed. Christopher Tolkien, HarperCollins, London, 2007.

—, *Beren and Lúthien*, ed. Christopher Tolkien, HarperCollins, London, 2017.

—, *The Fall of Gondolin*, ed. Christopher Tolkien, HarperCollins, London, 2018.

'Tolkien: The Lost Recordings', *Archive on 4*, BBC Radio 4, 2016.

Turner, A., (ed.), *The Silmarillion: Thirty Years On*, Walking Tree, Zurich, 2007.

Woodward, D., 'Medieval *Mappaemundi*', in *The History of Cartography*, vol. 1, *Cartography in Prehistoric, Ancient, and Medieval Europe and the Mediterranean*, ed. J.B. Harley and David Woodward, University of Chicago Press, Chicago, IL, 1987, pp. 286–370.

Zumthor, P., *Toward a Medieval Poetics* [1972], transl. Philip Bennett, University of Minnesota Press, Minneapolis, MN, 1992.

INDEX

Illustrations appear in italics

Isengard 74, 157–9
Isildur 140–42
Italy 16, 170, 176
Ithilien 44–5, 86, 126
I Vene Kemen (Ship of the Earth) 105–9

Jackson, Peter 162
John Barleycorn 173
Jones, Gwyn 10

Kane, Douglas 64–5
Kay, Guy Gavriel 17
Kilby, Clyde 62
Kili 86
Kinder-und Haus-Märchen (Grimm)
    198
King Edward VI School, Birmingham
    16
King Sheave (poem) 24, 166, 168, 170,
    173–7, 180
Klass, Baillie *see* Tolkien, Baillie

Lake-town (Esgaroth) 116, 188, 190
Lang, Andrew: *The Arabian Nights
    Entertainments* 198
languages, invented 8, 77, 89–90, 92–8,
    102, 105, 107–9, 133, 135–9, 142–4, 147
Laws and Customs Among the Eldar 59
Lays of Beleriand, The 57–8
Lay of Leithian, The 7
Leeds 8, 26
Leeds, University of 107, 166
Legend of Sigurd and Gudrún, The 57
Legolas 74, 155, 157, 159, 164, 168, 203
Letters from Father Christmas 17–18, 19,
    47, 48, 49
Lewis, C.S. 10, 14, 146, 149, 161, 172
Lewis, W.H. 'Warnie' 14
Lhammas, The 58
Lincoln, Abraham 168
Lindo 97
Linqil *see* Ulmo
Lombards (Longobards) 167–8, 170,
    173–4, 176
Lonely Mountain 72–3, 113–18, 121,
    188–92, 197
Long Lake 72–3, 114, 117
Lord of the Rings, The:
    abandoned ending 81–2
    accents of characters 147, 150–51,
    160–61
    Christianity 180
    doorways 193–204
    dramatization, film 162–3
    dramatization, radio 145–65
    elegiac 75–6, 82, 86
    foreword to the second edition 100
    'immensely long' 70–71
    inscription in Christopher Tolkien's

copy 231
    interrupted by work on the 'Lost
    Road' 166–7
    levity 74, 193, 196
    maps 14, 71–3, 119–28
    drawn by Christopher Tolkien 14,
    43–5, 123, 126
    music 147–9
    the 'new hobbit' 9–10
    publication in conjunction with *The
    Silmarillion* 70
    'rather bitter' 70–71, 74–6, 86
    read to the Inklings, 14
    'reared to be destroyed' 75–6, 86
    references to Gondolin 21
    reviews 74–5, 160–62
    sequel to *The Hobbit* 70–71, 80, 113,
    120
    sequel to *The Silmarillion* 20, 22, 70
    type of paper used 134
    use of word 'heathen' 173
Lost Road, The (unfinished story) 166–8,
    173, 177, 180
Lothlórien (Lorien) 21, 72–3, 200
Lowdham, Alwin Arundel 168
Lowdham, Edwin 168
Lúthien 60, 64, 79, 135, 142–3

Mablung 158, 164
McGill University, Montreal 16
McKellen, Ian 162
Magic Isles 107
Manitoba, University of, Winnipeg 16
Manwe Sulimo 92–3, 95–6
*Map of Beleriand and the Lands to the
    North* 110
Maps:
    Ambarkanta maps 110, 112–3
    drawn by Christopher Tolkien 14,
    43–5, 120, 123, 126
    earliest map of the Shire 123–5
    earliest version of Thror's map
    114–16, 119
    first large *Silmarillion* map 109–11
    first *Lord of the Rings* map 121–2
    Hobbit 113–19, 166
    I Vene Kemen 105–9;
    Lord of the Rings 14, 43–5, 71–3,
    119–28, 146
    *Map of Beleriand and the Lands to
    the North* 110
    Númenor 110
    Rohan, Gondor and Mordor, 43–5,
    122–3
    north-west of Middle-earth 71–3
    rough map of the world 103, 105–7
    rough map of Middle-earth 139–40
    second large *Silmarillion* map 110
    Silmarillion 106–13

A Part of the Shire 120, 122–3, 126–7
Thror's Map 116, 118, 190–91
Thror's Map. Copied by B. Baggins
    116–17
Wilderland 114, 116, 121
    The World about V Y 500 112–13
Mappaemundi 110, 113
Market Drayton, Shropshire 10
Marquette University, Milwaukee 61,
    114, 201–2
Masters, Anthony Smith- 156
Melko *see* Morgoth
Menegroth 64
Meneltarma 56–7
Merry (Meriadoc Brandybuck) 75, 119,
    147, 151, 154–5, 157–9, 164, 196, 204
Middle-earth 7–8, 17, 20, 22, 53, 60, 71,
    76, 78, 81, 89, 106, 110, 112–14, 121–3,
    126, 128, 134, 140, 180, 184, 188
Middle English Vocabulary, A 91
Milne, A.A.: *Winnie-the-Pooh*; *The
    Green Door* 114, 184
Milton, John: *Paradise Lost* 52
Mim the Petty-dwarf 64–5
Minas Morgul 44–5, 201–2
Minas Tirith 44–5, 106, 126, 157–9,
    202–3
Mirkwood 113–14, 116–17, 122, 185–7
Misty Mountains 72–3, 113–14, 185, 197
Mitchison, Naomi 120–21
Monde, Le 55
Monsters and the Critics, The 60, 69
Morannon *see* Black Gate
Mordor 44–5, 122–3, 154, 156, 158–60
Morgoth (Melko/Melkor) 22, 138–9
Moria 21, 76, 155, 197–200
Morris, William 71
Morwen 86
Mounds of Mundberg 86
Mount Doom (Orodruin) 44–5, 159
Music of the Ainur, The (Ainulindalë) 23,
    79–80, 82, 90–100, 102–5, 134, 138–40
Name-list to The Fall of Gondolin 96–8

Nandorin (invented language) 144
Nargothrond 21, 64, 76
Narqelion (poem) 133, 136–7
Nauglamír 65
Nazgûl (Black Riders) 71, 152–5, 158,
    163, 193
New College, Oxford 16–17, 26–7
Nienna 138–9
Nienor 86
Niggle 21
Norse sagas 7, 14, 16, 31, 39, 71
Notion Club Papers, The 167–8, 207
Númenor 22, 56, 59, 76, 100, 110, 167–8
Númenóreans 22, 168

Note to the reader

References to 'The Silmarillion', 'The Hobbit', etc. are to the unpublished work but references to the 'Silmarillion' refer to the wider legendarium. Name-forms used are appropriate to the particular text under discussion (for example, Melko rather than Melkor in the first versions of *The Book of Lost Tales*). References to the races of Middle-earth have been capitalized, except for hobbits, following Tolkien's practice in *The Lord of the Rings*. As there are many different editions of *The Hobbit* and *The Lord of the Rings*, references to the former are given by chapter and to the latter by book and chapter. Unless otherwise credited in the caption, the author or artist is J.R.R. Tolkien.

C·J·R·Tolkien

from JRRT
1955

Sínen randa nyarne metta ar taina andaurenya na quanta; mélima yondion, lenna antanyes mélio cenwa.

'With this the long tale ends and my extended long day is complete; dear [one] of sons, to you I give it to be read with love.' Inscription in Quenya by J.R.R. Tolkien in Christopher's copy of *The Return of the King*. From a private collection.